P9-DTC-470

HAL⊙®
CRYPTUM

HALO®
CRYPTUM
BOOK ONE OF THE FORERUNNER SAGA

GREG BEAR

TOR®

A TOM DOHERTY ASSOCIATES BOOK · NEW YORK

This is a work of fiction. All of the characters, organizations, and events portrayed in this novel are either products of the author's imagination or are used fictitiously.

HALO®: CRYPTUM

Copyright © 2010 by Microsoft Corporation

All rights reserved.

Microsoft, Halo, the Halo logo, Xbox, the Xbox logo, 343 Industries, and the 343 Industries logo are trademarks of the Microsoft group of companies.

A Tor Book
Published by Tom Doherty Associates, LLC
175 Fifth Avenue
New York, NY 10010

www.tor-forge.com

Tor® is a registered trademark of Tom Doherty Associates, LLC.

ISBN 978-0-7653-8038-8

Our books may be purchased in bulk for promotional, educational, or business use. Please contact your local bookseller or the Macmillan Corporate and Premium Sales Department at (800) 221-7945, extension 5442, or by e-mail at MacmillanSpecialMarkets@macmillan.com.

First Edition: January 2011
First Mass Market Edition: November 2015

Printed in the United States of America

0 9 8 7 6 5 4 3 2 1

AI Translator Note: The best tactical translations involve automatic conversion to immediately understandable terms and phrases, including colloquialisms. That tradition has been followed in this work.

HALO®
CRYPTUM

The peaceful one is at war without and within.

—*The Mantle, Fifth Permutation*
of the Didact's Number

THE FORERUNNER STORY—*the history of my people—has been told many times, with greater and greater idealization, until I scarcely recognize it.*

Some of the ideals are factually true. The Forerunners were sophisticated above all other empires and powerful almost beyond measure. Our ecumene spanned three million fertile worlds. We had achieved the greatest heights of technology and physical knowledge, at least since the time of the Precursors, who, some say, shaped us in their image, and rewarded that image with their breath.

The tugging threads of this part of the tale—the first of three—are journey, daring, betrayal, and fate.

My fate, the fate of a foolish Forerunner, was joined one night with the fates of two humans and the long world-line of a great military leader . . . that night on which I put in motion the circumstances that triggered the final wave of the hideous Flood.

So be this tale told, so be the telling true.

ONE

THE BOAT'S CREW banked the fires, disengaged the steam engine, and raised the calliope horn from the water. The bubbling clockwork song died out with a series of clicks and sad groans; it hadn't been working well to begin with.

Twenty kilometers away, the central peak of Djamonkin Crater rose through blue-gray haze, its tip outlined in ruddy gold by the last of the setting sun. A single brilliant moon rose bright and cold behind our boat. The crater's inland lake rippled around the hull in ways no tide or wind had ever moved water. Under the swells and whorls, sparkling with reflected sunset and moon, pale merse twisted and bobbed like the lilies in my mother's pond. These lilies, however, weren't passive flowers, but sleeping krakens growing in the shallows on thick stalks. Ten meters wide, their thickened, muscular edges were rimmed with black teeth the length of my forearm.

We sailed over a garden of clannish, self-cloning monsters. They covered the entire flooded floor of the crater, skulking just below the surface and very defensive of their territory. Only boats that sang the lulling song the merse used to keep peace among themselves could cross these waters unmolested. And now it seemed our tunes were out of date.

The young human I knew as Chakas crossed the deck, clutching his palm-frond hat and shaking his head. We stood side by side and stared out over the rail, watching the merse writhe and churn. Chakas—bronze-skinned, practically hairless, and totally unlike the bestial image of humans my tutors had impressed upon me—shook his head in dismay. "They swear they're using the newest songs," he murmured. "We shouldn't move until they figure it out."

I eyed the crew on the bow, engaged in whispered argument. "You assured me they were the best," I reminded him.

He regarded me with eyes like polished onyx and swept his hand through a thick thatch of black hair that hung in back to his neck, cut perfectly square. "My father knew their fathers."

"You trust your father?" I asked.

"Of course," he said. "Don't you?"

"I haven't seen my real father in three years," I said.

"Is that sad, for you?" the young human asked.

"He sent me *there*." I pointed to a bright russet point in the black sky. "To learn discipline."

"Shh-*shhaa*!" The Florian—a smaller variety of human, half Chakas's height—scampered from the stern on bare feet to join us. I had never known a species to vary so widely yet maintain such an even level of intelligence. His voice was soft and sweet, and he made delicate signs with his fingers. In his excitement, he spoke too rapidly for me to understand.

Chakas interpreted. "He says you need to take off your armor. It's upsetting the merse."

At first, this was not a welcome suggestion. Forerunners of all rates wear body-assist armor through much of their lives. The armor protects us both physically and medically. In emergencies, it can suspend a Forerunner until rescue, and even provide nourishment for a time. It allows mature Forerunners to connect to the Domain, from which all Forerunner knowledge can flow. Armor is one of the main reasons that Forerunners live so long. It can also act as friend and advisor.

I consulted with my ancilla, the armor's disembodied intelligence and memory—a small bluish figure in the back of my thoughts.

"This was anticipated," she told me. "Electrical and magnetic fields, other than those generated by the planet's natural dynamics, drive these organisms into splashing ıury. That is why the boat is powered by a primitive steam engine."

She assured me that the armor would be of no value to humans, and that at any rate she could guard against its misuse. The rest of the crew watched with interest. I sensed this might be a sore point. The armor would power down, of course, once I removed it. For all our sakes, I would have to go naked, or nearly so. I halfway managed to convince myself this could only enhance the adventure.

The Florian set to work weaving me a pair of sandals from reeds used to plug leaks.

———

Of all my father's children, I was the most incorrigible. In itself this was not an ill mark or even unusual. Manipulars of promise often show early rebellion—the stamp in raw metal from which the discipline of a full rate is honed and shaped.

But I exceeded even my father's ample patience; I refused to learn and advance along any of the proper Forerunner curves: intensive training, bestowal to my rate, mutation to my next form, and finally, espousal to a nascent triad . . . where I would climb to the zenith of maturity.

None of that attracted me. I was more far interested in adventure and the treasures of the past. Historic glory shined so much brighter in my eyes; the present seemed empty.

And so at the end of my sixth year, frustrated beyond endurance by my stubbornness, my father traded me to another family, in another part of the galaxy, far from the Orion complex where my peoples were born.

For the last three years, the system of eight planets around a minor yellow star—and in particular, the fourth, a dry, reddish desert world called Edom—became my home. Call it exile. I called it escape. I knew my destiny lay elsewhere.

When I arrived on Edom, my swap-father, following tradition, equipped my armor with one of his own ancillas to educate me to the ways of my new family. At first I thought this new ancilla would be the most obvious face of my indoctrination—just another shackle in my prison, harsh and unsympathetic. But she soon proved something else entirely, unlike any ancilla I had ever experienced.

During my long periods of tutoring and regimented exercise, she drew me out, traced my rough rebellion back to its roots—but also showed me my new world and new family in the clear light of unbiased reason.

"You are a Builder sent to live among Miners," she told me. "Miners are rated below Builders, but they are sensible, proud and strong. Miners know the raw, inner ways of worlds. Respect them, and they will treat you well, teach you what they know, and return you to your family with all the discipline and skills a Manipular needs to advance."

After two years of generally impeccable service, guiding my reeducation while at the same time relieving my stultifying existence with a certain dry wit, she came to discern a pattern in my questions. Her response was unexpected.

The first sign of my ancilla's strange favor was her opening of my swap-family's archives. Ancillas are charged with the maintenance of all records and libraries, to ease access to any information a member of the family might need, however ancient and obscure. "Miners, you know, delve deep. Treasure, as you call it, is frequently in their way. They recover, record, settle the matter with the proper authorities . . . and move on. They are not curious, but their records are sometimes *very* curious."

I spent happy hours studying the old records, and learned much more about Precursor remnants, as well as the archaeology of Forerunner history.

Here it was that I picked up hints of lore discouraged or forgotten elsewhere—not always in actual evidence, but deduced from this and that odd fact.

And in that next year, my ancilla measured and judged me.

One dry and dusty day, as I climbed the gentle slope of Edom's largest volcano, imagining that in the vast caldera was hidden some great secret that would redeem me in the eyes of my family and justify my existence—my common state of pointless fugue—she broke ancilla code in a shocking manner.

She confessed that she had once, a thousand years ago, been part of the retinue of the Librarian. Of course, I knew about the greatest Lifeworker of all. I wasn't completely ignorant. Lifeworkers—experts on living things and medicine—rank below both Builders and Miners, but just above Warriors. And the highest rank of Lifeworker is Life-shaper. The Librarian was one of just three Lifeworkers ever honored with that rank.

The ancilla's memory of her time with the Librarian had supposedly been expunged when the Librarian's foundation traded her to my swap-family, as part of a general cultural exchange; but now, fully reawakened to her past, it seemed she was prepared to conspire with me.

She told me: "There is a world just a few hours' journey from Edom where you might find what you seek. Nine thousand years ago, the Librarian established a research station in this system. It is still a topic of discussion among the Miners, who of course disapprove. Life is ever so much more slippery than rocks and gases."

This station was located on the system's third planet, known as Erde-Tyrene: a forsaken place, obscure, sequestered, and both the origin and final repository of the last of a degraded species called *human*.

My ancilla's motives, it seemed, were even more deviant than my own. Every few months, a craft lifted away from Edom to carry supplies downstar to Erde-Tyrene. She did not precisely inform me of what I would find there, but through hints and clues led me to decide it was major.

With her help, I made my way through the labyrinthine hallways and tunnels to the shipping platform, smuggled myself onto the cramped craft, reset the codes to conceal my extra mass—and lifted away to Erde-Tyrene.

I was now much more than just a rebellious Manipular.

I had become a hijacker, a pirate . . . And was astonished at how easy it was! Too easy, perhaps.

Still, I could not believe an ancilla would lead a Forerunner into a trap. That was contrary to their design, their programming—everything about their nature. Ancillas serve their masters faithfully at all times.

What I could not foretell was that I was not her master, and never had been.

———

I stripped down reluctantly, unwinding the torso spiral, then the shoulder and arm guards, and finally the leg guards and boots. The thin pale fuzz on my arms and legs prickled in the breeze. My neck and ears suddenly itched. Then, *everything* itched, and I had to force myself to ignore it.

The armor assumed a loose mold of my body as it slumped to the deck. I wondered if the ancilla would now go dormant, or whether she would continue with her own inner processes. This was the first time I had been without her guidance in three years.

"Good," Chakas said. "The crew will keep it safe for you."

"I'm sure they will," I said.

Chakas and the little Florian—in their own language, specimens, respectively, of cha*manune* and ha*manune*—scrambled to the bow, where they joined the five crew members already there and argued in low whispers. Anything louder and the merse might attack whether or not the boat sang the proper song. Merse hated many things, but they especially hated excess noise. After storms, it was said they were upset for days, and passage over the inland sea became impossible.

Chakas returned, shaking his head. "They're going to try pumping out some songs from three moons past," he said. "Merse rarely invent new tunes. It's a kind of cycle."

With a sharp lurch, the boat spun about on its mast axis. I dropped to the deck and lay beside my armor. I had paid the humans well. Chakas had heard strange tales of ancient forbidden zones and secret structures within Djamonkin Crater.

My researches among the Miners' files had led me to believe there was a decent chance there was real treasure on Erde-Tyrene, perhaps the most sought-after treasure of all, the Organon—the device which could reactivate all Precursor artifacts. It had all seemed to fit together—until now. Where had I been guided wrong?

After a jaunt across sixty light-years and a second, trivial journey of a hundred million kilometers, I might never get any closer to my ultimate goal.

Merse broke the surface on our starboard side, flexing gray-purple fans and shedding ribbons of water. I could hear long black teeth gnawing at the wooden hull.

———

The journey from Edom to Erde-Tyrene took a long and boring forty-eight hours, entry into slipspace being deemed unnecessary for a routine supply trip across so short a distance.

My first live view of the planet, through the open port of the supply craft, revealed a glowing, jewel-like orb of greens and browns and deep blues. Much of the northern hemisphere was lost in cloud and glacier. The third planet was passing through a period of deep cooling and expanding ice floes. Compared with Edom, long past its best eon, Erde-Tyrene was a neglected paradise.

Certainly wasted on humans. I queried my ancilla about the truth of their origins. She responded that to the best of Forerunner research, humans had indeed first arisen on Erde-Tyrene, but over fifty thousand years ago had moved their interstellar civilization outward along the galactic arm, perhaps to flee early Forerunner control. Records from those ages were sparse.

The supply ship landed at the main research station north of Marontik, the largest human community. The station was automated and empty but for a family of lemurs, who had set up residence in a long-abandoned barracks. It seemed the rest of civilization had forgotten about this place. I was the only Forerunner on the planet, and that was fine with me.

I set out on foot across the last stretch of grassland and prairie and arrived at midday on the trash-heaped outskirts of the city.

Marontik, located at the confluence of two great rivers, was hardly a city at all by Forerunner standards. Wooden shacks and mud huts, some three or four stories tall, were arranged on either side of alleys branching into other alleys, winding in no particular direction. This crowded collection of primitive hovels spread over dozens of square kilometers. It would have been easy for a young Forerunner to become lost, but my ancilla guided me with unerring skill.

I wandered the streets for several hours, a minor curiosity to the inhabitants but no more. I passed a doorway opening to underground passages from which rose noxious smells. Urchins in rags poured up through the door and surrounded me, chanting, "There are parts of Marontik only for the eyes of such a one . . . The dead in review! Ancient queens and kings preserved in rum and honey! They have waited centuries for you!"

Though that gave me a vague tingle, I ignored the urchins. They went away after a time, and never did I feel in danger. It seemed these rudely dressed, unkempt, shambling beings had some experience of Forerunners but little respect. This did not bother my ancilla. Here, she said, the genetically impressed rules of the Librarian included docility toward Forerunners, wariness toward strangers, and discretion in all else.

The sky over Marontik was frequented by primitive airships of all sizes and colors, some truly horrendous in their pretension—dozens of corded red, green, and blue hot-air balloons tied together, from which hung great platforms of woven river reed, crowded with merchants, travelers, and spectators as well as lower beasts destined, I assumed, to become food. Humans ate meat.

The balloon platforms provided a regular, dizzying means of conveyance—and so, of course, my ancilla instructed me to pay for passage to the center of the city. When I pointed out I had no scrip, she guided me to a stash hidden in a nearby substation, hundreds of years old but unmolested by the humans.

I waited at an elevated platform and paid the fare to a skeptical agent, who looked over the ancient scrip with disdain. His narrow face and darting, beady eyes were overshadowed by a tall cylindrical hat made of fur. Only after chattering with a colleague hidden in a wicker cage did he accept my payment and allow me to board the next creaking, swaying, lighter-than-air conveyance.

The trip took an hour. The balloon platform arrived at city center as night fell. Lanterns were lit throughout the devious streets. Long shadows loomed. I was surrounded by anthropoid rankness.

In Marontik's largest market, my ancilla informed me, there had in years past been a collective of human guides, some of whom might still know the routes to the centers of local legend. Soon, the humans would all be asleep—a condition with which I had had little experience—so we had to hurry. "If it's adventure you seek," she said, "here is where you are most likely to find it—yet most likely to survive the experience."

In a rambling sloven of alleys, which served both as

walkways and gutters, I found the ancient river-stone store-front of the matriarch of guides. Half-hidden in shadows, illuminated by a single candle dangling from a hook in the wattle, an enormously fat female, tented in a loose robe of white fabric, embarrassingly sheer, regarded me with open suspicion. After making a few offers I found offensive, in-cluding a tour of underground catacombs filled with human dead, she took the last of my scrip and passed me through a rag-hung arch to a young member of the guild who, she said, might be able to help.

"There *is* treasure on Erde-Tyrene, young Forerunner," she added in a dulcet baritone, "as you have no doubt de-duced through careful research. And I have *just* the boy for you."

It was here, in the humid shadows of a reed shack, that I met Chakas. My first impression of the bronze-skinned, half-naked human, with his greasy shock of black hair, was not favorable. He kept looking at me, as if we had met before—or perhaps he was seeking a weak spot in my armor. "I love solving mysteries," Chakas said. "I, too, seek lost trea-sure. It is my passion! We will be friends, no?"

I knew that humans, as lower beings, were deceitful and tricky. Still, I had few choices. My resources were at their limit. A few hours later, he led me through pitch-black streets to another neighborhood, filled with ha*manune*, and intro-duced me to his partner, a gray-muzzled Florian. Sur-rounded by a mob of diminutive youngsters and two stooped, elderly females—I think—the Florian was cheek-stuffing the last of a supper of fruit and plates of pounded, shapeless raw meat.

The Florian said that his ancestors had once frequented a ring-shaped island at the center of a great, flooded crater. They called it Djamonkin Augh—Big Man's Water. There, he said, a marvelous site still hid many antiquities.

"From the Precursors?" I asked.

"Who are they?"

"Ancient masters," I said. "Before the Forerunners."

"Maybe. Very old." The Florian looked me over shrewdly, then patted his lips with the furry back of his hand.

"The Organon?" I asked.

Neither Chakas nor the Florian were familiar with that name, but did not dismiss the possibility.

———

The crew separated and opened the hatch on the calliope's box. The ha*manune*—his head barely level with my waist— waggled his raised hands. With the help of his small, dexterous fingers, they inserted a different wooden placket set with tiny horn pegs, then reset the mechanism of plucked and bowed gut strings, cranked out the horn that broadcast the music into the water, attached the steam tube, and rewound the spring that powered it all.

Chakas walked aft, still worried. "Music soothes the savage flowers," the cha*manune* said, callused finger to lip. "We wait now and watch."

The Florian ran back to squat beside us. He looped a

hand around his friend's bare ankles. The little man's brain-case held less than a third the volume of young Chakas's, and yet I had trouble deciding who was more clever—or more truthful.

———

In my quest for treasure, I had focused my studies on old Forerunner records, and what little I had learned about human history I did not feel comfortable revealing to my guides.

Ten thousand years ago, humans had fought a war against Forerunners—and lost. The centers of human civilization had been dismantled and the humans them-selves devolved and shattered into many forms, some said as punishment—but more likely because they were a natu-rally violent species.

The Librarian, for some reason, had espoused the hu-man cause. My ancilla explained that either as a form of penance, or at the Librarian's request—the records were vague—the Council had given her charge of Erde-Tyrene and she had moved the last humans there. Under her care, some of the humans had stubbornly reevolved. I couldn't tell whether that might be true or not. They all looked de-graded to me.

From that seed stock, over nine thousand years, more than twenty varieties of humans had migrated and formed communities around this water-soaked world. Husky ocher and brown k'ta*manune* wandered the northern latitudes and skirted massive grinding sheets of ice. These dwellers in glacial shadows wrapped themselves in harsh woven fiber and fur. Not far from this inland crater sea, over an imposing range of mountains, skinny, lithe b'asha*manune* scampered across equatorial grasslands and leaped into thorny trees to avoid predators. Some chose to build crude cities, as if struggling to reacquire past greatness—and failing miserably.

Because of strong similarities in our natural genetic structure, some Forerunner sages thought humans might be a brethren species, also shaped and given breath by the Precursors. It was possible the Librarian was intent on testing those theories.

Very shortly, evolved or not, there might soon be seven fewer humans in the Librarian's collection—and one less Forerunner.

———

We sat near the widest spot in the deck, away from the low rail. Chakas formed his fingers into a cradle, then swapped them in an exercise he adamantly refused to teach me. His wry smile was so like that of a Forerunner child. The little Florian watched us with some amusement.

The merse made a sad, damp whistling noise and squirted jets of water. Their spray smelled like rotted seaweed. Looked at from afar, the creatures that surrounded our boat were laughably simple, little more advanced than the comb jellies that swam in the glassy walls of my swap-father's palace, on that russet spot a hundred million kilometers away. And yet, they sang to each other—spoke in soft, musical murmurs through the long nights, then basked silent in the dappled sun as if sleeping.

On rare occasions, the crater ocean roiled with brief sea-merse wars, and shreds of glistening flesh washed up on far beaches for weeks. . . .

Maybe there was more to these blind krakens than a Manipular could judge. The Librarian might have had a hand in bringing them to Erde-Tyrene—to grow in Djamonkin Crater, where they also served her ends, perhaps by solving biological riddles in their own strange way, using their own genetic songs. . . .

Was I imagining it, or was the grinding beneath and the churn around us slowly subsiding?

The moon set. The stars were thick for a time. Then fog rolled back in, filling the crater bowl from brim to brim.

Chakas claimed he heard the gentle lap of waves on a beach. "The merse are quiet now, I think," he added hopefully.

I got up to retrieve my armor, but a bulky, strong-looking human blocked my way, and Chakas shook his head.

The crew decided it might be time to drop the screw and engage the engine. Again we made forward progress. I couldn't see much beyond the rail except little bursts of phosphorescence. The water, what little I could see of it, appeared calm.

Chakas and the Florian murmured human prayers. The Florian ended his prayers with a short, sweet melody, like birdsong. Had I been faithful to my upbringing, I would even now be contemplating the dictates of the Mantle, silently repeating the Twelve Laws of Making and Moving, allowing my muscles to flex according to those rhythms until I swayed like a sapling. . . .

But here I was, following false hopes, associating with the discredited and the low . . . And I might yet swim in a toothy sea, my undeveloped body shredded by mindless monsters.

Or walk on a deserted beach around a sacred island in the middle of an old asteroid crater, flooded ages ago with cold water so pure it dried without residue.

Challenge, mystery, unbridled danger and beauty. It was all worth whatever shame I might be wise enough to feel.

As a Manipular, I still resembled Chakas more than my father. I could still smile but thought it beneath me. Despite everything, in my thoughts I could not help visualizing myself as taller, broader, stronger—like my father, with his long, pale face, crown hair and nape fur bleached white with lilac roots, fingers capable of surrounding a shrop melon . . . and strong enough to smash its tough shell to pulp.

This was my contradiction: I mistrusted everything about my family and my people, yet still dreamed of mutating into a second-form—while keeping my youthful, independent attitude. Of course, it never seemed to happen that way.

The pilot strode aft with renewed confidence. "The merse think we're one of them. We should reach the ring island in less than a flare."

Humans counted time using waxy wicks tied with knots that flared when touched by an ascending flame. Even now, two of the crew were lighting lanterns with crude sticks.

———

In the fog, something big bumped the bow. I caught myself in mid-lurch and steadied against a wide, slow swing of the stern. Chakas jumped to his feet, grinning ear-to-ear. "That's our beach," he said.

The crew dropped a board onto the black sand. The Florian scampered ashore first. He danced on the beach and snapped his fingers.

"Shhh!" Chakas cautioned.

Again I tried to retrieve my armor, and again the bulky crewmember blocked my way. Two others approached slowly, hands out, and guided me toward Chakas. He shrugged at my concern. "They fear that even from the beach, it might anger the merse."

I had little choice. They could kill me now, or I might die from some other cause later. We crossed the ramp through the fog. The crew stayed on the boat—and so did my armor. As soon as we were disembarked, the boat backed water, swung about, and left us in the drizzle and darkness with nothing but three small bags of provisions—human food only, though edible enough if I held my nose.

"They'll be back in three days," Chakas said. "Plenty of time to search the island."

When the boat was gone and we could no longer hear the chugging pump of its song, the Florian danced some more. Clearly, he was ecstatic to walk once again on the ring island of Djamonkin Augh. "Island hides all!" he said, then chittered a rolling laugh and pointed at Chakas. "Boy knows nothing. Look for treasure and *die*, unless you go where I go."

The Florian pushed out expressive rose-colored lips and raised his hands above his head, thumb and forefinger circled.

Chakas seemed unaffected by the Florian's judgment. "He's right. I know nothing about this place."

I was too relieved to have escaped the merse to feel much irritation. I had known humans could not be trusted; they were degraded forms, no doubt about it. But something felt authentically strange about this beach, this island. . . . My hopes refused to wink out.

We walked inland a few meters and sat on a rock, shivering in the damp and cold.

"First, tell us why you're *really* here," Chakas said. "Tell us about Forerunners and Precursors."

In the dark, I could see nothing above the palms, and beyond the beach, nothing other than a faint glow from the breaking wavelets. "Precursors were powerful. They drew lines across many skies. Some say that long ago they shaped Forerunners in their image."

Even the name we gave ourselves, "Forerunner," implied a fleeting, impermanent place in the Mantle—accepting that we were but a stage in the stewardship of Living Time. That others would come after us. Other—and better.

"And us?" the Florian asked. "Ha*manune* and cha*manune?*"

I shook my head, unwilling to encourage this story—or believe it.

"I'm here to learn why the Precursors went away," I continued, "how we might have offended them . . . and just possibly find the center of their power, their might, their intelligence."

"Oh," Chakas said. "Are you here to discover a great gift and please your father?"

"I'm here to learn."

"Something to prove you're not a fool. Hm." Chakas opened the bag and handed out small rolls of dense, black bread made with fish oil. I ate but enjoyed none of it. All my life, others had judged me to be a fool, but it stung when degraded animals reached the same conclusion.

I flicked a pebble toward the darkness. "When do we start looking?"

"Too dark. First, start a fire," the Florian insisted.

We gathered branches and half-decayed palm chunks

and built a fire. Chakas seemed to doze off. Then he awoke and grinned at me. He yawned and stretched and looked out over the ocean. "Forerunners never sleep," he observed.

That was true enough—as long as we wore armor.

"Nights are long for you, no?" the Florian asked. He had rolled his fish-oil bread into round little balls and placed them in lines on the smoothness of a glassy black rock. Now he plucked them up and, one by one, popped them into his mouth, smacking his broad lips.

"Better that way?" I asked.

He made a face. "Fish bread stinks," he replied. "Fruit flour is best."

The fog had lifted but overcast still lay over the entire crater. Dawn was not long off. I lay on my back and looked up at the graying sky, at peace for the first time I could remember. I was a fool, I had betrayed my Maniple, but I was at peace. I was doing what I had always dreamed I would do.

"*Daowa-maad*," I said. Both humans lifted their eyebrows—it made them look like brothers. *Daowa-maad* was a human term for the roll and tug of the universe. It actually translated rather neatly into Forerunner Builder-speak: "*You fall as your stresses crack you.*"

"You know about that?" Chakas asked.

"My ancilla taught me."

"That's the voice in his clothes," Chakas told the Florian, all-wise. "A female."

"Is she pretty?" the little one asked.

"Not your type," I said.

The Florian finished the last rounded ball of fish-oil bread and made another remarkable face. So many expressive muscles. "*Daowa-maad.* We hunt, we grow, we live. Life is simple—we do." He poked Chakas. "I begin to like this Forerunner. Tell him *all* of my names."

Chakas took a deep breath. "The ha*manune* sitting right next to you, whose breath smells of fish oil and stale bread, his family name is *Day-Chaser.* His personal name is *Morning Riser.* His long name is *Day-Chaser Makes Paths Long-stretch Morning Riser.* Long name for a short fellow. He likes to be called Riser. There. It is done."

"All good, all true," Riser said, satisfied. "My grandfathers built walls here to protect and guide us."

"You will see after sunup. Now—too dark. Good time to learn names. What's *your* real name, young Forerunner?"

For a Forerunner to reveal his actual *using* name to anyone outside the Maniple . . . and to humans, at that . . . Delicious. A perfect thumb-crook to my family.

"*Bornstellar,*" I said. "*Bornstellar Makes Eternal Lasting, Form Zero, Manipular untried.*"

"A mouthful," Riser said. He opened his eyes wide, leaned in, and made that full-mouth, lip-curled, leering grin that indicated vast Florian amusement. "But it has a good rolling sound."

I leaned back. I was getting more and more used to his fast, piping speech. "My mother calls me Born," I said.

"Short better," Riser said. "Born it is."

"Day is coming. Warmer soon, and bright," Chakas said. "Shuffle and scuff. Don't want anyone to find tracks."

I suspected that if anyone from Edom was searching for me, or if the Librarian's watchers decided to check from orbit, from a drone, or with a direct flyover, they would find us no matter how we hid our tracks. I didn't say anything to my companions, however. In my short time on Erde-Tyrene I had already learned an important truth—that among the poor, the downtrodden, and the desperate, foolish bravery is to be savored.

I was obviously foolish, but, apparently, my two companions now believed I might be brave.

We swept away our tracks using a palm frond from the shoreline vegetation. "How far to the center of the island?" I asked.

"Long legs, shorter trip," Riser said. "Fruit along the way. Don't eat. Gives you the scoots. Save it all for me."

"It'll be fine," Chakas confided to me. "If he leaves any for us."

"We're not going to the mountain," Riser said. He pushed through the vegetation. "No need to cross inner lake. A maze, some fog, a spiral, then a jump or two. My grandfather used to live here, before there was water."

Curiouser and curiouser. I knew for a fact—again, from my ancilla—that the crater had been flooded and the lake planted with merse a thousand years ago. "How old *are* you?" I asked.

Riser said, "Two hundred years."

"For his people, just a youngster," Chakas said, then made a clicking sound with tongue and cheeks. "Little folk, long lives, longer memories."

The Florian whickered. "My family grew up on islands everywhere. We made walls. My mother came from here before she met my father, and she told him, and he told me, click-song and stare-whistle. That's how we'll know the maze."

"Click-song?"

"You are privileged," Chakas said. "Ha*manune* do not often reveal these truths to outsiders."

"If they are true," I said.

Neither took offense. The humans I had met seemed remarkably thick-skinned. Or more likely, the pronouncements of a Forerunner meant little on a world they thought was theirs.

Daylight finally arrived, and swiftly. The sky went from mellow orange to pink to blue in a few minutes. From the short jungle came no sound, not even the rustling of leaves.

I had experienced few islands in my short existence, but had never known any of them to be as quiet as a tomb.

TWO

FOLLOWED THE little human's persistent, quick pace through low brush and past the naked, scaly trunks of many palms, topped with bristling, branching crowns. The undergrowth was not thick but it was regular—too regular. The pathways, if any, were invisible to me.

Chakas followed a few steps behind, wearing a perpetual light smile, as if preparing to unleash some joke upon us both. I had not yet learned how to read human expressions with confidence. Grinning might mean mild amusement. It might also be a prelude to aggression.

The air was humid, the sun high, and our water—carried in tubes made from a kind of thick-stemmed grass—was warm. It was also running out. The ha*manune* passed one of the last tubes around. Forerunners can't catch human diseases—or any diseases, if they wear armor—but only reluctantly did I share the warm liquid.

My good mood faded. Something odd and unexpected was in the air. . . . Without my armor, I was discovering instincts I didn't know I could trust. Old talents, old sensitivities, hidden until now by technology.

We paused. The Florian noticed my growing irritation. "Make hat," he told Chakas, wiggling his fingers. "Forerunner has hair like glass. Sun burns his head."

Chakas looked up, shading his eyes, and nodded. He glanced at me, sizing up my head, before shinnying up a naked trunk. Halfway, he husked off a dried branch and tossed it down.

The little one chuffed.

I watched Chakas finish his inchworm ascent. At the top, he pulled a knife from his rope belt and hacked loose a green branch, also letting it drop. Then he shinnied back down, leaping the last half and landing on bent legs with a wide-armed flourish. In triumph, he raised his hand to his mouth and lipped a musical blatting sound.

We paused in the shadow of the tree while he wove my head cover. Forerunners are fond of hats—each form, rate, and Maniple has their own ceremonial designs, worn only on special occasions. On one day during Grand Star Season, however, all wear the same style of headgear. Our hats were much more dignified and lovely than what Chakas finally handed me. Still, I placed it on my head—and found that it fit.

Chakas put his hands on his hips and surveyed me with critical mien. "Good," he judged.

We continued on for hours until we came to a low wall assembled from precisely cut lava stones. The wall pushed between the trees. From above, it would have ascribed a sinuous curve like a serpent crawling through the jungle.

Riser sat on the wall, crossed his legs, and chewed on a green blade left over from my hat. His head turned slowly, large brown eyes shifting right and left, and he pushed out his lips. The ha*manune* had no chin—nothing at all like the prominent feature that made Chakas bear a resemblance to my kind. But the little human more than made up for this with his elegant, mobile lips.

"Old ones did this, older than grandfather," he said, patting the stones. He tossed aside the green shred, then stood and balanced on the wall, arms out. "You follow. Only ha*manune* walk on top."

Riser ran along the top. Chakas and I followed on either side, pushing aside brush and avoiding the occasional pugnacious land crustaceans that stood aside for nobody, waving their powerful claws. I almost walked through them . . . until I remembered I had no armor. Those claws could take off a part of my foot. How vulnerable I was to everything! The excitement of adventure was starting to wear thin. The two humans had done nothing overtly threatening, but how long could I count on that?

We had a tough time keeping up with the little Florian.

A few hundred meters later, the wall branched. Riser paused at the juncture to study the situation. He swung his arm right. The chase resumed. Through thicker trees on our left, I saw the inland beach. We had crossed the ring. Beyond loomed the central peak, surrounded by the ring island's inner lake, the whole shaping a kind of archery target within the crater.

I wondered if merse lived in those waters as well.

My mind wandered. Perhaps a powerful, ancient Precursor vessel had crashed down from space, and the central peak was an effect of waves of molten rock lapping inward before solidifying. I wished now I had spent more time listening to my swap-father's tales of how planets formed and changed, but I didn't share his Miner's fascination with tectonics, except where it might conceal or reveal treasure.

Some Precursor artifacts were old enough to be cycled again and again through hundreds of millions of years, dragged down with subsumed crust and pushed up again through volcanoes or vents. Indestructible . . . Fascinating. And for now, useless.

Chakas was bold enough to poke me. I flinched away. "You wouldn't do that if I still had my armor," I said.

His teeth gleamed. Was he becoming more aggressive, or was this just his way of showing affection? I had no way of judging.

"Over here," Riser called from where he had run ahead. We broke through a particularly dense patch of twiggy green trees with bright red trunks and branches. The Florian was waiting for us where the long, low wall came to an abrupt end. Beyond lay a flat white plain, the inner lake on one side, its beach forming a line of black and gray, and jungle on the other. Once again the central peak was revealed, naked of vegetation, like a dead black thumb thrusting from the pale greenish blue center of the target.

"Okay, young Forerunner," Chakas said, coming up behind me. I turned swiftly, believing for a moment he was about to knife me. But no—the bronze-colored human simply pointed across the white waste. "You asked. We brought you here. Your fault, not ours. Remember that."

"There's *nothing* here," I said, looking across the flats. Heat waves broke the outline of the far side of the waste into velvety shimmers.

"Look again," Riser suggested.

At the base of the shimmers, what seemed like more water was in fact refracted sky. But through the shimmers, I thought I saw a line of large, hulking apes . . . great white apes, no doubt from the low end of the Librarian's folly. They came and went with the mirage—and then steadied, not alive but frozen: carved from stone and left to stand out on the flats like pieces on a game board.

A cooling wind whispered outward from the black peak, brushing away the rising heat, and the ape figures vanished.

Not a mirage after all. Something more deceptive.

I bent to pick up a bit of the soil. Coral and white sand

mixed with fine hard volcanic ash. The whole area smelled faintly of ancient fire.

I looked between the human guides, speechless.

"Walk," Riser suggested.

The walk to the center of the white waste took longer than I expected, but soon enough it dawned on me that we were crossing a baffler—a place protected by geometric distortions—or at the very least a dazzler, protected by delusions.

A Forerunner had apparently long ago decided the waste should be hidden from curious eyes. I shaded my eyes and looked up at the blue lid of sky. That meant it probably couldn't be seen from above, either.

Minutes passed into an hour. We couldn't keep to a straight line. We were most likely walking in circles. Still we kept on. My feet, shod in ill-fitting human sandals, crunched lightly. Sharp grains dug at my sensitive soles and crept between my toes.

The two humans showed great patience and did not complain. Chakas lifted the ha*manune* to his shoulders when it became apparent the little one's bare feet were suffering from the hot sand.

The last of our water tubes gave out. Riser tossed it aside with a resigned whicker, then looked back at me, covering and uncovering his eyes with one hand. I thought this was a sign of embarrassment, but he did it again, then gave me a stern look.

Chakas explained. "He wants you to blinker yourself. It helps."

I covered my eyes.

"Keep walking," Chakas said. "If you stop, we might lose you."

I couldn't help lifting my hands to peek. "Don't look. Walk *blind*," Riser insisted.

"We're walking in circles," I warned.

"*Such* circles!" Riser enthused.

The sun was affecting them. I felt like I was in charge of a pair of heat-stroked humans.

"Left!" Chakas shouted. "Left, *now*!"

I hesitated, lifted my hands, and saw my two guides— several paces ahead of me—abruptly vanish, as if swallowed by empty air. They had abandoned me in the middle of the flat, surrounded by white sand and distant jungle. Off to my right rose a lumpy blur that might or might not be the central peak.

I braced myself for the worst. Without armor, without water, I'd die out here in days.

Chakas reappeared on my left. He took my arm—I shook him loose instantly—and he stood back like a flattened cutout, his edges loose and seeming to flap. Blinking did not clear this apparition. "Suit yourself," he said. "Turn left, or go home. If you can find your way out of here."

Then he vanished again.

I slowly turned left, took a step . . . and felt my entire

body shiver. I now stood on a low black walkway curving to the right and then back to the left, surrounded on both sides by gritty white sand. So it *had* been a baffler and not a dazzler. A Forerunner had hidden this place long ago, using outdated technology—as if expecting that the old tech would be penetrated by clever, persistent humans.

Ahead, clearly visible now, not white apes but twelve midsize Forerunner fighting suits, arranged in a wide oval about a hundred meters across the long axis. I had spent long hours studying old weapons and ships, to better distinguish them from more interesting finds. Swallowing back disappointment, I recognized them as war sphinxes—flown into battle by Warrior-Servants in ages past but now found only in museums. Antiques, to be sure, and possibly still active and powerful—but of no interest to me whatsoever. "Is that all you have to show me?" I asked, indignant.

Chakas and Riser kept out of reach, posing in postures of reverence, as if engaged in prayer. Odd. Humans praying to antique weapons?

I turned my eyes back to the frozen circle. Each war sphinx was ten meters high and twenty long—larger than contemporary Forerunner suits that served the same function. An elongated tail contained lift and power, and from that, at the front, rose a thick, rounded torso. Atop the torso, smoothly integrated with the overall curvilinear design, perched an abstract head with a stubborn, haughty face—a command cabin.

I took a step forward, deciding whether to cross the remaining stretch of flat between the walkway and the white "giants" arranged around the center of the waste.

Chakas lifted his crossed arms and sighed. "Riser, how long have these monsters been here?"

"Long time," Riser said. "Before grandfather flew away to polish the moon."

"He means, more than a thousand years," Chakas interpreted. "You read old Forerunner writing?" he asked me.

"Some," I said.

"This place doesn't like humans," Riser said. He pulled back his lips and shook his head vigorously. "But grandfather caught bees in a basket. . . ."

"You're telling him the *secret*?" Chakas asked in dismay.

"Yes," Riser said. "He's not smart, but he's good."

"How can you tell?"

Riser showed his teeth and shook his head vigorously. "Grandfather put bees in a big basket. When they buzz loud, stop and wave the basket this way, then that. When they stop buzzing, go that way."

"You mean, there are markers—infrared markers?" I asked.

"What you say," Riser agreed with a pout. "Bees know. If you live, you drop rocks so others can follow . . . as far as you make it."

Now that I knew what to look for, I saw—through the dazzle—that there were indeed broken, veering lines of small pebbles marking the otherwise smooth white sand.

Riser guided us along this jagged path, pausing now and

then to chitter to himself, until we stood just a few meters from the nearest sphinx. I paused in its shadow, then leaned over and reached out to touch the high, white surface, pitted with centuries of battle debris and stardust. No response. Inert.

Towering over me, the scowling features were still impressive. "They're dead," I said.

Riser's voice took on a tone of some reverence. "They sing," he said. "Grandfather heard."

I drew my hand back.

"He said these are trophies from war. Important to old, big guy. Somebody put them here to guard, watch, wait."

"Which war, I wonder?" Chakas asked, and looked at me as if I might know.

I *did* know. Or strongly suspected. The sphinxes were about the right age to be from the human-Forerunner wars, ten thousand years or so. But I still did not feel comfortable discussing this with my guides.

Riser left the walkway and walked carefully around the fighting unit. I went next, observing the smooth points of the suit's forked tail, the gaping tunnels on each fork leading, no doubt, to thrusters. There were no visible guidance points. On the opposite side, I noticed the outlines of retracted manipulators and folded shields.

"Locked down for thousands of years," I said. "I doubt they're worth anything."

"Not to me," Riser said, looking up at the younger, taller human with pouched lips.

"To *him*, maybe," Chakas said softly, waving at the center of the oval—an empty stretch of distorted sand. "Or *her*."

"Him or her?" I asked.

"Who chose you? Who guided you?" Chakas asked.

"Do you mean the *Librarian*?" I asked.

"She comes to us when we're born," Chakas said, his face dark with indignation and something more. "She watches over us as we grow, knows good and bad. She joys at our triumphs and sorrows at our passing. We all feel her presence."

"We all do," Riser affirmed. "We've been waiting for just the right time, and just the right fool."

No doubt under her protection, these humans had grown arrogant and presuming. But there was nothing I could do. I needed them. "She's out there?" I asked, pointing at the central peak.

"We never see her," Chakas said. "We don't know where she is. But she sent you, I'm sure of that."

My ancilla. They were more right than they could possibly know. "She must be a great power indeed, to arrange all this," I said. But my voice lacked conviction.

"Luck is her *way*," Chakas said.

Once again, old Forerunners were conspiring to guide my life.

Riser bent and waved his hand over what appeared to be an empty span of sand. This motion pushed aside a low mist, revealing for a moment a single large, flat lump of black lava. "Good for walls."

We stepped over the rock onto the central oval bordered

by the sphinxes. Suddenly, I felt a chill—an awareness that I was on a space sacred not to humans, but to some other power. Something great and old was nearby—a Forerunner, of that I was sure—but of what rate? Given the sphinxes, a Warrior-Servant seemed most likely.

But how old?

From the human wars. Ten thousand years ago.

"Don't like it here," Riser said. "Not brave like grandfather. You go on. I stay."

"Follow the pebbles and the rocks," Chakas said quietly. "Where the rocks stop, no human has ever stepped—and lived. What needs to be done, I can't do—nor can Riser." The young human was sweating, his eyes unfocused.

The Forerunner universe has a rich history of impossibilities that became truth. I considered myself a pragmatist, a realist, and found most such stories unsatisfying, frustrating, but never frightening. Now I was not only irritated, I was frightened—far more frightened than I had been on the boat.

When Forerunners die—usually by accident or, on rare occasions, during war—elaborate ceremonies are enacted before their remains are disposed of in fusion fires associated with the activities of their rates—a melting torch or planet cutter.

First, the Forerunner's last memories are abstracted from his armor, which preserves a few hours of the occupant's mental patterns. This reduced essence—a spectral snatch of personality, and not a whole being—is placed in a time-locked Durance. The body is then torched in a solemn ceremony attended only by close relations. A bit of plasma from the immolation is preserved by the appointed Master of the Mantle, who secures it along with the essence in the Durance.

The Durance is then given to the closest members of the dead Forerunner's family, who are charged with making sure that it is never abused. A Durance has a half-life of more than a million years. Families and rates are very protective of such places. In the treasure-hunting manuals I had read over the years, seekers are frequently warned to observe the signs and avoid such locations. Stumbling upon such a family Durance would definitely be considered sacrilege.

"This is a *disgraceful* world," I murmured. "No Forerunner would want to be buried here."

Chakas set his jaw and glared at me.

"It's all nonsense," I persisted. "No high rate would be buried here. Besides, what treasure would possibly be kept near a *grave*?" I continued, drawing my arrogant words to a stronger point. "And if you never met the Librarian, how . . ."

"When I first met you, I knew you were the one," Chakas said. "She comes to us at birth—"

"You said that."

"And tells us what we must do."

"How could she know what I'd look like?"

Chakas dismissed this. "We owe our lives to the Librarian, all of us."

A Lifeworker as powerful as the Librarian certainly had the means to impose a generations-long genetic command upon the objects of her study. Such a compulsion in past times would have been called a *geas*. Some students of the Mantle even believed that the Precursors had imposed a *geas* upon Forerunners. . . .

I was regretting more and more leaving my armor on the boat. I desperately needed to ask my ancilla how these humans would know to expect *me*. "What will you do if I go home now and give up this quest?"

Behind us, Riser snorted. Chakas smiled. This smile displayed not humor, nor a prelude to aggression, but contempt, I think. "If we are so weak and our world is so disgraceful, what are you afraid of?"

"Dead things," Riser said. "Forerunner dead. *Our* dead are friendly."

"Well, my ancestors can stay in the ground and I'd be happy enough," Chakas admitted.

Their words stung. With an abrupt hitch of confidence, and perhaps even a slight swagger, I began walking toward the center of the circle, parting the mist with swings of my foot, looking for the pebbles laid by earlier generations of ha*manune*. I must have seemed to be dancing my way toward the center, watched with sullen disapproval by the oval of inward-facing war sphinxes. Ancient weapons, ancient war. The sphinxes bore the scars of ancient battles, wars that no one cared about anymore.

I looked over my shoulder. Chakas leaned casually

against the prow of a sphinx. The machine's stern visage glowered over him like a disapproving priest.

It takes a great deal to provoke my people to war, but once provoked, the war is carried out ruthlessly, totally, by our Warrior-Servants. There is a kind of embarrassment in that slow rise to total fury that Forerunners do not like to acknowledge. It goes against the very Mantle that we so strive to inherit and hold, but to defy the Forerunners is after all to show contempt for the Mantle itself.

Perhaps that was the case here. Monuments of the past. Hidden passions, hidden violence, hidden shame. The shadows of forgotten history.

About twenty meters from the center of the circle, a sidewise kick of my sandaled foot revealed another low black wall. Beyond the wall there were no more pebbles—no more markers. I knelt to push my hand into the sand and sift it between my fingers. The sand flowed back, smooth again, unmarked. But in my palm, the sand had left a bizarre gift.

I turned it in my fingers.

A chip of bone.

My footprints had made no trace. The sand did not cling to my shoes or my feet, and not one grain stuck to my palms, my skin, anywhere. A sand pit built to withstand storms and intrusions, built for the ages, never to be erased, never to be completely forgotten.

Designed to kill any intruder who did not follow precise rituals. Anyone not wanted here.

Above me, something blotted out the sky. I had been

studying the sand so intently that I neither felt the ground effect nor heard the subtle rushing sound of a ship, until its shadow passed over and I jerked my gaze upward.

As I had feared, one of my swap-father's mining ships had found me. Reluctant to face the shame of losing me, my surrogate family had sent search parties throughout the system, looking for their ward.

I stood straight, waiting for the ship to descend, waiting to be lifted into the hold and swifted away before I even had an inkling why I was here. I spun about and looked out at the circle of war machines. Chakas and Riser were nowhere to be seen. They might have dropped below the mist, or run back through the dazzler, heading for the trees.

The mining ship was an ugly thing, sullen, entirely practical. Its belly was studded with unconcealed grapplers, lifters, cutters, churners. If the master of this craft so desired, its engines could easily convert all of Djamonkin Crater into a steaming tornado of whirling rock and ore, sifting, lifting and storing whatever components it wished to carry back.

I hated what it stood for.

I hated it all.

The vessel continued its slow, steady glide over the crater. The sand did not dimple beneath the pressure of its lifters, the rocks did not shiver; I heard nothing but a subtle rush, like wind through the trees. I dropped my shoulders and knelt in submission; no choice. I might escape again, but I doubted it.

After a while, the opposite blurred edge of the ship's shadow crossed my body and sunlight spread again to the other side of the sandy waste. The mining craft rose slowly, with lumbering grace, then sped up and flew over the peak. Moving on.

I could not believe my good fortune. Perhaps the island's deception could hide us from the deep-seeking probes of a mining ship . . .

My relief was short-lived. I heard a melodic wail. Chakas and Riser had joined in hideous song. That made no sense at all. The sand, which had withstood the immense pressure of the miner, now whirled under my feet and upended me. Ripples pushed out, lifting me like a wave. I fell on my side and was swept around in a spiral toward the stone wall. I scraped up hard against the rough lava. The motion stopped, but a precisely hemispheric hollow dropped in front of me. At its center, a white cylinder topped with a black stone capital slowly rose to a height of more than fifty meters.

Chakas and Riser stopped their wailing. The island fell silent. It had no opinion, made no comment.

The Miner vessel had dropped out of sight behind the peak, then turned north, and was now almost over the horizon.

My companions reappeared, standing up through the low mist. Riser ran out along the markers, arms held out in swinging balance, and stood on the inner wall, looking down on me. He squatted, toes poking over the edge.

"Big," he said. "Looking for you?"

"It's not easy concealing anything from a Miner ship," I observed. "They scan hard and deep."

"Special place," Riser said.

Chakas was striding toward us, picking his teeth again with a palm fiber—a gesture he seemed to think revealed sophistication. "It worked," he said, shading his eyes.

"You sang to make it go away?" I asked.

"No song," Riser said. They looked at each other, shrugged their shoulders.

I turned back to examine the column sticking up from the hollow. Definitely Forerunner but far too prominent for a Durance. In color and shape, it seemed to fit the severe style of a marker one might find outside a temple of battle, commemorating regret and eternal sorrow. A military monument was certainly more in tune with the war sphinxes.

I walked toward the hollow and stood on the rim for a moment, considering my options. The island had been visited frequently by ha*manune*. They had explored, built walls, laid down trails, kept defying the dazzler.

I rolled the bone chip in my fingers.

Then, as if giving up, the humans had departed—leaving the island to brood on its own enigma. Of late, however, visitors—mostly Florians, I guessed—had again begun to cross the merse-filled lake, as if in anticipation of a change, an awakening. Following their *geas*. The Librarian had obviously tuned these peoples for a particular, very difficult task.

And now—song.

We were all being set up. I could feel it. But to what purpose?

The pair watched with curious expectancy from the inner wall. "Any ideas?" Chakas called.

"Go ahead," Riser suggested, waving his fingers. "It welcomes you."

"You don't know that," Chakas said to the Florian.

"I know it," Riser insisted. "Go down. Touch it."

I had studied just about every source on Precursor myths and treasure. But now I was working hard to remember other tales . . . tales I had heard in my youth of the strange practices of a high class of Warrior-Servants known as *Prometheans*: practices antiquated and rarely seen today—that is, in the times of my family. Practices involving sequestration and self-exile.

In the archives of treasure-seekers, such tales were inevitably followed by warnings. If one should come across something called a *Cryptum*, or a *Warrior Keep*, one should leave it alone. Violating a Cryptum, whatever it was, came with nasty consequences, not the least of which involved angering the highly protective guild of Warrior-Servants.

That could also explain why the Miner ship had moved on.

For possibly the first time in my life, I decided to do a little thinking before taking any reckless action. I stepped back from the hollow, joined the humans at the wall, and sat beside Chakas. He lifted his palm-frond hat and wiped his forehead.

"Too hot for you?" he asked.

"Your yelling . . . your song. Where did you learn that?"

"No song," Riser said again. He looked puzzled.

"Tell me more about the Librarian," I said. "She protects you. She marks you at birth. How does she mark you?"

"She doesn't *mark* us. She visits us," Chakas said. "We're told who we are and why we are here. Even if it's not secret, it's hard to remember."

"How many young Forerunner chumps have you brought to this place?" I asked.

Chakas grinned. "You're the first," he said, and then backed off as if I might hit him.

"The Librarian told you to bring a Forerunner here, didn't she?"

"She watches over all," Riser said and smacked his lips. "Once we were great and many. Now we are few and small. Without her, we would be dead."

"Riser, your family has known this island for a long time," Chakas said. "How long? A thousand years?"

"Longer."

"Nine thousand years?"

"Maybe."

Since the time the Librarian had been given charge of Erde-Tyrene. Since humans had been devolved and exiled here.

A Warrior Keep, if that was what it was, hidden on a

planet of exiles. I was detecting a pattern but could not bring it into focus. Something about Forerunner politics and the human war . . . I had never cared much for that sort of history. Now I really missed my ancilla. She could have retrieved what information I needed almost instantly.

The sun was westering. Soon it would fall behind the central peak and we would be in shadow. Now, however, the ring island's heat was at its most intense, and I was getting uncomfortable, sitting on the black wall, surrounded by glaring white sand—disciplined sand, made to stay here for the ages.

I stood, my mind made up, and walked away from the hollow and the pillar. "Take me back to the beach. Call the boat."

The pair looked uncomfortable. "The boat won't return for days," Chakas said.

I suppose they would have been glad to strand a silly Forerunner youth out here, making off with his armor, sneaking back to Marontik. But it did not make sense for them to be stuck out here with their hapless victim.

I squinted. The sun hurt my eyes. "You didn't actually plan any of this, did you?" I asked.

Riser shook his head. Chakas made a breeze on his face with his hat. "We thought you'd do something exciting."

"We're still waiting," Riser said.

"Where we live is boring," Chakas said. "Out there . . ." He swept his hand up and around the vast, hot blueness.

"Maybe you and me, we get crushed by sameness. Maybe you and me, we think alike."

Something stiffened my neck, then made my head hurt, but it wasn't the last flashing glare of the sun. I could *feel* the two humans beside me, sitting quietly on the rock wall, patient, bored—heedless of danger. Like me in so many ways.

Too much like me.

There are points in life when everything changes, and changes in a big way. The old sophistic texts refer to these points as synchrons. Synchrons supposedly tie great forces and personalities together. You can't predict them and you can't avoid them. Only rarely can you *feel* them. They are like knots creeping forward on your string of time. Ultimately, they tie you to the great currents of the universe— bind you a common fate.

"This whole crater is a mystery," Chakas said. "I've dreamed about it all of my life. But if I step inside this circle, or away from the maze lines, it will kill me. Whatever it is, it doesn't like humans. The sand climbs down our throats. When we are dead, the sand climbs back out. Now, we bring you, and everything changes. This place recognizes you."

"Why would anything valuable or even interesting be stuck out here, on a world covered with *humans*?"

"Go ask," Riser suggested, pointing to the column. "Whatever happens, we'll sing your story in the market."

Dusk was upon us, but the air stayed hot and still. I

knew that I had to go out to the pillar. If I couldn't handle a Cryptum, then almost certainly, when the time came, my courage would fail me when I faced something much older and far stranger.

I pushed off the wall and took a step. Then, I looked back at the two humans.

"Do you feel it?" I asked.

Riser circled two fingers and waggled them—yes— without hesitation, but Chakas asked, "Feel what?"

"The ties that join us."

"If you say so," Chakas said.

Liars. Cheats. Low beings suitable only for being kept as specimens. Of course the sand would choke them.

But not me.

THREE

CLIMBED OVER the lip and descended the hollow. First step. The sand did not sink but held me upright, as if each footfall made its own stair step. Second step. No mishap.

In a few seconds, I stood beside the pillar, its wide black cap looming over me. The tropical dark that had slipped across the island was profound, but the clouds parted and stars in a diffuse, glittering belt illuminated the sand, the hollow, the pillar. I knelt. Around the base scrolled a single line of text in old, sweeping Digon characters, used almost exclusively by Warrior-Servants—and in recent history only by their most powerful class, the Prometheans. I was far from family, rate, and class, but what I read in those characters practically defined my attitude toward existence:

You are what you dare.

Everything fell into place. This confirmed what I had felt earlier. A Forerunner youth, a low Manipular, had been expertly recruited by the Librarian's ancilla—on instruction of the Librarian herself. He had been deposited on the ring island within Djamonkin Crater and guided to a strange patch of white sand guarded by stolid war sphinxes. His guides had urged him to cross a deadly, barren ground of sand and stones, then, all unknown to themselves, had sung a preprogrammed song, and for the first time in a thousand of years, the site had changed—reacted, responded.

You are what you dare.

The synchron was definitely upon me. By the sensations that crept up and down my back and my neck, I sensed that a connective loop of world-lines would bind me for a long time—perhaps forever—to the two humans waiting in the dark, back at the stone circle. I wondered if they knew.

I stretched out my hand and laid it on the pillar's smooth surface. The cold stone seemed to shiver beneath my fingers. A voice vibrated up my arm and echoed in the bones of my jaw.

"Who summons the Didact from his meditative journey?"

I was stunned into immobility. My thoughts flashed with panic and wonder. The stories still echoed over thousands of years. . . . The *Didact*! Here, surrounded by the last population of humans in the galaxy . . . Not even a fool such as myself could believe such a thing. I had no idea what to do or say. But out of the dark behind me, the humans began singing again. And with that wailing, wavering song, the tone of the voice from the pillar changed its challenging tone.

"A message from the Lifeshaper herself, conveyed in a strange manner . . . but the content is correct. Is it time to raise the Didact and return him to this plane of existence? A Forerunner must give answer."

There was really only one sensible answer: *No. Sorry. Leave him be! We're leaving now. . . .*

But you are what you dare, and the chance to meet this hero, enemy of all humans . . . Only the most foolish of young Forerunners would dare this, and so, once again, I had been well chosen.

"R-r-raise him," I said. "You mean, bring him back . . . ?"

"*Bring him back.* A Forerunner commands this. Stand aside, young messenger," the voice instructed. "Stand well back. This is a millennial seal, held by the wisdom of Harbou, hardened by the strength of Lang—and the force of its breaching will be great."

FOUR

THE SAND WITHIN the hollow whirled outward in spiral ridges, washing around my feet but not upsetting me. The pillar seemed to melt down, flow away into the sand. The movement dug deeper, revealing a large ovoid vessel originally buried meters below the surface. I backed away, not to stumble and get caught up in the excavation.

The two humans and I again waited on the wall, dodging the sand as it hurled itself over and formed neat conic piles on all sides.

Eventually, the pit became a well.

The great copper and steel vessel, over ten meters high and at least that wide, gleamed as if freshly forged.

Riser was chattering to himself, no doubt singing little prayers to little gods. Or perhaps the ha*manune* had greater gods, huge gods, to compensate. Chakas did nothing but watch and jump aside when necessary.

Bad enough that a Forerunner of another rate would disturb the Didact's Cryptum, but if indeed this vessel carried the great Promethean warrior, he might be severely displeased to find himself in the presence of the descendants of his old enemy.

Again the voice buzzed in the bones of my skull.

"Minimum safe distance, fifty meters. Stand aside. Millennial seal will be breached in five, four, three, two . . ."

"Look away," I said to the two humans. As one, we all averted our eyes.

I heard a crackling rumble and saw even through my palms a flash of transchronic blue. It revealed the bones of my hand. I felt it in my viscera. It made me feel immensely old, as if I might crumble to dust. I seemed to sense deep pulses of memory from all who had ever chosen to enter a Cryptum and were still sealed in profound meditative transcendence, united, brothers and sisters in timeless *xankara*.

The night was illuminated by another flash, this one pure white, shot through with arcs of green fire. Behind us, through the jungle, palm leaves swung wildly, caught in changing winds. I looked everywhere but directly at the Cryptum vessel.

Then it was over. The pit fell silent. Afterimages danced across the darkness and faded. Now appeared the first striations of dawn. It seemed that mere seconds had passed, and yet, the morning was upon us. Soon it was bright, and we were allowed to see clearly what we had done.

The ovoid vessel had parted in three sections above its midline belt. The sections had opened outward like the protecting calyx that falls to unveil a flower. But the great figure so revealed was not nearly as pretty as a flower. In fact, curled up like some monstrous, wrinkled embryo, it resembled a great corpse shriveled by time—mummified.

Back in the town, I had been offered tours of catacombs filled with human dead, a disgraceful performance typical, I thought, of these degraded beings. There are things of which I have no curiosity. Yet now, I was looking upon the mortal shame of a Promethean. I had no idea what happened within a Cryptum or why any Forerunner of such fame and rank would choose such an exile, whether in penitence or insanity. . . .

At first, I did not hear the approach of the sphinxes. From their frozen circle, three of the machines had unfolded great curved legs and now walked over the low black rock walls. Between the swinging legs and grapples hard blue light sparked and flowed. The closest of the sphinxes unfolded four arms from just below the port of its empty control cabin and spun silvery cords into a loose net. Then, the sphinx stepped over us and descended into the pit. On the other side of the circle, another sphinx also descended, and reached into the opened Cryptum to gently lift the Didact's shriveled body.

With infinite patience, the machines shrouded the body in the net, then withdrew from the pit, the net and its contents swinging slowly between. They carried the Didact right over us, and I looked up at the wrinkled hide, the minimum of clothing concealing the body's bony hips. I could not see the face or the head, but I remembered Warrior-Servants who had visited my family in Orion . . . Powerful, fiercely handsome, giving me in my cool, calm nursery both visions of strength and nightmares of great destruction.

As a full-rate Promethean of the Warrior-Servants, the Didact, revived and uncurled, might have risen to twice my height and weighed in at four to five times my mass. His shoulders by themselves might once have been as broad as my outstretched arms. But now, lacking armor, alive or dead, he looked as vulnerable and ugly as a hatchling bird.

With a humbled, shift-footed gait, I followed the machines and jumped over the walls, ignoring the prescribed path. Chakas said nothing as he walked behind me. Riser kept to the ceremonial tracks of his ancestors and fell behind.

"Truly, is this treasure?" Chakas asked dubiously.

"Not treasure," I said. "Disaster. Any Forerunner who disturbs a Cryptum . . . Sanctions. Disgrace."

"What's a 'Cryptum'?" Chakas asked.

"A vault of ages. In search of wisdom, or to flee punishment, a mature rate might choose the path of endless peace. It is allowed only for the most powerful, whose punishment might prove troublesome to the Forerunner hierarchies."

"You know this, yet you opened it? Will they punish humans, too?"

No defense, no excuse. I felt both embarrassment and misery. "It wasn't me—not just me. You sang the right song, and it heard you," I said.

"You're happy to share the blame?"

Riser had caught up with us, running along and balancing, arms out. "We sang nothing," the little human said. Chakas shrugged and looked away.

I wondered at their foolhardiness, that they did not vanish into the jungle. The war sphinxes breached the ellipse of their still-frozen companions and, without slowing, passed through, then shoved and crashed into the jungle.

Two more out of the original twelve sphinxes then lifted up on blue-sparking limbs, joints alive with hard light, and followed the others through a cleared path of shredded greenery.

"What are we going to do?" Chakas asked as we picked our way over broken palms and bushes.

"Await retribution," I said.

"Us, too? Truly?"

I looked upon them and felt pity. These war sphinxes had likely killed many of Chakas's ancestors. . . . Humans must have sinned greatly against the Mantle to deserve such a fate.

FIVE

THE SPHINXES CIRCLED east on the ring island, gradually trending outward from the inner shore. Following in their cleared wake, we finally reached the opposite beach and looked across the broad outer lake, toward the distant crater rim.

The sphinxes conveyed their burden to a low, flat building constructed of bare blast metal, gray and angular. This structure lacked the nodes and projectors that created the ornate outer shells common in Forerunner architecture. Indeed, from the sky, it might have looked like a forgotten storage depot, and against the line of tall palms, from the lake, it would hardly have been noticed at all. More and more mysterious.

The four sphinxes approached in ranks of two. The pair carrying the Didact paused before a wide descending ramp—the entrance. I heard the sound of huge doors swinging wide. The sphinxes sidled down the ramp into the building.

The other two sank to the ground outside and folded their legs and arms with faint whirrs and sighs. The blue glow of their joints dimmed and vanished.

We walked slowly past the immobile pair, skittish, uncertain whether they were guardians or just monuments once again. Bravest of all, Riser stopped to pat the pitted surface of the nearest machine, drawing an exclamation from Chakas—"Don't do that! They could vaporize us."

"Don't know that," Riser said, eyes narrow, ears up, lips straight. No doubt this was his courage face.

Indeed, the sphinxes looked as stolid and ancient as ever. I peered down into the entrance. Sand had drifted down the ramp, marked by the dimpling steps of the other sphinxes. Darkness lay at the bottom.

The doors were still open. *You are what you dare.*

"Stay here," I told Chakas, and started down the ramp. He reached to grab my shoulder.

"Not your business," he said, as if concerned for my safety. I gently pulled away his hand. The touch of his flesh was not as repugnant as I had thought. It felt little different from the skin of a young Forerunner—my own.

Surely we could not actually be brothers, both shaped by the Precursors. . . .

"I think the Librarian wanted *all* of us here," I said. My fear had merged with my boldness and some other quality I mistook for courage, forming foolish resolve. I was like an insect flying toward a flame, certain it promised, if not complete justification and salvation, at least supreme adventure. "Someone slipped messages into your brains before you were born. Someone told you to lure a Forerunner. You sang the proper codes, and the Cryptum opened."

Chakas formed his mouth into an O, then knelt and held his arms over his head, facing away from the ramp. Riser joined him, glancing up at me as if unsure this was the proper way to observe the ritual. "The Librarian touches all," Chakas said, and together they lapsed into whispered chants.

I continued down into the darkness. The first chamber within the building was wide and dank, four times my height—just barely enough to admit the sphinxes. Coolness pooled while warm air swirled above my waist. A dim greenish light grew in the darkness and I saw, in outline, the sphinxes facing each other over a broad pit filled with silvery liquid. The sling containing the Didact draped between the sphinxes, mere centimeters above the pool. I squatted as close as I dared to the edge.

Around me, for the next few minutes, all was still.

Then, the jarring voice again addressed me:

"Forerunner, do you witness this return?"

I tried to retreat, but a brilliant white light shot down from the roof of the chamber and held me. The light shimmered and removed my will to move.

"Do you witness?"

"I witness," I said, my voice low and tremulous.

"Do you speak for this one about to be recalled?"

"I . . . I don't know what to say."

"Do you speak?"

"I speak . . . for this one."

"Do you defend the decision to bring the Didact back from ageless peace?"

To me, the shriveled body looked dead. I wondered if that meant the Didact was about to be resurrected—something I had been taught was impossible. Clearly, I understood nothing of what was happening, but by now I knew the drill well enough to simply say, "I defend the decision."

From the roof of the chamber, four ribbon sections of personal armor, big enough for a full-rate Promethean, dropped slowly through dilations. The pieces hovered on both sides of the sling, and from them depended long tentacles transparent as glass which quickly filled with three colors of liquid—the basic electrolytes and nutrients required for long journeys. Most Forerunner armor was equipped to keep the wearer alive for years without outside sustenance.

"*Approach*," the voice instructed. "*The Didact is unaware of this realm. Administer the reviving fluids.*"

My whole body shook, but I stepped into the pool and waded through the silvery liquid. My legs warmed. The tentacles curled toward me, not aggressive, simply offering, waiting.

The sphinxes had spread the net in such a way that it opened at the top, revealing the coiled form. The Didact's face was now visible for the first time. It was indeed a strong face, the skin drawn tight against the natural skull beneath.

"Apply the electrolytes," the voice told me. Obligingly, the red-filled tentacle pushed forward, and I grasped it.

"To his mouth?" I asked.

"Push through the lips. Dehydration will be reversed. Rigor will be suspended."

I leaned in, trying not to touch the shriveled arms and not succeeding. The skin was not cold, but warm. . . .

The Didact was not dead.

I bumped the end of the tentacle, a narrow spigot, against the Didact's dried lips, then pried them apart, revealing wide, grayish white teeth. The spigot released a flood of red liquid between the clenched jaws. Most of it spilled down the shriveled cheeks and drained into the pool.

I then applied two shades of blue fluid. Came a rustling within the net—the large body actually stirring. The sections of armor flexed above the Didact as if eager to embrace and protect him.

"Timelessness is deep. He returns, but slowly. Lift and stretch his arm, *gently*," the voice instructed. Had the arm not been shriveled, the weight might have defeated me. But I did as I was told. I walked around the sphinxes, lifted and rotated the other arm, then straightened and flexed the legs—almost as stiff as wood—until the skin took on a different sheen and a kind of suppleness returned.

I followed all of the instructions of the voice that vibrated through my jaw, massaging and cleansing the Didact with handfuls of the silvery liquid as he took in more renewing fluids. For the next four hours, I helped painstakingly restore the shriveled Promethean from his long slumber, from that profound, meditative exile that was a dim legend among Forerunners my age.

Return him from the joy and peace of timeless space.

His rheumy eyes opened. Two protective lenses fell away and he blinked, then looked up at me with a terrible scowl. "I *curse* you," he murmured, his voice like rocks grinding on the floor of a deep ocean. "How long? How long have I been here?"

I said nothing. I had no idea how long.

He twitched and struggled, but the net restrained him, that he might not move too quickly, too soon. After an awkward time, he fell back, exhausted, and fluids leaked from his nose and lips. He tried to speak, but it was difficult.

He managed one more utterance—a question. "Has the damned thing finally been fired?"

"Go now. It is done," the voice told me.

I scrambled out of the pool and left the chamber. The humans waited for me, but I was too moved and too frightened to speak.

SIX

TIME ON THE ring island seemed suspended.

Something in the silvery fluid, in the splash from the restoring liquids—in the aura of disturbed peace that had surrounded the Didact—had deeply affected me. I felt I had been bathed in history, waded through time itself.

Suns rose and set, but I was not sure they were the same sun, nor that the night sky was the same sky—everything seemed different. The two humans stayed close, like worried pets. We dozed together. Their touch was no longer repugnant. They helped keep me warm. Given time, I would never understand humans, but I might feel a certain affection for them. I actually slept for the first time since infancy, confirming to myself that it was armor that relieved Forerunners from this natural act.

After ten days, the Didact ventured out of the chamber to take exercise. His skin had lost most of its wrinkled character and taken on a more natural grayish pink color. He still wore no armor, perhaps because he was intent on full recovery, without assistance. Silent, morose, he did not ask for company, and we avoided his pathways. Still, I made note of the changes his return from eternity had brought to this place.

All the war sphinxes were now active. They moved purposefully about the island, blazing fresh trails through the trees, though they always left the green, leafy canopies intact. I assumed they were establishing points of observation and lines of communication between possible defensive positions. Such preparations seemed antique and peculiar, to say the least. Perhaps the Didact had not returned with his wits intact.

Once, we observed two sphinxes merging to create a larger unit, yet with the same stern, judgmental expression carved into the forward surface.

From near the ramp, where Chakas and I lunched on fruit and coconuts, we watched the Didact return from a hike that had begun with movement east, and now ended with his return from the west—a complete circuit of the island, following the new trails.

"What's he *doing*?" Chakas asked, his mouth full.

"Reconnoitering. Preparing for his defense," I guessed.

"Defense against what?" Chakas asked, incredulous.

I wondered if these humans knew how lucky they were, that he hadn't already crushed them with his great hands, or had the sphinxes burn them to ashes.

The Didact descended the ramp, paying as little attention to us as he might a windblown shrub or a wayward scatter of birds.

"Why are we here?" Chakas asked me, his voice hushed. "What is he to the Librarian?"

"Her husband," I said. "In the old legends, they were married."

Chakas looked shocked, then disgusted. "Forerunners *marry* each other?"

To be honest, I was equally incredulous. How could such an intimate alliance form between the supreme enemy of humans and their last and greatest protector?

I explained simply to pass the time. "Forerunners marry for many reasons, but the lower rates are said to marry more often for love. This allows strange liaisons. Humans will never understand. Your own customs are much too primitive."

Chakas received this with less than perfect grace. He swore under his breath and took off through the jungle. I thought him remarkably obtuse, unwilling as he was to accept his station in life.

Riser was constantly venturing into the jungle alone, and brought back more fruits and a few coconuts. He seemed unconcerned about what might happen next.

The Didact stayed in the chamber that evening while I hiked through the jungle with my humans. (Ownership seemed a more seemly relation than brotherhood.) We then gathered on the inner beach under a brilliance of stars. My apprehension and numbness had dissipated and were now—too typically, I fear—being replaced by boredom.

We had served our purpose. We weren't needed anymore, obviously. If we weren't to be killed or arrested, if the Didact ignored us, then perhaps we could make our way to the outer shore and find a boat.

But Chakas didn't think so. He pointed out that the profile of the crater's central peak had changed. "They'll see it from the rim. That will stop any boats from coming here."

I hadn't deigned to be so observant. Generally, personal armor kept track of life's little details, leaving Forerunners free to engage in elevated thoughts. "What's changed?" I asked, irritated. "It's dark. It still has trees around its base and bare rocks up to the top."

"I think the machines are crossing over and working there," he said. "Anyway, something is moving rocks."

"Sphinxes are war machines, not excavators."

"Maybe there are other machines."

"We don't see them," I pointed out. "And I don't hear anything."

"Tomorrow," Riser suggested, and vanished into the trees, not to return for hours. Chakas and I made our way to the outer shore.

The next night, we tried to follow Riser on one of his excursions. The little human was apparently allowed to roam freely, but a solitary war sphinx dropped swiftly through the trees and planted itself on curved legs, blocking Chakas and me.

"What are we, *prisoners*?" I shouted.

It made no answer.

Chakas shook his head, grinning.

"What's funny?" I asked as we trudged back the way we had come, followed by the hovering sphinx. Riser darted past us with a small pile of nuts.

Chakas shouted after him, not in anger, but in humor. "Ha*manush* are free to come and go," he said. "He'll boast about it if we get home. Looks like he's our superior here."

"His brain is smaller than yours," I said.

"And yours is smaller than the Didact's, I'll wager."

"No," I said, and was about to explain the ways of mutation from Manipular to higher rates and greater forms, while we returned to the clearing around the half-buried chamber.

But my words were choked off.

The Didact sat in a posture of quiet thought atop the left wall of the ramp. His dark-hooded eyes tracked us for the first time as if we were worthy of some small attention.

He grunted and dropped from the wall with newfound agility. "Manipular," he said. "Why are these humans here?"

Chakas and I stood before the Promethean, locked into awed silence. This was it, I thought—the time of judgment and punishment.

"Tell me, why *humans*?"

"This is *our* world," Chakas said, in a fair imitation of the Didact's exalted grammar and tone. "Perhaps we should ask why *you* are here."

I wanted to clamp my hands around his mouth, and turned to reprimand him, but the Didact raised one powerful arm. "*You*," he said, pointing to me. "How came this to be?"

"The human is telling the truth," I said. "This is a planet reserved for their occupation. I came here seeking artifacts. These humans showed me to your resting place. They have a *gea*—"

"A Cryptum is not to be violated," he interrupted, looking off at the sky. "One of you found a way to open my vessel. Who? And how?"

His sadness was like a pall over the beach and the jungle. For me, in the presence of such a senior Forerunner, it seemed as if the very air filled with his weary gloom.

"The humans sang songs," I answered. "The Cryptum opened."

"Only one Forerunner would ever be so devious," the Didact said, his voice softening. "Or so clever. You were about to say, the humans have a *geas*. Someone infused them with codes in their infancy, or earlier—genetically."

"I think that might be so."

"How much time has passed?"

"Perhaps a thousand years," I said. "A very long sleep."

"Not *sleep*," the Didact said. "I entered the Cryptum on another world. Someone brought me here. Why?"

"We are tools of the Librarian," Chakas said. "We serve her."

The Didact examined the human with distaste. "With my sphinxes, someone helped revive me."

"I did," I confirmed.

"I had hoped to rise in triumph and recognition of my judgment—but instead, I find myself facing young fools and the offspring of ancient enemies. This is worse than disgrace. Only one other reason . . . one other provocation would make the Librarian revive me under these humiliating circumstances."

He raised one arm, then executed a brief wave in the air with his fingers. The pieces of armor floated out of the chamber, and the Didact assumed a position of robing, arms extended. The armor sections surrounded his limbs, his torso, and finally, the top of his head, in shimmering pale bands that floated centimeters above his skin. I was surprised by the humbleness of the armor's design. My father's armor was far more ornate, yet he was not the stuff of legend. Such were the sumptuary rules of

Forerunners—even a great Promethean must dress below the style of any Builder.

"There must be a reason my wife is not here to greet me," the Didact said when he was fully clothed. He stretched his arms to the stars. Beams shot from his fingers, and he sketched out several constellations, as if commanding the stars to move. I felt strangely surprised when they did not.

The beams dimmed and went out, and he curled his fingers into fists. "You know nothing."

"So I've been told," I said.

"You are a mere Manipular, and a reckless one at that." He pointed to Riser. "Little human, I know your kind. You are of ancient form. I asked you be preserved, because you are peaceful yet full of cleverness. Worthy pets to amuse and by low example to instruct our young. But *you* . . ." He swung his finger around to Chakas. "You are too much like the humans who nearly wrecked my fleets and murdered my warriors. My wife has taken liberties. She provokes me." He stretched out his arms. The armor flashed. "*You* provoke me."

Chakas's face clouded but, wisely, he said nothing.

The Didact seemed to rethink any violent action. His arms dropped and the armor returned to a state of protection.

"Manipular, where did you see first light?" he asked.

I explained that my venerable Builder family had long inhabited systems in and around the Orion nebular complex, near the Forerunner core.

"Why are you naked?"

"Merses surround this island," I said. "They won't tolerate complex machines. My ancilla—"

"My wife raised merses in our garden shallows," the Didact said. "Never liked them much myself. Show me."

SEVEN

IN A FOUL mood, Chakas lagged behind the Didact, Riser, and me as we hiked along the outer shore, following one of the new trails blazed by the sphinxes—which were, indeed, acting as excavators, apparently to the surprise of the Didact as well. In truth, he seemed more often dismayed than in control of his surroundings—more often confused than enlightened by what we found.

He had no explanation for the reshaping of the central peak.

"I am lost here," he said as we looked over the outer lake of Djamonkin Crater. He studied the wallowing merse. He found a low boulder and sat again in that contemplative posture that also seemed to reveal exhaustion. "No one can tell me why I am not still in timeless peace."

"In exile," I said.

He glowered. "Yes, exile. Forced to retreat for speaking truth, tactical and strategic wisdom, useless against the bold assertions of the Master Builder . . ."

He stopped himself. "But those matters are not for the ears of a Manipular. Tell me—are the weapons finished? Have they been used?"

I told him I knew nothing of weapons.

"That means little. As a Manipular, you have no need to understand your greater circumstances. Worse, however, you apparently focus on personal gain and *treasure*. Precursor artifacts. No doubt you seek the Organon."

His words stabbed deep, not just because they were true. "I am honest to my goals. I seek diversion," I said. "Excuses for adventure are means to an end." I quoted, "*You are what you dare.*"

"Aya," the Didact murmured, shaking his great head. "So I told *her*, once, and she's chided me with it ever since." He looked out over the lake and the clear cloudless morning sunrise. A breeze sallied from the west into the crater's wide bowl and dappled the blue waters, eliciting circlets of foam from agitated merse.

"Ugly, mean brutes," the Didact observed, his rancor cooled. "What ritual allowed you to come here without being attacked?"

I explained about humans and their wooden boats, powered by steam, but even then requiring soft watery songs to cross safely.

"Humans making tools . . . again. . . . I have been well and cleverly hidden. No other Forerunner would seek me here."

"Long time," Riser confirmed. He seemed comfortable around the Didact—as if from instinct. I saw it clearly. A servant species favored for ages . . .

No wonder Chakas was in a foul mood. His own instincts were likely either blank—long erased—or filled with much darker memories.

"Your Cryptum killed any human who approached," I said. "At least, any stupid human."

"A selection process," the Didact said.

"But there was a safe way in, partly. Someone made a puzzle that would stick in the human imagination. So humans came time and again and sacrificed themselves, and the survivors erected walls and laid pebbles to show the way. Someone wanted you to be found—when the time was right."

This seemed to sink the Didact into deeper gloom. "Then it is almost over," he said. "All we have tried to do as inheritors of the Mantle—all *that* will be violated, and the galaxy will be murdered . . . because *they* do not understand." He let out a grating sigh. "Worse, *it* may already be loose. Join your human friends and sing sad songs,

Manipular. There is judgment, and just doom is upon us all."

"It is what you all deserve, no more," Chakas said, throwing down a shred of palm.

The Promethean paid him no attention.

EIGHT

THAT NIGHT, IN the dark, the profile of the central peak altered abruptly. Thousands of sparking fires and bluish glows burned around the jutting prominence like the flitting of lightning insects, until the dawn snuffed them with the sun's first yellow rays.

Riser accompanied me to the inner shore, sharing parts of a coconut and the sour green fruit he favored. He also offered a piece of raw meat from some animal he had snared in the darkness, but I of course refused. The Mantle forbade the eating of the flesh of unfortunates.

Chakas was nowhere to be found.

What the sun revealed of the former peak was a circle of slender pillars, rising a thousand meters out of a remnant base of mountain and surrounded by sloping chutes of scoria. I had never seen the like before, and vaguely wondered if here, finally, was a Precursor machine fully active, ready to unleash mischief.

I was very confused. My curiosity about all manner of things historical had been sparked by the example of the Didact. If he was indeed the Didact . . . for how could a great warrior and defender of Forerunner civilization, how could a true Promethean, feel such a depth of defeat and gloom? What passions—what *adventures*—had this Warrior-Servant known in his long life, and what could have possibly forced such strength and accomplishment to cower in meditative exile?

I put little store in his condemnation of other Forerunners. Truly, the concept of an end to Forerunner history had never occurred to me. I found it ludicrous. And yet . . .

The idea of Warrior-Servants laying low entire species—now that I had actually met humans—seemed to violate all the precepts of the Mantle. Did not the Mantle give us dominion to allow us to uplift and educate our lessers? Even humans, so degraded, deserved that much respect. . . . After all, I had learned much about Chakas from observing him, and my opinions of his degraded status were changing. The Didact's guilt alone might account for his deep sense of darkness and failure.

I looked from the inner shore at the revealed pillars and wondered what they were meant for, what would rise through or up and around them. Was it something for the use of the Didact? An architectural beacon announcing his return? Or the final instrument of his punishment?

I understood nothing about Forerunner politics. I had always disdained this concern of mature forms. Now I felt weak in my ignorance. What shattered my youthful naïveté most powerfully was the realization that the world of my people—a world of ageless social order and regimentation, of internal peace against external challenge—might not be eternal, that rising through the forms from Manipular to Builder, or whatever other destiny I fled so blithely—

All that might soon not be a choice.

This morning, I felt true mortality for the first time. And not just my own. I now understood the deep old symbol for Time—the sweeping opposed hands with lightning between, extended fingers triangulating the pinch of most efficient fates from which there is no return.

Chakas interrupted my thoughts with a touch on my shoulder. I turned and saw him standing behind me, looking out at the pillars with a look of bitter dread.

"They're coming from the east," he said.

"Across the lake, over the merse?"

"No. The sky is filling with ships. The Librarian no longer protects us."

"Does the Didact know?"

"Why should I care?" Chakas said. "He's a monster."

"He's a great hero," I said.

"You *are* a fool," Chakas said, and ran back through the trees.

NINE

T **HE SHIPS MOVED** slowly in a great, waving gray and black line from east to west, like a ribbon of steel and adamantium slicing the sky. So many!—I had never seen so many ships in one place, even on ceremonial days on my family's homeworld. What I could not understand was the reason so many were necessary, if in fact they were here to capture and incarcerate just one old Warrior-Servant.

Even a Promethean, it seemed to me, did not merit such a show of force.

But everyone around me seemed to think I was a fool, even a simpleton. I kept to the inner beach, lying on the sand, watching the ships arrange themselves in tight whorls spiraling in toward Djamonkin Crater. At the center of the whorl, a great Builder ship—the largest I had ever seen—and a great Miner vessel, easily outmatching anything owned by my swap-family, held steady in a dyadic cloud of buffer energies. The air itself began to feel stiff and harsh with the pressure of so many ships hanging in slow suspension.

A shadow of a nearer, darker sort crossed my face, and I angled my head to see a war sphinx just a few meters away, rising on its curved legs.

"The Didact requests your presence," it announced.

"Why?" I asked. "The entire galaxy is coming to a bitter end. I'm just a piece of waste matter not worth flushing."

The sphinx took a step closer, unfolding upper arms tipped with tangles of flexible grapples. Hard light flashed blue along all its joints.

"So it's not a request, eh?" I said, and pushed to my feet. "Do I walk? Or are you offering me a ride?"

"Suck it up, Manipular," the sphinx intoned. "Your presence will be useful."

I felt for the first time that there might be more than just a mechanical intelligence under its pitted skin. "He wants me to witness him being arrested," I said. "Is that it?"

The grapples flashed like the agile fingers of a *pan guth* master. "These ships are not here to arrest the Didact," the sphinx informed me. "They are here to demand his help. He will of course refuse."

I had no response to this. Instead, I followed the sphinx quietly through the trees to the inner shore. Since the sphinx seemed to have found a new purpose—telling me what was what—I ventured another question.

"What's with the mountain? Why tear it down?"

"It is the Librarian's doing."

"Oh." That told me nothing, of course—but it was intriguing. Something big was happening, that much was obvious. Without my armor, I wasn't fit to meet my superiors—or even other Manipulars, for that matter—but the fact that the Didact still knew I existed and required my presence was also intriguing.

I looked around the inner shore. Then a glint caught my eye, and I looked up toward the base of the mountain, the cloud-piercing pillars—and saw the other war sphinxes flying across the inner lake, climbing rapidly to several hundred meters.

I looked around. The inner beach was deserted. "Where is everybody?" I asked.

The sphinx's control cabin hatch pulled aside with a fluid sigh. "You will join the Didact. Get in."

I knew enough about the protocol of warriors and their machines to understand that I was not being recruited into a glorious, defiant fight to the finish. And then it dawned on me—the *humans* might be riding in sphinxes as well.

Why were we so important?

I tried to crawl up the pitted ancient surface. The grapples extended around and aft, providing stirrups. I climbed in through the rear hatch, and it sealed behind me. The cabin inside was spacious enough for a mature Warrior-Servant, only slightly smaller than the Didact himself— giving me plenty of room but no comfort because nothing was shaped to accommodate a much smaller and almost completely naked Manipular.

There were a bare seat, a variety of antiquated displays, and control tubes designed to hook up with armor. Standing on the seat, I could see through the slanted, forward-looking direct-view ports that gave the sphinx's features the illusion of a disdainful, downward gaze.

I felt only a little bump, and then we were away, wheeling about to join the general migration toward the dismantled mountain and the mysterious pillars. Above the island, the spiral of ships held position and did nothing—perhaps locked in some sort of dispute.

Wherever the Didact was, there was likely to be trouble. I could not imagine the power he had once wielded—that he could still, after a thousand years, provoke legions of Foreunners to seek him out and assemble their ships above the island.

We crossed the inner lake in minutes, a leisurely pace for craft designed to drop from high orbit, sweep continents, and decimate cities. The only thing these old machines lacked, I thought, was a direct connection to slipspace. But I didn't know that for sure.

The sphinxes circled the lower reaches of the pillars, then passed between and dropped to a central, octagonal platform. There, they settled in a protective ellipse, just as I had first seen them only a few days before.

The hatch opened. I emerged and slid off the rear curve. From another sphinx, Riser poked out, clearly agitated. Not tall enough to see out the ports, I thought.

The Florian ran over and stood close, wringing his hands and trembling. "*Something* in there with me," he muttered, then smirked up at me and wiped his forehead with one hand. "Not alive. Not happy. Very bad!"

The greater, doubled war sphinx arrived last and settled in the center of the ellipse. As if at its touch, the platform vibrated under my feet, then began to rotate. All around, the pillars and the base of the mountain—and the ships in formation high above—also seemed to turn. The spiral of ships took on a hypnotic, whirlpool fascination.

We felt none of this motion, but still, Riser grunted in dismay.

The Didact descended from the doubled sphinx and walked on his trunklike legs to confront us. "You're being kidnapped, young Manipular," he grumbled as the pillars sped up. "The humans have to come as well. Apologies to all."

I looked down to avoid getting dizzy, even without the sensation of spinning. . . .

"Why apologize now?" I asked.

The Didact's expression did not change—he did not react in the least to my insubordination, whelp that I was, agitating against the Promethean's thousands of years of life and experience. He simply looked outward, drew his brows down in concentration, and asked, "Where's the other human?"

"Still hiding," Riser said. "Sick."

Chakas chose this moment to poke his upper body out of the hatch of his transport. He looked woozy. His descent down the sloping back of the machine lacked any dignity, and he landed on bent legs, then slumped to one side and vomited.

"*Bad* sky," Riser said stoically.

The Promethean regarded this sign of human weakness with the same emotion he had shown to my insubordination. "In a few hours, all signs of my stay here will be erased. No one will be able to prove I was ever here."

"Can't the ships see us?"

"Not yet. But they obviously know something."

"Why so many?" I asked.

"They've come to ask my help—or arrest me again. I think the former, and I think I know why—but I *must not help them*. I've stayed here too long already. It's time to leave. And all of you will come with me."

"Where? How?"

My answer arrived even as I spoke. The platform was still rising. The circling pillars sprouted bulkheads, beams, and stanchions—all the necessary parts. The skeleton of a slipspace voyager was growing around us, almost too rapidly to track—until the pillars were walled in, the sky and the swirling ships vanished, and we were completely enclosed.

Chakas stumbled over to stand on my other side. Clearly, he might throw up again. A disgusting practice and to little purpose, I thought.

I was flanked by humans, with the Didact before me, his back turned and arms extended, as if commanding the voyager to rise and grow by the very gestures of his hands—which might have been the case.

"They might notice *that*," I suggested.

"From where they are, they see only a solid island and the water of the lake," the Didact said. "The ship will grow and launch—and *then* they will know. The Librarian designs beyond her station. She has always planned well."

"She made this for you?" I asked.

"For our greater cause," the Didact said. "We fight for the grace of the Mantle."

The Didact turned to face me as our chamber finished, and I saw we were within a large, fully equipped command center. My father himself could not have designed a more advanced ship. I could easily imagine the outer hull, a gray, gleaming, elongated ovoid, at least a thousand meters in length. The power and the expense had to be enormous—but, cleverly enough, rather than hiding a finished ship, the Librarian must have left a Builder's design seed under the central peak, updating it as new technology was revealed. Forerunner technology still grew in spurts, even after millions of years.

She must have traded great favors for such an installation.

Displays flashed into action around the command center and showed views in many frequencies and aspects of the outer island, the distant walls of the crater, and above, I saw as I craned my neck back, the assembled, searching ships.

A single bright star gleamed just outside the circle of vessels at the center of the fleet spiral. That star marked our voyager's calculated point of departure. In early slipspace, we did not want to pass through anything as massive as another ship.

We lifted from the island. The command center displays revealed our motion; we felt nothing. At this point, the ships *must* see us, I thought. Such a large vessel must leave a definite trail!

I felt that brief sensation of unencumbering—of all history and memory being cut loose, and then painstakingly reassembled, as every particle of our ship and our bodies was wrenched from the doubled hand of time, and had to find new scalars, new destinies, far, far away.

"Aya," the Promethean said. "We are away. It is done."

The displays tracked our course. We were moving outward along the great spiral arm that held both the Orion complex and Erde-Tyrene—just a few tens of thousands of light-years.

Hours at most would pass for us.

Had I known where we were fleeing, and what we would find . . . Against the greatest and most solemn instructions of the Mantle, I might have killed myself then and there.

TEN

I KNEW ENOUGH about interstellar travel to realize that time frames and reference-level fates were also adjusting. There would be no paradoxes, no curling or bunching-up of world-lines in slipspace. The secrets that lie between the streaking particles and waves that make up atoms are said to be vast. From those inner secrets, Forerunners have prodded sufficient power to change the shape of worlds, move stars, and even to contemplate shifting the axes of entire galaxies. We have explored other realities, other spaces—slipspace, denial of locale, shunspace, trick geodetics, natal void, the photon-only realm called the Glow.

But the vastness between suns is great and mysterious in a very different way. Our familiarity with these distances has, I think, almost been lost because we cross them so blithely, but no Forerunner memory would be great enough—perhaps not even the combined memories of all the Forerunners who ever lived—to remember the second-by-second events of a simple *walk* between two neighboring stars, this far out in the galactic arm.

We fly over and above but just barely *through* all that. And yet—this journey, in this ship, seemed to me to last forever. I felt it in my unarmored flesh and bones. I was naked to space for the first time in my life. I hated it.

We arrived. And then, perversely, I regretted that it was over.

———

We looked down over a huge, bleak, rocky gray world, a slagged and singed corpse which must have recently supported life, for it still wrapped itself in an atmosphere sufficient to allow armored Forerunners to survive—if not our humans.

Chakas and Riser lingered in a corner of the command center. Riser tossed in restless half-sleep. Chakas looked out at us with a frightened, angry expression. He knew he was far from home. He suspected he would never return. He owed nothing to Forerunners, least of all to the Didact.

I actually worried for him—strangely enough.

"This used to be a Precursor hub world," the Didact said. "Once, it was covered with tremendous structures—mostly intact. Extremely impressive."

I looked down, prepared to be awed. I had never heard of such a place. It made sense that the higher forms would conceal real treasure.

The Didact's voice deepened. "It's changed," he said.

"How, changed?" I asked.

We walked around the command center, past the humans, the Didact leading the way, as we surveyed hundreds of magnified images gathered from our first orbit.

"No orbital arches. Looks as if they've collapsed out of orbit. Look at those long, linear impacts. Everything's corroded. I recognize hardly anything—not the arena, not the Highway, not the Giant's Armory. Nothing, really."

"That can't happen," I said. "Precursor artifacts are eternal. They are with us as reminders of our littleness, forever."

"Apparently not," the Didact said. He seemed to be formulating a theory. Then he clapped his hands—massive, booming slams of armor and flesh—and pointed one arm up. The command center complied and began to search and magnify the sky across a broad spectrum.

"You've studied the basic principles of Precursor technology, what little we know?" the Didact asked.

"What little we think we know. No one has ever seen Precursor technology in action."

"*I* have," the Didact said, and gave me a look from the

corner of his dark, slitted eyes. "Once. Tell me what you know, what's changed in our understanding in the last thousand years . . . and I'll judge whether you might be of use to me."

"The basic principle was called neural physics," I said. "Precursors felt the Mantle extended to the entire universe, energy and matter as well as living creatures . . . some say. The universe lives, but not as we do."

"Some say. Since my exile, have we cracked their techniques, acquired their learning?"

"No. That is why I seek the Organon."

"Well, it doesn't exist," the Didact said. "Not as such."

Another layer of disappointment fell over my thoughts. "I suppose I knew that," I said. "But the quest is the joy of it."

"Aya. Ever so. The quest, the fight—never the finding or the victory."

I looked up at the Didact, surprised.

The voyager's sensors scanned heat and other radiation signatures in the sky, latencies in cosmic ray patterns from the inner galaxy and outer reaches of the spiral arm.

"Our humans should feel right at home here," he said. "Once, they knew these worlds better than Forerunners. They fought and died here, surrounded by Precursor ruins . . ." He slowly turned, the displays silently precessing with him. Then he pointed out a void in the system's magnetic flux. "There was recently a huge construct nearby, no more than three hundred million kilometers from here."

"Precursor?" I asked.

"No. Forerunner—but big enough. The size and mass were sufficient to create a persistent distortion in the system's field. See that—it even leaves a mark in the stellar winds."

"How recently?"

"Judging by the diffusion of its magnetic shadow, four or five decades ago. Portal technology has grown enormously more powerful, but to move such an object, they must be slowing other traffic throughout the galaxy."

He swept out his hands like a sculptor and tugged down virtual charts, diagrams, simulations based on the sensor's measurements. What they revealed was a circular gap in the interstellar medium, and a drawn-out loop in the star's vast, slowly wobbling magnetic field, its patterns smearing outward for hundreds of millions of kilometers.

"This world was recently used as a test subject," the Didact said. "I can guess by whom."

"Test for what?"

"They transported a great, *sinful* weapon into the system—and fired it. Then they left and took it with them. The Builders are going ahead with their plan—complete neural destruction. When I entered my exile, the designs had not been finalized. Apparently, that's changed. This time, they tried it on a limited scale. However . . . there has been an unfortunate side effect, one I hope they did not anticipate. We must act quickly."

The displays quivered and vanished. "The Librarian

heard about the test. Knowing she would try to alert me, the Builders set up surveillance to watch her. She could not come to release me herself, but she had made other arrangements by using what she loves most . . . our more problematic brethren." He glanced at the humans. "Ultimately, they helped save me from being captured. They are her servants, whether they know it or not."

"They know," I said.

"And whether I like it or not, she knew they must become my allies," the Didact said. "You as well. We are going down to the planet. All of us. You'll require armor. The ship will outfit you."

ELEVEN

THE ARMOR TOOK an hour to grow up around me, with numerous half-visible engineering units, small and large, flitting from the bulkheads to adjust and connect the necessary parts, then to activate—and then cut me and my fresh armor lose.

At first, the humans refused, but after being chased around the command cabin by rippling bands, they were finally cornered—and forced to submit. Chakas seemed more willing than Riser, even curious, but the poor Florian was mortified, growling to himself and trembling. The Didact tried to reassure him with a finger-stroke across his cheek. Riser bit him.

The Didact withdrew, then waited impatiently.

As there was nothing else to do except wince at some minor pinching, I observed my Promethean kidnapper with what I hoped was more discernment and sophistication, based on the experience I had gained in the last few pentads.

I had never met anyone like the Didact.

Warrior-Servants as a rule kept to themselves, except to respond to commands from political leaders, most often Builders. A few Warriors, among them Prometheans, had once served on various councils but only in an advisory capacity. Skill at war, however necessary at times, has always seemed shamefully contradictory to the basic principles of the Mantle. Still, Forerunners had used Warriors many times and likely would again.

Hypocrisy is its own collapsing mineshaft, my swap-father was fond of saying.

The Didact walked around me, punching my shoulder and torso ribbons, poking a darkly shielded finger into the interstitial at my neck, and generally putting my armor through a series of forceful tests, none of which I felt was strictly necessary. My armor—smoothly curved and silvery gray, helmet edges sweeping back from my facial features, with trim-lines of white and green—was already sufficiently functional to provide me with lists of command structures, such as would be made available to Manipulars. But here, on this ship, access seemed to be expanded—as if I were tapping into the Didact's own stores.

And then I heard a familiar voice.

The little blue feminine shape reappeared in the back of my head. I felt subtle tendrils establish the necessary connections with memory and thought. My ancilla . . .

"I am here, Manipular," she said. "I cannot establish a connection with your previous ancilla. Until that connection is made, may I serve you to the best of my ability?"

"You're from the Librarian's staff," I said.

"That seems to be the case."

"An ancilla like you got me into this situation. Are you here to serve *me*, or the Librarian?"

"Are you disappointed by your present circumstances?"

That took me aback. I looked across the command center. The humans were clumsily adjusting to their outfits. Riser was much taller than he was used to, walking stiffly on long legs that put him on a level with Chakas.

The Didact was deep in study of the system's trace in the photonic realm of the Glow, which might reveal even more evidence of what had happened here.

"I'm in way over my head," I said to the ancilla. "I don't like being twisted around and held against my will—even to compensate for my foolishness."

"Do you feel foolish?" the voice asked.

Chakas approached. "I also have a woman in my clothes," he said with a wry twist of his mouth. "She says she will help me. She's *blue*. Where is she, really?"

"She doesn't exist except in your armor and your head . . . and wherever she gets her information from, perhaps the ship."

"Can I sleep with her? Marry her?" Chakas asked.

"I'd like to see you try."

Chakas was not much enlightened by this answer. "What kind of help do I need?" he asked.

Riser walked about with increasing confidence and joined us, eyes darting as if he were being shown things only he could see. "Doesn't itch. Pretty in here, but I can't see my family—only *her*. She looks like ha*manush*, but she is not part of my family."

I found it interesting that the ancilla would adopt Riser's physical form.

Chakas turned to me. "Ha*manush* live with ancestors in their heads. Cha*manush* do not."

"She will answer your questions," I said, "both of you, if you figure out what to ask."

Riser nodded. "Perhaps she is *somebody's* ancestor." And he closed his eyes.

The Didact broke from his study and approached us. "They look silly," he said of the humans. "You look . . . What's wrong?"

"My ancilla was programmed by the Librarian."

"So is mine," the Didact said. "We're here at her request, to fulfill a mission we set for ourselves a thousand years ago. It's not starting at all well."

"I don't feel free to ask what I need to ask, or study what I need to study," I said.

"You are certainly *not* free, if by that, you mean free to act like a selfish Manipular."

"You mean, suck it up," I said.

"Exactly." He drew down more displays. "From orbit, I can't make the necessary inspection. We're going down to the surface. All of us."

"The humans are just animals—they're not ready for this," I said.

"I fought those *animals* once," the Didact said. "Believe me, they're capable of surprising you. Make sure they're prepared. This will not be an easy landing."

Chakas put on a statue-like expression of calm disdain as I passed along this information. "There's a barren planet below," I said. "We're going to land."

"What's *he* want with us?" Chakas asked.

"I'd sell him for a bag of fruit," Riser said.

I was dismayed by how much sympathy I felt for these two inferiors. Animals, perhaps—but not fools. What then was my excuse?

Atmosphere sang against the hull. The ship shuddered at the new strains on its fresh construction. It hadn't yet integrated—hadn't tested itself under all conditions, especially planetfall.

"The Librarian protects you," I told them. "But the Librarian looks after *him*, too. Something big happened here—something other Forerunners have kept secret."

I returned to the Didact. He was lost in research, his armor connecting with the ship to take on new volumes of knowledge. Somewhat to my surprise, my ancilla synced with his, and I accessed an intricately stepped and footnoted chart of relationships concerning the Didact himself.

He wanted me to know more about him.

Ten thousand years ago . . .

The Librarian and the Didact had first met on Charum Hakkor, the political center of the human-San'Shyuum empire. The final battle of Charum Hakkor had broken the human-San'Shyuum alliance and destroyed the last reserves of human resistance. That battle had been notorious, a great victory—but from the point of view of Mantle orthodoxy, of course, supremely disgraceful.

Victory did not bring joy for the Didact.

The limb of the barren gray planet expanded. Our ship took on an aerodynamic configuration, bowing out at the sides, altering its propulsion, growing huge landing pads and radiating fluxor shields against blowback.

We were about to land on a dead world in a dead system. The horizon was rugged in the extreme.

"Below . . . This is Charum Hakkor, isn't it?" I asked.

The Didact did not answer, but I sensed the truth.

"The fools," he murmured. He looked at me with a deep sadness. The contrast between his face and mine—the depth of experience, sorrow, character . . . "And they claim that *Warriors* violate the Mantle."

Slowly, we descended through the last few kilometers of atmosphere. Our armor locked itself to the deck. Behind me, Riser chirruped bitterly about being unable to move.

The command center shifted its bulkheads and opened a direct view port to the surface. We were landing in darkness.

"Humans made Charum Hakkor the center of their empire to be close to one of the greatest collections of Precursor structures," the Didact said. "They believed they were the true inheritors of the Mantle."

"Heresy—right?" I asked.

"It was one cause of our war," the Didact said. "Not the primary cause, however. Humans resented Forerunner expansion outward. For fifty years, scattered through the galactic arm, humans probed our settlements and positions. Then they allied with the San'Shyuum, combined their knowledge, and created weapons against which my warriors had little defense."

"Settlements? I thought Forerunners didn't need new planets—that we'd achieved maximum growth."

The Didact sighed. "There are many things Builders do not teach to their young," he said. "Earlier displacements around Orion and in toward galactic center forced us to move native populations from their home regions to new, outer systems. The Librarian and her staff cataloged and searched for the most appropriate matches, those stars most like native suns . . ."

"You shuffled planets?"

"Yes," the Didact said. "Humans are naturally purists. They resent having to live with other species. In fact, they're among the most contentious, bigoted, self-centered . . ." He looked back at Riser and Chakas. "I never understood how my wife tolerated them."

"Forerunners don't like living with other species, either," I observed.

"Yes, but for good reason," the Didact said. "We enforce the Mantle. We must focus and protect and preserve all life—including ourselves."

I had been taught this principle often enough, yet now it rang incredibly hollow. "The humans wanted to be left alone," I said.

"Oh, they were expanding as well, and happily displaced and destroyed on their own. The San'Shyuum are not naturally inclined to war. They are a handsome, intelligent race, besotted with eternal sexuality and youth. They hoped to spend their lives in luxury. For all that, their science was extraordinary. I suspect that given a few more centuries, humans and San'Shyuum would have fallen out with each other. . . . Humans would undoubtedly have devastated their more effete allies. We saved them that trouble."

"You devastated both," I said.

"We made a pact with the San'Shyuum. For the humans, there was no pact. The Librarian managed to save some. More than I suspected."

"Pardon the insolence, but your relationship with the Lifeshaper does not seem ideal."

"You don't know the half of it. Brace yourself, Manipular. This ship is still young."

There were several more groaning shudders and then a

great, shivering bounce—which must have been impressive outside our cabin buffers.

The ship settled and all sense of motion ceased.

The horizon outside appeared grayer and more rugged. Strange, spiky mountains rose everywhere, but closer scrutiny revealed these could hardly be natural formations. The outlines were slumped, rounded, decayed, but still monumentally artificial. Once, these ruins had formed the anchors and foundations for the superstructures of an ancient Precursor world—their system-linking, unbending filaments. But something had reduced those supposedly irreducible foundations and the filaments themselves to slag. The very thought chilled me. Precursors built for eternity!

"Atmosphere is not optimal," my armor reported as we descended the egress tube. What the ship sensed and measured, we all knew instantly. Riser and Chakas were not happy. Riser tried to climb back up the wall of the tube, but it rebuffed him.

"You should have seen this world in its prime," the Didact said. "It was magnificent. A center of mysterious, dormant power that humans could live among, look at, but never begin to comprehend. Now . . . *look* at what we've done." Anger and dismay mixed in his tone.

"How?" I asked. "How do you destroy Precursor artifacts? They're inviolate, eternal."

"They understood the universe in ways we never will. We can't unlock their secrets—but now, apparently, we can destroy all they ever made. *That*'s what I call progress."

TWELVE

THE SHIP HAD come down near the perimeter of an arena many kilometers wide. The irregular walls of the arena consisted of huge chunks of rubble, tens of meters in size, broken along crystal planes. The planes glinted in the low light of a blue-white sun, a blinding point near the horizon.

The atmosphere on the surface was cold, thin, poor in oxygen—the sky above thick with clouds of stars in one direction, almost empty in the other. Out there, beyond the diffuse edge of the galaxy, was the emptiness of intergalactic space, a void that Forerunners found unattractive—a vastness of few or no resources between far-flung islands of great wealth and energy.

We were satisfied with the resources of *this* galaxy, for the time being, and rarely looked outward. So I had been taught. But, as the Didact was so quick to point out, there are many things Builders do not teach their young.

Armor protected us against the harsh conditions and supplied our personal needs without difficulty, but that was not immediately obvious to the humans. They clutched at the apparent openness of their wraparound helmets, slowly realizing that both fingers and faces were covered with a thin, adjustable film of energy.

The Didact walked west, toward the blue star, his shadow long behind him. I followed his diminishing figure. Hundreds of meters across the arena we came to a broad, circular pit. Targets upon targets . . . This reminded me of the ring island and the sandy field around the Didact's Cryptum. Eerie to say the least. I did not like this place. Once I would have welcomed a chance to visit this world, but all my ideas of what the Precursors had to offer had changed.

Everything about my ideas was changing.

Chakas and Riser, I noticed, had decided to follow me, if not the Didact. That was foolish. I had nothing to offer anyone. I was an empty husk. I was trying to rebuild something of my personality, reshape myself into a defiant and discerning ego—but it was hard. What did Forerunners possess that could *do* this?

How could the Precursors have left their heritage so vulnerable?

The vast pit dropped several hundred meters to a smaller version of the arena. Then I noticed a thin overburden of slagged, charred material, crunching like cinders beneath our feet: not gray-silver, not broken along crystalline planes—and therefore not Precursor. We walked with slow precision down the slope, balancing gingerly on smaller chunks of rubble, leaping from chunk to larger slab, stepping around more dangerous jumbles. This entire area must have been paved at one time. Someone had overbuilt the arena. The Precursor structures were at the bottom, possibly tens of millions of years old. The higher, charred ruins were likely human or San'Shyuum.

We were descending through layers of awful history.

My ancilla chose this moment to reassert her presence. "May I attempt to reconstruct your relationship with the prior ancilla? I will need to access your memory."

"I don't care," I said, irritated at the interruption—but also relieved. The silence among these atrocities of war had become almost poisonous.

"I can better serve if there is continuity, of a sort," she said.

"All right. Tell me what I'm seeing," I said.

"This is Charum Hakkor, though not as the Didact left it, nor as the Librarian last saw it."

"What happened here?"

She fed me a series of vivid images. "The Didact's fleets

cut off this system from the replenishing armadas of the San'Shyuum. Humans had laid their strongest fortifications on foundations of Precursor ruins. They used unbending filaments to link their orbital platforms, and fought for fifty years against repeated Forerunner assaults, until finally they were defeated. Most of the humans, and not a few of the San'Shyuum who were here, committed suicide rather than submit and be removed to another system."

"What can destroy Precursor artifacts?"

"That is not in my base of knowledge."

"The Didact knows. Query his ancilla."

"Not yet permitted. He has, however, supplied you with the necessary information to assist him, should you agree to do so."

"He doesn't seem to be giving me much of a choice."

"Soon you must make a significant choice, but we have not reached that point."

"I *chose* to follow him."

The Didact interrupted. "No wonder they sought me out," he said in what for him passed for an awed whisper.

We stood before a broad cylinder capped with a shattered dome, blown up and out like a ragged crown. Part of the wall had collapsed, and we were able to enter the interior of the cylinder through that breach.

We picked through rubble—what seemed to be both human and Precursor walls and thick containment structures—until we came to a staircase rising to a circular walkway five meters wide, the far side about fifty meters away. This had apparently once served as a gallery designed to look down upon something contained below, within the core of the cylinder. The inner parapet consisted of angled panes of transparent material, hazed and starred by impacts from some long-ago explosion. Little more than the walkway and the inner cylinder below were intact.

Overhead, the shattered crown of the dome allowed the last of the blue daylight and a few unwinking stars to light our path. The Didact approached the inner parapet, his armor actually glowing at his inner turmoil—as if preparing to deflect major damage. This was what he must have looked like going into battle. . . .

Below, half-hidden in shadow, an intricately shaped mold filled most of the pit. The mold had once snugly encapsulated something about fifteen meters tall, ten or eleven meters broad and almost as thick—far too large to be any variety of human or any rate of Forerunner.

The armor's ancilla made no comment, supplied no information.

I thought I discerned what might have been cushions or braces for a number of long, multiply jointed arms, ending in shackles or gloves designed to grip hands bigger than my own body. Hands with three thick digits and a central clasping thumb . . . or claw.

Two pairs. Four arms, four hand-claws.

Pushed up and aside, three meters wide, like a huge hat

tossed on a table, was a restraining headpiece. A ridged conduit flowed down one side, presumably the back. Apparently, the head confined by that helmet had once trailed a thick, sinuous, articulated tail.

A cage. A prison.

Empty.

The Didact said, "In the name of the Mantle and all I honor—I hope it is dead, I fear it is not. They have unleashed it."

"What did they keep here?" I asked, standing close to the Didact, like a child cleaving to his own father for protection.

"Something the Precursors left behind long ago," the Didact said.

"Yes, but what *was it*?"

I broke my entranced gaze long enough to see that the humans had followed us onto the walkway. They stood beside me, staring into the pit, eyes searching, jaws agape.

The Didact gave them a narrow glance, then walked around them to another point on the parapet. "An ancient construct . . . or a captive," he said. "Nobody knows its origins, but what was confined here terrified all who saw it. Millions of years ago, it was confined in a stasis capsule and buried thousands of meters below the surface. Humans found the capsule and excavated it, but fortunately could not break it loose . . . not completely. They did devise a means of communicating with the prisoner. What it said to them frightened them deeply. With surprising wisdom, they stopped all attempts to communicate, then added another layer of protection, a San'Shyuum time bolt almost as effective as anything built by Forerunners. And they placed the capsule here, in the arena, as a warning for all to see."

Chakas's expression, behind the faint mask of his helmet field, was stiff, his forehead covered in moisture. Every few seconds, another expression broke through this stiffness, grief mixed with inexpressible pain. I wondered what memories of their history the Librarian had passed along with her *geas*—memories only now being reawakened. What had his ancestors witnessed here? I could not know.

The Didact turned away from the emptiness. His armor lost its glow. "How could it travel?" he asked. "Who would come here . . ." Then his face reflected a darkly obvious theory. "Those who conducted the test," he said. He turned back and walked toward the staircase. "We must leave immediately."

Chakas continued to gaze into the pit. Riser said nothing, but the fur on his cheeks was wet with tears. Not sad tears—tears of rage.

"Let's go," I said. "The Didact is leaving, and there's nothing for us here."

"Once, there was *everything* here," Chakas said, looking around wildly, seeing ghosts.

"When we get back to the ship, tell me what you're learning," I suggested. Slowly, he broke from his spell, and he and Riser followed me down the stairs, across the arena, to the lift tube of the Didact's ship.

Minutes later, we were in space, looking down over Charum Hakkor.

"We must examine other planets in this system," the Didact said. "Whatever happened may have spread. Tell your humans—"

"They're not *mine*," I said.

The Didact looked me over critically. "Tell your *shipmates* that the Librarian, in her perverse wisdom, tried to create a team capable of helping me to explore and understand. That isn't much, granted, but it's what we have—ourselves, this ship, our ancillas and armor."

"There's nothing down there," I said. "Whatever you sought, it's gone. Forerunners have moved on without you—and they must have their reasons. We should go back and turn ourselves in—"

"Your ancilla hasn't begun to fill in the gaps in your education," the Didact said.

"There's hardly been time."

"This system has fifteen worlds. Precursor ruins are found only on Charum Hakkor. Humans settled two more: Faun Hakkor and Ben Nauk. The other planets were mined for ore and volatiles. We'll try Faun Hakkor next. Tell your . . . tell the humans."

The Didact vanished into the lower hold. I stayed in the command center, close to Chakas and Riser, who huddled together, then hunkered down. Chakas seemed angry and confused—as much as I had learned to read human emotions. Riser I could not read at all. The Florian sat with eyes crossed, lips slack, hands folded, motionless.

"Why does she curse us with these stolen memories?" Chakas asked, looking up at me. "I remember so many things I could not have lived!"

"When you see old worlds, hear old tales, that brings up deep memories," I said. "Part of your *geas*, I imagine."

"What is that killer going to do with us?"

"I'm wondering the same thing myself," I said.

Chakas rotated to face away. Riser still did not move.

"What *do* you remember?" I asked Chakas, kneeling beside him.

"It's all tangled. We were a great power. We fought long and hard. I can feel what they went through . . . ancient humans. Those feelings *hurt*. We lost everything. *He* defeated us and took revenge." He bent over, tears dripping on the deck.

Whatever I thought about the Didact, however much he impressed and frightened me, I could not bring myself to believe he had ever acted out of malice. "The Librarian must have equipped you with human essences from those times."

"What does that *mean*?"

"Memories gathered from captives, mostly. You aren't those people, of course."

Chakas swung his arm out to Riser. "His ancestors have come back to sing to him, and he doesn't know how to stop their pain."

There was nothing more I could say or do.

Leaving the humans, I took a tour of the ship with the goal of learning why the Librarian felt her husband needed such a large means of conveyance. Energies of the vacuum be damned.

The ship having returned to space, its shape was once again an ovoid, at least eight hundred meters from stem to stern. All visible hatches opened for me. Nothing blocked my way. Lift entrances and transit corridors brightly illuminated at my approach, their walls and floors immaculately clean—and no wonder. They were newborn. It was a young vessel, not even fully acquainted with its own nature; like me.

I had spent enough time watching my father and his Builders design ships like this to understand the basics. Most of the ship's interior was shaped from hard light of one cast or another, creating an adjustable decor subject to the will of the captain. I guessed that half of the ship was matter and perhaps a third fuel, reaction mass, and of course the central flake of the slipspace drive, chipped from the original core, still closely held in a location known only to the Master Builder, chief of rate and all guilds, the greatest of the great in engineering . . . possibly the most powerful Forerunner in the ecumene.

I impressed myself with a sudden deduction. The Librarian—if indeed she provided the seed for this vessel—must have connections to senior Builders. Only they could authorize the cleaving of a slipspace core.

For one of them to have given her that core, to fit that

necessary device into the ship's seed—hiding for all that time on Erde-Tyrene—could mean only one thing. There was division among the Builders at the very highest level.

I felt a brief moment of pride at my cleverness, before it was overwhelmed by a thousand other questions—to each of which my ancilla professed that such information was "outside of my present range."

Of course there would be no uplinks, because all entangled communication had to pass through proprietary encryption and could thereby be traced. The Didact was surrounded by silence, unable to update, unable to communicate what he had learned on Charum Hakkor. No wonder he was brooding.

To convey what he knew, he had to reveal his location, and of course he would have to reveal that he had been revived, he had escaped and was actively engaged in whatever he and the Librarian were planning.

That left the Domain, of course—not often used as a means of communication. There was always the slight chance that crucial messages might be altered, even twisted. As a Manipular, I knew very little about the Domain, and the ancilla was unlikely to inform me about things forbidden to my youthful form.

More and more complicated.

I descended on the axial lift below the command center. The ship's living spaces were a maze of cubicles and service facilities: empty mess chambers and galleys, empty libraries and assembly spaces, training docks, armor repair, automated shops for refit and expansion. It could easily have accommodated five thousand Warrior-Servants and support crew.

The aft spaces, above the drive chambers, were filled with machines of war—hundreds of them, in compact storage as well as fully activated form, all far more modern than the sphinxes. Here were armed scouts and orbital picket cruisers to lay cordons and screens around larger vessels, thousands of anonymous, condensed combat wraps to convert personal armor, hand weapons . . . tens of thousands of hand weapons of all varieties, for any situation.

Enough to fight a major battle, if not a war.

What was the Didact planning? Was he truly thinking of rebelling against the council that ruled the ecumene?

He had taken me along—taken *us* along—perhaps to avoid killing us, but at all events to keep us close, to keep us quiet. I was in the middle of something too enormous to contemplate. Something far beyond the abilities of a Manipular, however clever, to comprehend.

All my young life I had lived on an invisible cushion of civilization. The struggles and designs of thousands of years of history had brought me to this pinnacle. I had had to exhibit only the tiniest minima of self-discipline to inherit the place my family had planned for me: the life of a privileged Forerunner, the very notion of which I found so restraining.

My privilege—to be born and raised all unaware of what Forerunners had had to do to protect their position in the galaxy: moving opposing civilizations and species aside, taking over their worlds and their resources, undermining their growth and development—reducing them to a population of specimens. Making sure their opponents could never rise again, never present a threat to Forerunner dominance, all while claiming the privilege of protecting the Mantle.

Mopping up after the slaughter.

How many species had collapsed beneath our hypocrisy, stretching how far back in time? What was myth, what was nightmare, what was truth? My life, my luxury—rising from the crushed backs of the vanquished, who were destroyed or *deevolved*—

And what did that mean, precisely? Had the humans defeated by the Didact and his fleets been forced into sterility, senescence without reproduction, or had they been forced to watch their children subjected to biological reduction, to becoming *lemurs* again?

The ancilla would supply only scattered images of a select few, under the protection of the Librarian, transplanted to Erde-Tyrene. Under her influence, equipped with her *geas*, these pitiful remnants had in a few thousand years grown into a population of hundreds of thousands and regained many of their ancestral forms. If Erde-Tyrene had been their true planet of origin, then these later transplants and interventions must have muddied the fossil record beyond all sense.

I stood on the outer perimeter of the largest of the

weapons bays, studying the slender, aerodynamic shapes racked overhead, the heavily shielded hulking transports beneath them, stacked on pallets and suspended in and silver and blue hard-light grips. I listened to the faint, almost inaudible tick, tick, tick of form-fit stasis fields maintaining the vessels and weapons in prime condition. The Librarian's ship-seed had been designed with far more than just escape in mind. The Didact once again had a full-blown ship of war at his command. A ship filled with death.

A planet-breaker—suited to a Promethean.

How could a Lifeworker, even one as great as the Librarian, have arranged for such awesome might? Not alone, surely. Not without the help of Builders.

I had always been taught that the most sophisticated and ornate intellectual abilities and social talents came with the first mutation—the end of youth, the end of being a Manipular. Out here, away from rate and family, mutation to first-form was impossible.

These problems were beyond my understanding, far beyond any solution. Wrapped in melancholy, I ascended to the command center, where the humans had stripped off their armor and fallen asleep. I stood over them, longing to shed my own armor, as well—longing for all of us to return to Djamonkin Crater and take our chances again on the merse-studded lake, lose ourselves on the ring island and recapture those all-too-brief moments of foolish adventure, wearing only rough sandals and crude hats, pointlessly hunting for improbable treasure.

The *real* pinnacle of my life to that point.

But there would be no returning to that innocence.

Never again.

————

The ship pushed away from the sad gray hulk of Charum Hakkor. The journey to Faun Hakkor would take just over thirty hours.

I compelled the humans to suit up if they wanted to live. Acceleration was extreme, of course. Riser and Chakas watched with me as the stars wheeled and the ship powered into full reaction drive, grabbing the vacuum energy and expelling a violet streak of virtual neutrons, which winked out as soon as their lives were discovered by the doubled hand of time.

We stayed within our armor until the ship found its proper orbit. Time slowed to a crawl. I tried to teach the humans how to access diverting games but they were not attentive. Finally, excluding me, they played mysterious finger games over and over. I was about to learn by long observation their rules and elements of strategy when the Didact rejoined us in the command center.

Our armor unlocked.

Faun Hakkor came into view. Our orbit adjusted to allow a looping pass. We would not linger, we would not land.

"I've inspected all the planets with long-range sensors," the Didact said. "The information they glean is not one hundred percent compelling at such distances, but . . ."

"Where did humans fight the hardest?" Chakas asked, approaching the Didact. He looked up at the Promethean with a clear gaze and without fear.

"Where their interests were most crucial, of course. Charum Hakkor saw some of the final and worst fighting." The Didact drew himself up before this accusing human. "Your people—if I may call them that—were most cruel when they savaged worlds where Forerunners had resettled other species. The pressure of their growing populations was strong. They annihilated fifty defenseless systems and sowed their conquests with human colonies before we coordinated and drove them back to the outer reaches of the spiral arm. They believed—"

"In creating many souls," Chakas said, eyes dull, as if looking inward, "I'm learning much about my ancestors."

"Makes unhappy," Riser commented.

"Switch to full view," the Didact ordered, perhaps to break out of this conversation.

Abruptly, we appeared to be suspended in space, the ship gone from around us. With some twitching and fumbling, getting used to this experience, we could all look down upon Faun Hakkor unfettered.

Almost a match in size for Charum Hakkor, this planet was covered with a mottled carpet of green and a few scattered, high oceans locked between mountains—completely different from Charum Hakkor, even beautiful . . . at first glance.

"I could live there," Riser said.

But the sensors were telling us a different tale. Only now did we see evidence of past destruction, highlighted by ancilla commentary—slash marks, craters, vast flattened and burned regions, now overgrown, but outlined in red and blue, with dates of strikes, counterstrikes, and lists of Forerunner ships engaged in the long-ago battle.

And then—beside those lists—other ships, other names. Human names. Chakas flinched at some of these names as his ancilla translated for him.

"Faun Hakkor was the origin of the Pheru which humans so deeply valued as pets and companions," the Didact said. "The reserve forces defended it fiercely but their numbers and installations were minimal, so the planet kept most of its original flora and fauna . . ."

"Something's changed," Chakas said. "It doesn't look right."

Riser walked around us—an outlandish figure in his armor, striding across an invisible deck. "Who lives here now?" he asked.

The Didact requested scans of the planet's present biota along with lists of the flora and fauna that had survived the battles nine thousand years before. In the records of the survey conducted by the Lifeworkers, likely after the end of hostilities, I saw hundreds of species of larger animals ranging in size from a meter to a hundred meters— some clearly aquatic, others huge land carnivores or sedate prairie-grazers. This list was compared with what the sensors could now locate.

One by one, the larger species dropped out.

"No animals larger than a meter," the ship's ancilla reported in a precise, clipped voice.

Next came a range of historic species less than a meter in size—tree-hoppers, burrowers, small carnivores, seed-eaters, flying creatures, arthropods, clonal sibling societies . . . the Pheru.

One by one, they dropped off the current list. None to be found.

Next came flora, including dense arboreal forests. Many of the original trees had acquired a kind of long-term intelligence, communicating with each other over centuries using insects, viruses, bacteria, and fungi as carriers of genetic and hormonal signals, analogous to neurons. . . . That list also quickly emptied. There were remnants—dead forests and jungles covered with a false green carpet of primitive plants and symbiotic species.

All that remained, apparently, were mosses, fungi, algae, and their combined forms.

"Nothing with a central nervous system or even a notochord," the ship's ancilla reported. "No fauna above a millimeter in scale."

"Where are the bees?" Riser asked. "What will bear fruit if bees are gone? No little meats to hunt. Where are *they*?" His voice rose to a sad squeak.

"Flowering plants are few and in decline," the ancilla continued. "All oceans and lakes and rivers are sour with decaying matter. Sensor results indicate extensive ecosystem collapse."

The Didact could stand no more. He cut off the virtual view, and we stood again on the deck of the command center, the fading lists flapping away if blown by discouraging breezes.

"We have become the monsters," the Promethean said. "It has returned in such force that Forerunners will destroy everything that carries even the smallest seed of reason . . . everything that thinks or plans. This is to be our last defense. A crime beyond all reason, surpassing all previous sins against the Mantle. . . . What will remain?"

I wondered what it he was referring to—the prisoner released from Charum Hakkor?

Something worse?

He called up a chair suited to his size and sat to think. "You wonder what forced me to enter the Cryptum. It was my refusal to agree to this plan even in its early stages. With all my being, I fought against the design of these infamous devices, and for thousands of years forestalled their construction. But my opponents finally won. I was reprimanded by the Council, bringing shame upon my rate, my guild, my family. Then I became the infamous one—the conqueror and savior who refused to listen to reason. And so, I vanished."

"No sympathy here," Chakas said, eyes sharp.

"Defiant to the last," the Didact observed, but without

anger—as if all his anger had been sucked away by the vision of these barren or dying worlds.

Riser lay down and curled up in misery. "No bees," he murmured. "Starving." Chakas knelt beside him.

"There is one more journey we must make," the Didact said after a time. "If that quest fails, we have no other option. Nothing more to contribute." He swiveled to face Chakas and Riser. "Humans refused to surrender in the face of overwhelming force, and so they were reduced. Their allies were less stubborn, less honorable, and were accorded a less severe punishment. The San'Shyuum were stripped of all weapons and means of travel and confined to a single star system kept in strict Forerunner quarantine. One of my former commanders oversaw that quarantine. Perhaps he is still in charge. . . ."

"We will go see how fares the last of the San'Shyuum. But first, I need time to think and plan. I will go below. The humans will be sequestered in their cabin." He looked them over dubiously. "I don't think they like me."

He gave the command and the ship complied. In minutes, we entered slipspace, and the Didact departed the command center.

THIRTEEN

HOURS LATER, WE emerged. The effects passed more slowly than usual, indicating we had gone a very great distance indeed, perhaps beyond the range of normal particle reconciliation. There might be dilation effects when we returned.

I stood alone in the command center, looking out across the tremendous, dim whirlpool of a galaxy, and called up a chart to see where we were. Spirals and grids spread quickly. At least this was our home galaxy. The ship was in a long, obscure orbit, high above the galactic plane, tens of thousands of light-years from any feasible destination.

I moved through the ship, seeking the Didact. He was

just a few decks down, in a medium-size storage bay separate from the larger weapons bays. Here, the war sphinxes had arranged themselves in their characteristic ellipse, each gripped by a gleaming hard-light buffer.

I watched him from behind a pressure arch that swept across the broadest dimension of the hold. He seemed to be speaking to an assembled group, like a commander addressing his warriors.

"I've never been naïve enough to believe following duty led to glory, or experience elevated one to wisdom among Forerunners," he said, his deep voice echoing through the chamber. "My young ones, I wish you were truly still here to counsel me. I feel weak and isolated. I fear what I will find when I walk among Builders again. Their rule brought us to this impasse. What we learned long ago from the humans . . ."

He saw me behind the arch, then stretched up his thick arm and gestured for me to join him. I did so.

The Didact was alone with his war sphinxes. I saw no others.

"Why have we traveled so far?" I asked.

"Multiple slipspace journeys can be tracked by core authority, if the journeys are rational. This is not a rational journey. For several more jumps, we will now be harder to track."

The Didact walked around the interior of the ellipse, touching one sphinx, then another. "These contain what is left to me of my warriors from long ago."

"They're *Durances*?" I asked. Beneath my armor, my skin crawled at the memory of a sphinx upbraiding me, telling me to *suck it up*, and my intuition that there was something more than an ancilla within. Riser had felt it, too.

"No. Warriors do not observe the niceties, as you may have noticed, Manipular. In battle, our dead are seldom in any condition to have their complete essences harvested. All I have left to me are the final interactions my children had with their machines—fleeting samples of their thoughts and memories, before they were killed in action . . . kept to be studied by their commander, to see what can be learned for future battles. I was their commander, as well as their father. . . . I have never had the heart to erase them."

"Do they still offer you their opinions?" I asked, regarding the sphinxes with a shiver.

"Some judgment remains," he said, looking down upon me. He laid a big hand on my shoulder. "You are not such a fool as you make yourself out to be. If I asked you what I should do," he said, "how would you answer?"

This caught me in a vise of contradictions. "I would think long and hard," I replied. "I have not the knowledge."

"The Librarian selected you and imprinted the humans—she seems to think you can help. And despite our many disagreements, I have rarely found her to be wrong."

He struggled inwardly for a moment, features flashing anger and sadness, confusion, then resolve. "My tactics before the Builder and Warrior councils were too blunt, my politics far too direct and naïve. The Librarian was always correct. That is not easy to admit."

A chorus of voices rose from the sphinxes—etched and hollow. I could understand only a few chopped phrases:

"They are out there, waiting . . ."

"Thousands of years wasted!"

"The solution was lost, Father . . . Lost!"

"If what the Old Ones made is loose . . ."

I stepped away from the ellipse, terrified.

The sphinxes fell silent. The Didact stood among them, shoulders bowed.

"Who *were* they?" I asked, suddenly feeling that here was much more than a commander and his dead soldiers.

"These were our sons and daughters. The Librarian's and mine," the Didact said. "They became warriors and served in my fleets. They died in battle. All of them."

I did not know what to say or do. His grief was palpable.

"Their final communications, their last commands and patterns and memories, stored in these machines, are all I have left. All that matters to me personally other than my oath . . . my duty. But I need *help*, more than they can even begin to give. The Librarian chose you to help me. But how?"

For a moment, he seemed lost, as if unable to decide which course came next—oddly indecisive for a Promethean. Then he asked a non sequitur question. "The humans . . . how much time did you spend with them . . . observing, before we left Erde-Tyrene?"

"Ten days," I answered.

"Do they still have their honor?"

"Yes," I said without hesitation.

"She's testing me, my wife, isn't she?"

"I know very little about the Librarian."

The Didact waved that off. "You'll never know her the way I did. She possesses a sense of humor rare in all Forerunners and impossible to find in Warrior-Servants . . . or in most Builders. It would be like her to summon me from my peace and set me this challenge."

"What does she want you to do?"

"When I served as commander in chief of Forerunner forces, I always had the support of an expert staff . . . dozens of fellow Prometheans, each backed by the very finest ancillas of long military experience. I'm not used to working alone, Manipular. I think better with a staff. But what she has given me . . . a Manipular and two humans . . . one of them docile and very small . . ."

Riser was not all that docile—the little Florian *had* bitten the Didact—but I did not contradict him.

"To reach full efficiency, a Promethean's staff shares most or all of the commander's knowledge. It's a tradition of long standing." He extended his armored hand. A dark red field spread along his fingers, as if the hand was dipped in glowing blood.

Here was something completely unexpected. Frightening, even. "I am not your equal," I objected. "I have not your experience. . . ."

"You saw what happened on Charum Hakkor and Faun Hakkor. Your ancilla will help you absorb my knowledge. You have only to ask and you will know all that I know."

Simple enough. The ancilla would absorb that knowledge, and I could study it at leisure. I hesitated, then extended my own hand. As I did, I saw the red field grow around my own fingers. The ancilla appeared in the back of my thoughts, not blue but red as blood . . . and hungry.

I had never felt the true, unfettered instinct—I might say *passion*—of an ancilla to gather knowledge.

Our fingers touched. He folded my much smaller hand in his own. "Close your eyes," he suggested. "Less disorienting that way."

I closed my eyes. Some time later—I lost track of time, but it might have been hours or days—I opened them again. My armor tingled against my skin. I felt hot inside, almost *burned*. The sensation slowly diminished, but I was still having difficulty focusing. The Didact wavered before me, little more than a shadow.

I tried to access my ancilla. She appeared in mingled red and blue, with an off-axis quiver. "Did it work?" I asked. "I don't feel very good. The ancilla seems broken, disconnected. . . ."

"It did *not* work," the Didact said, pulling back his hand. Only minutes had passed. "It's too much for a Manipular. I should have known. Only a first-form might be capable of absorbing so much."

"Then what can I do? What's left for me?"

The Didact did not immediately respond. "Go tend to the humans," he finally. "We will travel again soon."

———

In their cabin, the humans appeared to be either asleep or absorbed in the Librarian's *geas*, I could not tell which. Their eyes were closed and they lay curled beside each other. I decided not to interrupt. Judging from my own recent experience, there was a hard kind of cruelty in subjecting them to so much information, so rapidly—from both inside and out. I wondered if they would emerge sane or anything remotely like their past selves.

The residual pain of the attempted transfer had left me miserable. Not even the armor could immediately dissipate my discomfort. Worse, the armor's ancilla deeply resented being overloaded. For now, she seemed to blame me rather than her own greed for knowledge. I acutely felt her broken pulses of disapproval.

I lay down beside the humans, then rolled over on the deck, clutching my helmet and gritting my teeth.

Riser stood over me, chittering his concern. "Did he hurt you, the killer of humans?" he asked. A few steps behind, Chakas loomed as well, his face pale and unhealthy-looking.

They are changing. I am not.

"No," I said, my thoughts slowly beginning to clear and my head to cease throbbing. "He asked for help. He offered me . . . his training, his war-subtlety, personal history." I simplified these concepts as best I could.

Chakas shivered his shoulders and shook his head. "Sounds stuffy. What if I go out there and spit on him?"

Riser gave a low *faa-schaaa*. I had learned enough about the Florian's expressions to see that he was up for this assault if Chakas was.

"He *fears* you," I said. "Well, he respects you. No. That isn't it, either. He remembers what you once were and what you did. You killed his children . . . in battle."

"Us, personally?" Chakas asked doubtfully. "I don't remember that."

"Our ancestors," Riser observed, squatting. "Back when your people and mine were the same."

"You've been learning from your *geas*," I said.

"And from the little blue woman," Riser said. "But I will not marry her. You are right about that."

FOURTEEN

OUR SHIP EMERGED from its next passage surrounded by a diffuse mist of icy dust, the remains of ancient cometary material enveloping the hereditary system of the San'Shyuum. Once this cloud had been much denser. The San'Shyuum had depleted it to supply their early starships with fuel. Now the last of the cloud served to mask our presence and allow the Didact to observe the inner system as best he could.

The sensor images were impressive and strange. I had never seen a quarantined stellar system before. Such capabilities were rarely displayed to young Builders. A planetary system is mostly empty, even the greatest of worlds being lost in the immensity of billions of kilometers of space. Like their former human allies, the San'Shyuum had evolved on a water-rich world not far from a yellow star, within a temperate zone that allowed only a narrow range of weather. Now, however, ten thousand years after their defeat, the system was surrounded by trillions of vigilants that constantly wove in and out of space-time, sometimes so rapidly that they seemed to shape a solid sphere. This sphere extended to a distance of four hundred million kilometers from the star, and thus did not encompass four impressive gas giants whose orbits lay beyond that limit. Several of the many moons orbiting those gas giants provided platforms for semiautomated maintenance stations, some of them populated by the Builder servant-tools known as Huragok. Huragok are more tools than organisms, and are rarely accorded personhood among Forerunners. Their pride derives from their service—and, to a certain extent, their buoyancy in whatever supporting atmosphere they find themselves. They enjoy being confined by gravitation or centrifugal force and staying within a meter of a solid surface. I found them boring, whenever I encountered them, which was never in polite society. Their anaerobic metabolism, and those gas bladders . . .

The Didact kept his sensor sweep passive for the moment, merely listening. Forerunner communications are never transmitted along electromagnetic wavelengths, but the San'Shyuum had given up all other methods. And so, he could study what was leaking through the quarantine boundaries. His ancilla translated.

"It's quiet," he said. "I hear little other than microwave pulses and transpositive signaling."

Stepping through the virtual display, calling up whatever information was being gleaned by the sensors across the system, it took the Didact several minutes to locate the lone Warrior-Servant outpost in the system, orbiting just within the inner boundary of the quarantine.

"They retired the *Deep Reverence* here," he murmured. A magnified image appeared and was enhanced by specifications and other data. The *Deep Reverence* was an impressive fortress-class vessel, fifty kilometers in length, its incept date before the human-San'Shyuum war. "I apprenticed on her when I was a cadet. A grand old hulk. These quarantine worlds are terrible duty. I almost hope my friends are no longer in service . . . I suspect they caught blowback from my own troubles. I suspect they were *punished*."

He waved off the display. "We have to break cover and move in closer. It's a risk, but I need to understand more. And I need all the help I can get."

"But we tried . . ."

"There's one more way. Your patrimony is buried deep, inaccessible to a Manipular. To absorb my knowledge, you must be able to access your patrimony and the full richness of the Domain. To do that, you'll have to expand your capabilities. If you are willing . . . if you volunteer."

"You mean . . . mutate to a higher rate."

"As close an approximation as we can manage out here," the Didact said. "It's called a brevet mutation. It's not common, but it is within the Warrior-Servant code. This ship is capable of supporting such a ceremony. Lacking that, I cannot supply you with my knowledge . . . and you cannot access what your ancestors stored within you, or access the Domain, which supplements all."

"I'm supposed to unlock my patrimony with my father's assistance."

"Traditionally, that's true. But since I'm the only Forerunner around and we're unlikely to find any Builders nearby . . ."

He did not need to lay out the details. I was being asked to mutate and grow without my family or even my rate being present to assist. He would be my mentor. And that meant I would receive the Didact's genetic imprint.

"I'd mutate to a Warrior-Servant," I said.

"At least in part. You could always petition for a correction, a reversion, once you returned to your family."

"I've never heard of such a thing."

I *had* heard of failed mutations, of individuals hidden in special family enclaves and restricted to menial tasks. Not an attractive prospect.

"It is a choice."

Under the circumstances, it didn't feel like a choice. "What . . . what would it feel like?" I asked.

"All mutation is difficult. Brevet mutations are particularly unpleasant."

"Is it dangerous?"

"We will have to exercise caution. But once we've succeeded, we can venture down and see what the situation is on the *Deep Reverence*."

"I haven't *volunteered*," I reminded him.

"No," he said. "But the Librarian has always been a great judge of character."

FIFTEEN

YOU DO NOT wear armor during a mutation. You do not
accept the opinions or advice of an ancilla. Everyone
and everything around you falls silent and does not
respond to your sounds of pain or need, except to provide
pure water when you cry out that you are thirsty.

Every Forerunner advances through at least two mutations over their life span. Many go through five or more. The
number helps determine your rank within the hierarchy of
family, Maniple, and guild. The collective of guilds can be
entered only after mutation to first-form. Which guild,
which rate, would I belong to . . . ?

The Didact led me to a small chamber the ship had prepared on the point of the bow, for such a mutation by ritual law must take place under the direct light of the stars—or a reasonable approximation.

The bow became transparent. I stripped off my armor, as did the Didact. The pieces were transported aft, and the deck closed up beneath us. We seemed to stand alone and naked on the highest point of a narrow mountain, awash in the ancient light of millions of suns. . . .

Intercepted only by me, the supplicant, and my mentor. For every Forerunner rate mutation had to be patterned after a mentor, and the Didact was the only Forerunner available.

None of the irony of this was lost on me. I had never consciously hoped for this moment and yet had always anticipated it, as if fully aware that at the end of my foolishness was yet more privilege and advancement—and perhaps new methods of having fun, seeking adventure.

Never the notion of duty or responsibility. Yet now they were awakening. I felt inadequate, immature in the extreme—ready for change.

Still, I could not stifle deep indignation at being mentored by a lower rate rather than one of my own Builders. In this, like my father, I was a true Forerunner after all.

"Brevet mutation entails risks," the Didact said. "The ship is equipped to stimulate the proper growth factors, but you will not be imprinted by your immediate relatives . . . some details of your development may be lost or distorted. Is this understood?"

"I accept . . . under pressure," I said.

The Didact stepped back. "There can be no misgivings," he said. "Mutation is a personal journey, not to be coerced."

"If I don't do this, you tell me the entire galaxy could be wiped out. . . . That isn't coercion?"

"Allegiance to duty is the Forerunner's highest instinct and purpose. It is what empowers us to defend the Mantle."

I wasn't about to argue the hypocrisy inherent in *that*. If the Mantle—the exalted preservation of life throughout the universe—was the core of our deepest philosophy, our reason for being, then why were Lifeworkers at the bottom of our rates?

Why did Builders, who worked mostly with inanimate matter, rank so high?

Truly, I was at least as fed up with Forerunner sanctimony as ever. . . . But if I could prevent my family from suffering, if I could prevent the devastation we had seen on Charum Hakkor and Faun Hakkor, if I could preserve the strange and compelling beauty of Erde-Tyrene from being extinguished . . . all too clearly these possibilities, inevitabilities, presented themselves to my imagination . . .

Then I would have to accept this procedure, no matter how clumsy or dangerous it might be.

The Didact looked me over through his narrow gray eyes. The pale fur on his scalp bristled. "You're enjoying being a victim," he said.

"I am not!" I cried. "I am ready. Proceed!"

"You still believe you should be uniquely privileged to

live your life in a certain fashion." He looked defeated, then relieved, as if all hope had finally gone—and he was glad. "There can be no rise in rate without a modicum of wisdom. You do not demonstrate that wisdom."

"I had no part in creating this disaster, but I'm willing to sacrifice my life to save my people! Is that not selfless and noble?"

"Mutation to a higher rate requires acceptance of the Mantle. The Mantle is in part awareness of what all life has sacrificed to allow you to *be*. That arouses a deep kind of personal guilt. You do not feel that guilt."

"I've violated the wishes of my family, I've involved these humans in my stupidity, and what will happen to them when you're done? I feel guilt! All through me, *guilt*!"

"Only arrogance," the Didact said. "To dare is to risk self-lessly, not to waste your life because you see no other purpose to your existence."

This struck me to my heart and I kicked at the deck, wanting to drop below the stars, go back, forget this awful-ness. I reached out as if to strike him, and then saw the difference in our sizes, in our situation—saw his weary sad-ness and thought of the pitiful memories still held in the war sphinxes that had protected his Cryptum for a thou-sand years . . . the last of his children.

The Didact knew no other duty but this. His wife was far away, he had not seen her in literally ages, did not know whether she was using him for ends that might not have been foreseen when he was forced into meditative exile. Yet he trusted.

He served.

I pulled back my tiny fist. "I don't want your sadness," I said.

"It is the Mantle."

"You *mourn*."

This set him back a little. "I spent thousands of years mourning and found no virtue in it." He settled, crossing his great legs, leaning his torso forward until there was very little room left for me under the unwinking stars.

I got down on my knees beside him and crossed my own legs. "Tell me about your exile."

"Not wise, perhaps, but rudely *curious*," he said with a sigh.

"What did you experience in the Cryptum?"

"Let us just say I did not find peace. What all the great, higher Domains of the universe mandate for Forerunners is never peace, never solace, never rest. Never consistency, logic, or even pure passion. Frankly, I envy your perversity, Manipular."

I did not know what to make of that. "Your difficulty is, you regret all you have done. And you mourn."

The Didact's arms dropped, his shoulders relaxed, and I saw a glint of more than just acknowledgment, more than just recognition. He spoke in a low, grinding voice. "My blood and seed . . . wasted. My life with my family, my wife, so brief. I felt so much hatred. Hatred is still with me. Perhaps you are right to reject my imprint. The Mantle is as far beyond me now as . . ."

"*You* weren't prepared to mutate either, were you? In combat, mutation was forced on you. A brevet mutation. Someone saw your potential even through your flaws."

The Didact inspected me and for a moment, in that great stone visage, carved or artfully mauled by history and grief, he lifted his lips and almost smiled as if he were still young. I did not know that was possible.

"Touched by your blade, Manipular," he said.

"I accept my flaws as you accepted yours, and I will transcend them . . . as you did. I am as ready as I'll ever be, Promethean." I was actually trembling, but not with fear.

The Didact heaved himself up and waved his hand. "So be it, aya—and *aya* again."

A column studded with small spherules rose from the deck and slowly rotated to press against my side. The spherules twisted on stalks to touch my skin, access my points of nervous and genetic energy, of metabolic and catabolic reserves. . . .

Memory, muscle, intent, passion, intellect, stability—and that peculiar connection to the Mantle that all have but seldom know or feel.

The points of my being, as embarrassing as having my organs of sex examined and outlined, more so—for Forerunners were never shy about sex.

"Mentor and sponsor," he said. Another column rose and more spherules surrounded and connected with his larger frame. "From my life let the best be taken. Let the growth inherent in this youth be examined and maximized. Let all that is potential and beloved of the Mantle be nurtured and encouraged. Let all that was past be put away, and all that is future brought forward, made real and physical. . . ."

The Didact's words moved on. I no longer heard them, but I felt them. Transfixed, I could not speak.

My body was already responding.

SIXTEEN

THE DIDACT REMOVED the spherules by hand, it might have been hours later.

The stars rotated slowly to a new position.

I seemed to be at the center of the universe. I could neither reason nor believe that it was our ship that had moved.

I was taken aft and placed in a large cubicle that could have comfortably contained a squad of warriors: gray, a single light in the rear wall, empty of all ornament, clean, slightly cool.

"Eat nothing for a time but drink when you are thirsty," the Didact told me, arranging my limbs on the bunk. The bunk was larger than I needed—for now. "Your body will be upset. Not all the changes will happen right away. It could take many days."

"I feel a shadow in my head," I said.

"The old you. Soon, you will experience a cleaner, swifter mind. You will feel an arrogant kind of exhilaration—and then, that, too, will pass."

In the solitude of that cubicle, I felt the first changes: a slow, careful ache throughout my limbs. My hands in particular hurt. I looked down upon them and thought they already looked larger, less pale, the skin grittier and grayer. I had always thought that higher rates were less attractive than Manipulars.

My youthful beauty was passing. I was growing uglier.

I did not care.

———

So, when did you realize that you had grown up?

I thought I saw Chakas stand beside my bunk, watching with a frown. How remarkable that I used to be like him. So much alike. I wondered whether the geas imposed upon him and Riser by the Librarian felt anything like this mutation.

I wanted to compare my experiences with his, but the room was empty.

I drank some water.

For a few minutes, I thought I experienced yet another

voice in my head, not me, not my past me or any future me. It seemed to contain a great deal of knowledge, none of it of any use. It was knowledge that belonged to others from very far away, other existences where life and death were meaningless, light and darkness twisted together, where the twin fists of time uncurled their fingers and joined in a clasp, so that nothing changed or ever would.

Of course that made no sense. Later, even thinking about it repulsed me.

The Didact checked in on me and tested my limbs, thumped my chest, hummed over my prone body. I assumed he would declare the mutation a failure. I did not feel like any sort of Forerunner, young or old.

"Be glad," he said. "You are not becoming a warrior. Not entirely. But you'll do."

"What *am* I becoming?" I asked. If I was to live, I needed to know where I might fit in, what rate would accept my hideously distorted body.

"In a little while you will be hungry," he said. "The ship will prepare special food. When you're ready, join me in the control center. We need to plan how we will approach the San'Shyuum."

"When will I access the Domain? When will I receive your knowledge?"

"The potential is already there, Builder. But take it slowly for now."

———

I walked on my own to the control center. Chakas and Riser were not present. I wondered if the Didact had locked them away during all the time I was out of action.

He stood by a direct view of the stars. The control center's wide curved floor had sprouted a number of instruments I did not immediately recognize. One of them, it turned out, was there to give me my special food.

The Didact pointed without looking at me. I sat and ate.

I ate a lot. And then the second round of pain began, but I was not allowed to hide away and lie down. Our work was beginning.

SEVENTEEN

I PUT MY armor on after I stopped being hungry and feeling terrible. It required some adjustments before matching my new, larger body. The little blue female in the back of my thoughts was still there but seemed reluctant to deal with me. I had to dig deep to even find her. I felt as if my armor were judging me.

The Didact observed, blinking with slow dignity. He rearranged himself on the floor and turned back to the steadiness of the stars.

"The armor's broken," I said.

"You're different. The ancilla knows that, but she won't cater to you. You're no longer a Manipular. You have to listen better." The Didact seemed remarkably patient. Perhaps he remembered his own brevet mutation, all those thousands of years ago.

"The Domain—I don't feel *anything*."

"I would say that is also your fault—but perhaps not this time. I, too, have difficulty accessing the Domain at present. It is a mystery—for now. Perhaps in time we will explore together and see if it can be solved."

Disappointed, I stood up, performed a quick diagnostic on my armor, watched everything chart up clear and fine—then focused, trying to will my thoughts to be more mature. Still, I couldn't get the ancilla to cooperate. She came and went in different places in my head but would not do anything I asked—perhaps because my internal speech was garbled.

"Where did the humans go?" I asked the Didact when I was sure this process was getting nowhere.

"I locked them in a room with plenty of food they seem to like."

"Why?"

"They asked too many questions."

"What sort of questions?"

"How many humans I've killed. That sort of thing."

"Did you answer?"

"No."

"The Librarian filled them full of knowledge they can't handle. They're like me."

"Yes, they're like you, but they seem to actually be *listening*. They just don't like what they're hearing."

EIGHTEEN

MY FIRST SUCCESSFUL though stumbling efforts to access the Didact's experiences produced scattered impressions of darkness, brilliance, rolling suns, grief and sickness and glory—complete chaos. My ancilla was still balky; I had to find my own way of accepting and interacting with the knowledge.

What I managed was a crude arrangement, missing fully nine-tenths of the subtlety and subtext and power, but at least the memories began to open to me.

Soon, I was jittering and plunging my way through a great space battle, events moving far too quickly for me to make much sense of it. I had no idea where or when this was—I could not correlate these events with any historical record. Complicating the recovery was many hundreds of points of view, threading through and around the central events, chopping and intercutting—and a remarkably different perception of objective reality. As a Promethean, the Didact simply saw things differently.

Clearly, a thousand years ago, when entering battle, the Didact had plugged into the full sensory experience of thousands of his warriors . . . something I could barely imagine and certainly not control.

My ancilla fell far behind, glowing between all the half-processed, crudely assembled information like a distant blue star, frantically seeking details which connected all this to real history.

What startled me as I explored the threads—and tried to collapse them into a usable narrative—was how pitiful objective reality was, all by itself. The combined threads—even the chaos of uncombined threads—were far richer, far more evocative and informative.

In my education as a Manipular, it had seemed to me that my teachers and even my ancillas had been intent on having me memorize the bare facts and not add my own interpretations. They did not trust me to enrich the whole; I was young and naïve. I was foolish. Even now, it was obvious the Didact's memories resisted my adding any coloring from my own experience. I had not been there.

Now I understood that no matter how sophisticated one became, the total richness was something no individual could ever capture or truly know. *It must not be constrained. It is ever raw, ever rich. . . .*

I tried to emerge from this pool of ecstatic excess. The so-called solid reality of the ship, of my armor, of the space and stars around us, was suddenly ominous, frightening. I had difficulty distinguishing these different states. I was drunk.

I fell back from the memories and tried to reengage with my core self.

And suddenly, as if everything had come into focus, I rode the whipsnap of over a dozen threads—warrior threads. They had a place, a name, a historical marker. I could not scramble free.

I plunged deep into the first battle of Charum Hakkor, one of the final engagements between Forerunners and humans. I saw thousands of war sphinxes spiraling in clouds around the planet like flocks of deadly sparrows, twisting and entangling human ships—

Sending them tumbling into the atmosphere to disintegrate, or slamming them against the unbending pillar of a Precursor ruin stretching high over the planet, or being slammed in return—the memory thread suddenly burning bright at the end, winking out, shriveling away.

Passion and the flow of a warrior's life . . . and, too often, death. The deaths jerked and whipped around me; the end of a warrior's life in a spreading, sparkling plume of molten metal, carbonized flesh, plasma and pure gamma rays, that flailing, crying, terrified abruptness felt as sharp as a plunging dagger.

I could not stop it.

I saw the implacable Precursor ruins of Charum Hakkor studded with human constructs, like ivy growing on great trees: vast cities and energy towers and defense platforms operating at geosync and equigravitation, little less sophisticated than Forerunner ships and platforms and stations.

Humans had been a great power, a worthy adversary—technologically. What about spiritually? How did they connect to the Mantle?

Were they truly our brethren?

I could not know. The Didact had been remarkably open to those ideas at the time. *You must know your enemy, and never underestimate or belittle them.*

No human threads in the Domain—no way of knowing their reactions—the Domain is not complete—

Was that my thought, or the critical observation of the Didact himself, realizing the greatness of his enemy?

I managed to lurch free and came to myself in my cabin, under the single wall lamp, gasping, crying out, my fingers scrabbling at the bunk and at the bulkhead, as if to dig myself free.

Truth was not for fools.

T HE HATCH TO the humans' quarters opened as I approached. I stepped inside and saw Chakas and Riser in the middle of the floor, sitting cross-legged, facing each other. Their armor lay beside them. Each had tucked a single foot into the leggings.

Chakas did not move, but Riser opened one eye and glanced at me.

"Blue lady is exploring us," he said.

"You're not wearing your armor," I said.

He moved his foot. The armor moved with it. "This is enough."

Chakas stretched up his arms with a cross expression. "What have we done to deserve this?" he asked.

"I had nothing to do with your *geas*."

"Blue Lady says we have many lives inside," Riser said.

"We're seeing some of what happened on Charum Hakkor," Chakas said. "Before the battles, before the war. I'm trying to see the caged prisoner. It's there somewhere, but why should I care?"

"I wish I understood," I told them. "I don't. Not yet. There's a greater story, something that brings glory to your people . . . but I don't see it. I think it is yours to see, not mine."

Chakas got to his feet, breaking the connection with the armor and the ancilla. "There's food. Forerunner food. You might as well have some."

Riser climbed onto a low bunk and brought forward a pair of trays covered with floating ampoules of grayish material. It looked little different from the "special" food provided after my brevet mutation. Clearly, Warrior-Servants were not tied to creature comforts. I tried to eat a little. "We're approaching a quarantined system," I said. "What have you learned—what do you remember about the San'Shyuum?"

"They are shadows," Riser said. "They come, they go."

"I don't think I like them," Chakas said. "Too charming. Slippery."

"Well, we're going to visit them, and I think the Didact is going to want you to meet and talk with them. We all seem to be part of a game he's playing with the Librarian."

"A tricky game?" Riser asked.

"A very serious game. I think she wasn't able to warn him about what's been happening since he entered the Warrior Keep. So we're his special tools. Few would suspect us."

"How does that work?" Chakas asked.

"We visit the places of history, we see, it stimulates us— we remember. Mostly, *you* see and you remember. Now that I have the Didact's memories, I think I'm supposed to link up with the Domain, but the Domain's not cooperating."

"*Domain* . . ." Riser held up his hand. "We don't know what that is."

"I'm not sure I do, either. You talk with your ancestors . . . in the memory the Librarian gave you, locked inside you, waiting to be activated. Is that a fair statement?"

Riser waggled his hand, meaning, I presumed, yes. His face relaxed and he cocked his head. Chakas looked at him curiously.

"The Domain is where we keep our deep ancestral records," I said. "They're stored there forever, available to any Forerunner, anywhere, no matter how far away."

"Not ghosts."

"No, but sometimes strange. The records don't always stay the same. Sometimes they change. It is not known why."

I flashed through some of the Didact's own experiences with the Domain, confused and unsatisfactory.

"Like real memories," Chakas said, watching me closely.

"I suppose. Such changes are regarded as sacred. They

are never reversed or corrected. And I learned something about the Didact's war sphinxes. They're all that's left of his children."

Riser whistled and squatted, then rocked gently, screwing up his face again.

"The war killed many . . . but humans fought well," I said. "I think we're about to face a common enemy—not the San'Shyuum."

Chakas and Riser focused fully on me. "Empty cage," Riser said, and folded his arms around his body, as if embracing and reassuring himself.

The ship's ancilla flashed before us. "The Didact requests your presence in the command center."

"All of us?"

"Humans will stay in quarters until the situation is better understood."

Riser chuffed, then sat cross-legged again and closed his eyes, lifting his chin as if listening to distant music. Slowly, Chakas sat as well, and they were as I had found them.

I took the lift to the command center.

TWENTY

'VE SENT A message to the *Deep Reverence* and revealed our location," the Didact confessed as we moved downstar, approaching the interlocking vigilants of the system's outer defenses. "We'll be destroyed if we don't communicate our intentions to the commander. Among Prometheans, he was known as the Confirmer."

On the deck of the command center, we again stood in virtual view, unsupported in wide space, surrounded by stars. One of the small outer worlds passed by: airless, rocky, lifeless. The displays conveyed updated information about the quarantine shield, along with what could be gathered about the three protected planets downstar—two apparently inhabited by San'Shyuum, the third a storage depot for stockpiled (and presumably outdated) Forerunner weapons.

I saw the San'Shyuum in my other memory as they had been ten thousand years before: a sleek, beautiful race, strong and sensual, intelligent but not overly impressed by intellect—capable of seducing other species with their almost universal beauty. Slippery indeed. Around the San'Shyuum, it seemed, all emotions melted into uncritical passion. The sole exceptions, in their historical experience— humans and Forerunner.

Our ship cruised on its long orbit downstar for a hundred million kilometers before a strong signal was received from the *Deep Reverence.*

"Aya, a Promethean interrupts our solitude, claiming to be the Didact!" a hoarse, deep voice said, accompanied by a visual of an old and nearly shapeless mass of muscle and scarred skin. Here was a Warrior-Servant who had undergone, it seemed to my newly informed eye, more battles and mutations than the Didact, some less successful than others. "Is it truly *you*, my old nemesis?"

The Didact revealed no dismay at what time had done to his fellow Promethean. "I told you I'd return. We have important business, and need your assistance. Are there traps laid here? Tell me true."

"Are you in trouble again?"

In an aside to me, the Didact said, "It *is* the Confirmer. But something feels wrong. The quarantine shield has been in battle mode for some time, I think."

"What would cause that?" I asked.

The Didact looked wary and grim. "Recent punitive action, possibly. . . . But the San'Shyuum were model citizens after they were brought here. Try to focus down-star on the San'Shyuum worlds." To the *Deep Reverence*, he said, "How long have you been stationed here without relief?"

My fingers worked quickly to draw up the required sensor data. I studied the two inner planets in the low-rez scan available through the quarantine shield. The surface features were mostly obscured. What I could make out deviated substantially from the ancilla records. The features had been *rearranged*. I thought immediately of Faun Hakkor. . . .

Nothing on the scale of a spaceship could be resolved, except of course for the *Deep Reverence*.

"Twelve centuries," the Confirmer said. "They have been years of blessed opportunity for growth and reflection. The Council assigned we old warriors to guard and protect our ancient enemies, now prostrate before Forerunner power. I do my duty and nothing less. You should see my collection of San'Shyuum carvings. Magnificent—I value it more because it's worthless. No Forerunner pays heed to the artifacts of vanquished foes. I presume you wish to visit my poor vessel?"

"That's my first intention," the Didact said.

"Just a moment . . . let me check with my staff. Oh, wait. I *have* no staff."

"You're alone?" The Didact gave me a look that might have asked, *Are all the old warriors alone?*

"Out here, the Domain is my only consolation," the Confirmer said. "I've been working my way through ancestors I never knew existed. But of late, the Domain has rebuffed me. . . ."

"I've come here on a mission for the Librarian," the Didact said. "We're traveling with two humans chosen by her. We need to question the leaders of the San'Shyuum."

"The Librarian—the Lifeshaper herself. . . . She was just through here on some mission or other. Caused some difficulties. Perhaps you've noticed the shield and vigilants are on alert."

"My wife has been busy," the Didact said.

I continued to study the inner planets. From what little we could see, through the filter of the quarantine shield, nearly all looked darker, probably damaged.

"Curious as to why anybody even cares about these remnants of our old wars," the Confirmer said. "Every now and then, I intercept a message about big events going on at the capital. I ignore them. They have nothing for me—no new orders. The Domain is all I have left—and now it's shut me out. Do you know why?"

"I'd like to view those reports."

"When you get here, we can rummage around in the ship's memory and look for them. But allowing the San'Shyuum to meet up with humans—that's forbidden. We separated them for a reason, old friend."

"May we approach and discuss?"

A pause. The Confirmer appeared to be turning a small sculpture around and around in his thick, coarse hands. Then, "For the Didact himself, of course. Adjust your orbit downstar, match your ship's ancilla to these codes, and the vigilants will avoid weaving a barrier where your orbit intersects. Glorious to hear from you! A living friend from the old days. So much to get caught up on!"

The transmission ended. Our ship altered its course and matched the codes. Displays revealed that the vigilants were indeed no longer flashing in and out of the sector where our orbit would penetrate the blockade.

"The Confirmer was a grand warrior and a good friend, but I never considered him much of an expert in the fine arts," the Didact said. "Keep the sensors trained on those planets." He appeared troubled

"Should I bring the humans forward?"

"Yes. Make sure they wear their armor."

I went aft and opened the cubicle assigned to Chakas and Riser. They emerged reluctantly, eyes thick with sleep. Riser dragged his armor behind him. "The blue woman and I argued," he explained. "I don't like her."

Chakas gave me a dirty look. He was far too involved in his own inner turmoil to pay attention to the slight physical changes I was already showing.

I told Riser, "We may be going into danger. The armor will protect you. I'll show you how to shut down the ancilla, if you want—for now."

"Make her quiet?" he said. "She gets upset with me."

"Exactly."

With a shudder, he allowed the armor to wrap him again, and stood of a height to match mine—almost. I was still growing.

"You look bigger," Riser said dubiously. "Smell different, too."

I showed them how to deactivate the ancilla, then queried my own blue woman about their complaints.

"What they remember makes them angry," she explained. "They ask questions I am not equipped to answer. I try to calm them. That only makes them angrier."

"Well, stop calming them," I told her. "There's got to be a reason for what they're experiencing."

———

The *Deep Reverence* appeared formidable in close sensor scans. I had first seen fortress-class vessels during ceremonies back in my early youth in the Orion nebular complex. The largest single Forerunner ships of war, fortresses were fifty kilometers in length, with a huge hemisphere on the forward end, a midlevel series of layered platforms equipped with launch bays and gun mounts, and below that, a long, weapon-studded tail. At their widest, they were ten kilometers across and could carry hundreds of thousands of warriors, as well as automated phalanxes that could be guided by warriors at a ratio of one to a million weapon-ships. . . .

It took me a moment to realize that I wasn't accessing

my own youthful experience or memory of those past ceremonies, but the Didact's.

Chakas looked miserably upon the *Deep Reverence*. "We're here to visit our old allies, aren't we?" he said. "Did you punish them like you did us?"

"They cut a deal," I said. "Let's talk about that later—"

The Didact lifted an arm as if in warning. "We're being brought into the quarantine," he said. "If there are any traps, we should learn soon enough."

The ship's ancilla appeared on a raised platform between us. "Ship's control has been handed over to the commander of the system," she said. "Within the shield, all sensors are limited to low-rez and close-in scans. We will be more than half-blinded."

"We know how to pick 'em, don't we?" Chakas asked Riser as they stood stiff and miserable.

Our armor had once again rooted us to the deck.

As we approached and then maneuvered to docking position, it became more and more obvious that the *Deep Reverence* had seen better days. It looked barely operational. The surface was a study in collisions, grooves, craters: unrepaired battle damage, worse by far than the stardust pocks on the old war sphinxes.

The launch ramps and bays were mostly empty. A token force of pickets and fast attack runners remained, and even these did not look as if they had been tended to recently.

Evidently, Forerunners had parked the fortress in its orbit and hoped to forget about it, about the old war, about this world—about the San'Shyuum in general. A pact had been made, but to nobody's pride or benefit. The fortress had been abandoned in place, out of shame.

Still, the old war platform remained impressive if only for its size. Compared with the fortress, our ship was a bit of fluff stuck on the sleeve of a giant.

Our ship's ancilla extruded a walkway. A few minutes after, we walked the fortress's cold, bare decks. Not to upset the Confirmer, for the moment, we left the humans behind.

The space across which we walked was almost void of atmosphere, the far reaches lost in violet shadow, the bulkheads and deck coated with a thin, crunchy rime of water ice. From all around came a shrill, wandering, whining sound, like vacant whistling, intermixed every few seconds with a pulsing *thump* like a soft mallet striking the outer hull.

"Long duty has not been good to the Confirmer," the Didact observed. "No warrior should allow his weapons to rust."

A lift dropped from the high arched ceiling and opened for us to enter. From all around came a crackling, poorly reproduced voice, filling and echoing through the vault:

"Come higher, old friend! We of the broken Domain await your inspection."

The Didact looked down upon me as the lift door closed. "This may not go well. No blame on your head, young firstform."

"I am patient, with a keen edge," I replied.

This impressed him. "You're starting to sound like a Warrior," he said. "But you still look like a Builder. Your strength . . . how is that progressing?"

"Bigger," I said, inspecting my hand. It no longer looked ugly to me. My thoughts were catching up with my growth. "I don't ache as much."

"The Confirmer once commanded legions. No more. I doubt there will be any sort of fight. Aya, I wonder why he did not choose the Cryptum over this."

"He wished to serve," I said.

"I served by my departure, not to provoke conflict," the Didact grumbled.

"He keeps talking of the Domain. Has that been his only connection with Forerunners?"

"Perhaps. That concerns me. Sometimes, there is a kind of broken-mirror aspect. . . ."

We reached a midlevel within the hemisphere of domiciles. The level was a confusion of half-made walls and labyrinthine channels, crossed by ghostly ramparts and bridges. Here, the atmosphere was still too thin—not safe without armor. The hard-light overlays were weak and inconsistent. The fortress's power situation had apparently been dire for many centuries. I would no more have trusted a stroll over these flickering, corrupt structures than if they had been made of frost.

"Stay close," the Didact said.

Ahead, a large, lumpish figure wearing what looked like

parts from three sets of armor stepped into a dim, snow-flecked shaft of light. This must be the Confirmer, I thought—but the Didact's features did not reveal gladness or even instant recognition.

"Permission granted to board the *Deep Reverence*," the figure said. He came closer, surrounded by a circling ring of ship's displays, conveying what seemed to be, from where I stood, almost useless information—or no information at all.

"We are honored to be received on your great ship," the Didact said. "Many served and are remembered."

"Many served," the Confirmer said. "Did you bring the Grammarian with you? The Strategos?"

"Not this time," the Didact said. "As I said, we come on an errand from a Lifeworker, my wife. . . ."

"And as *I* told you, she came through here recently," the Confirmer said. "If you ask me, she was too full of herself. But she had the stamp of the Council, so I asked no questions. I do not interfere in the politics of higher rates."

"Aya," the Didact said. "We ourselves do not have the stamp of the Council."

"I thought as much. Ever in difficulty. First you marry a Lifeworker, then you oppose the Builders. . . . Makes me wonder whether you deserved my brevet mutation." The Confirmer stepped forward and clasped the Didact in a thick, clanking embrace.

The Didact glanced at me in some embarrassment. I pointed and mimed, *Him?*

The Didact raised his eyes. Snow circled them for a moment, until the Confirmer let go and held the Didact at arm's length.

The old Promethean now turned to regard me. Never before had I seen an uglier, more gnarled and broken Forerunner of any class. His skin, what I could make out through the almost cancerous overweave of armor, was mottled gray spotted with unhealthy veins of paleness, tinged with pink. He had none of the patches of bluish white bristling fuzz on crown or shoulders that marked the Warrior-Servants I had known, including the Didact. In his mouth, I saw two solid ridges of stone-black teeth—grown together—with a hint of darting tongue between.

"Not yet, old friend. Amuse me. Tell me again tales of the strife we have seen, the victories we marshaled. I am lonely here, and time stretches to intolerable lengths."

TWENTY-ONE

TRULY, THE DEEP *Reverence* seemed like a great tree riddled through by the wandering whimsy of a single, awful termite. The higher we progressed within the fortress—and *progress* is not the correct word—the deeper the sense of undisciplined decay. I wondered if the Confirmer had for the last thousand years spent his time building useless follies throughout the decks, above and below, draining the ship's resources and perverting its original design.

We came finally to a space warm enough and with sufficient oxygen to relieve the burden of our armor. The hiss of replenishment was like a gasp as our ancillas sucked in reserves for what they, too, seemed to think might be a desperate time.

The Confirmer's command center was hung with tattered draperies of a design I could not recognize. Within the drapes, pushing up through or rising between, were dozens of sculptures made of stone and metal, some quite large, and all wrought with a grace and skill that was evident whatever their subjects might have been—abstractions or representations, who could tell?

But as a command center, this space was no more functional than the empty vault we had first entered. Clearly, the fortress had become a cluttered ghost of its former might.

The Confirmer ordered up seating arrangements. With creaks and groans, the deck produced only two chairs suitable for Prometheans, plus a small bump that might have been meant for me. Some of the drapes drew aside, ripping and falling in dusty shreds . . . and three sculptures toppled, one of them nearly striking me before it landed on the deck with a solid *thunk* and split in two.

The Confirmer carried bottles from a broad cabinet half-hidden in the drapes, walking with a left-leaning lurch. "The best I have to offer," he said, and poured out three glasses of a greenish liquid. He sat and offered a glass to the Didact and one to me. Neither of the glasses were clean. "You remember *kasna*," he said, lifting his own glass in toast. The liquid inside smelled sweet and sour—pungent— and left a stain on the glass. "The San'Shyuum have always excelled in the arts of intoxication. This is from their finest reserves."

The Didact looked at his glass, then downed it in a gulp—to the Confirmer's dismay.

"That's rare stuff," he chided.

"You allow the San'Shyuum to travel between their two worlds?" the Didact asked, returning the glass to the dusty tray.

"They are confined within the boundary of the quarantine," the Confirmer said. "There's no reason to hold them fast."

"In many ways, they were worse than humans," the Didact said.

"Misled and misguided, they now claim."

"No matter, at this late date," the Didact said. "You've not had contact with any other warrior in how many years?"

"The living? Centuries, centuries," the Confirmer said. "The last shipment of . . ." He stopped himself, looked about with curtained chamber with eyes that had lost nearly all focus. "Many colleagues are brought here, you know. Exiled with less dignity than the Council allowed you. They've fought, and lost, many political battles since you vanished."

"Where are they?"

"A few were allowed their own Cryptums. The rest . . . the Council shipped us their Durances."

"The *Deep Reverence* has become a *graveyard*?" the Didact asked, the last color departing his already pale features.

"An acre of Mantle. A Memorial. It's what is allowed to our class, now that they have been decommissioned and banished from Council action. The San'Shyuum come here every little while to repair and tend to the displays, and I am grateful. I have neither the staff nor the energy to do the job myself."

"Our enemies *tend our dead*?" The Didact stood and seemed to be looking for something to pick up and throw. I moved away—still no match for his strength.

"The war is long over," the Confirmer said with a feeble attempt at dignity. "We face greater enemies. . . . And yet, *you* have chosen exile rather than argue with the Council and face the inevitable. And relying on a Lifeworker to hide you and no doubt provide for your return . . . *I* have nothing to regret, my friend." The Confirmer moved with that awkward gait toward the nearest sculpture, a dark green, overarching shape patterned with what might have been foliage. His hand stroked the smoothly carved surface. "The San'Shyuum ambassador leaves these as a form of respect for their esteemed conquerors. He arrives in a strange chair, on wheels. . . . I do believe they now require their leaders to be paraplegics. I also believe they hold me in some affection. The San'Shyuum are not much like they used to be."

"Decadent seekers after sensual gratification, you mean? Clever frauds who betrayed their alliances?"

"Indeed, they once worshipped youth and beauty. Not so now. Elders rule, and the youth serve their bidding.

True, there is still much celebration about procreation. . . . Unseemly, but their populations are contained, they breed selectively, and so they do not outgrow their planets, as once they threatened. . . ."

"Who leads them now?"

"There have been many titles, many names. Many assassinations. I've lost track of who or what speaks for their two worlds."

"Find out," the Didact said. "Tell them a senior Promethean needs to question them about Charum Hakkor and what was imprisoned there."

Now was the Confirmer's turn to lose all the color in his face. He slowly lowered the glass. "The timeless one?"

"The Master Builder has finished his supreme weapon. It was tested near Charum Hakkor," the Didact said. "No one seems to have anticipated the effect on Precursor structures. The arena has been breached."

"Impossible," the Confirmer said. I thought for a moment that the possibility of a new challenge brought a stiffer carriage to the old warrior, a return of proud bearing, but after a moment's thought, he looked around the half-hidden chamber, the dusty, tattered drapes, the dozens of sculptures, some still seated on their transport pallets . . . and seemed almost to deflate within his patchwork armor. "Impossible," he repeated. "If the cage is broken and the prisoner is missing—where could it have gone? We never understood what it was to begin with."

The Didact spoke with it. . . .

But that part of the Didact's memories were not at all clear to me. Too dangerous for a newly mutated first-form? Was I not trusted after all? But he had transferred so much!

"That's why it's imperative we question the San'Shyuum."

"I won't stop you. Your ship is heavily armed, however. The weapons must be left with me."

"All except my war sphinxes. They are no longer lethal and serve me as remembrance."

"Aya, I understand."

"We also have two humans."

"Forbidden."

"Necessary to our mission."

The Confirmer held the Didact's gaze. Again, a shadow of the old strength seemed to return. "If the Council has not formally decommissioned your rank, you are my superior. The humans are your responsibility. The weapons cannot pass, however."

That seemed to settle the matter. An understanding between two old warriors. They drank again, and this time the Didact sipped rather than gulped. "The Librarian . . . Did she explain her mission?"

"She selected individuals from the San'Shyuum and other species and took them away. I understand that's what she does now all over the galaxy. Maybe she collects species the way I collect sculptures."

"Where did she take them?"

"An installation called the Ark. She was escorted by

these new Builder security types. Haven't you spoken with her?"

An awkward silence.

"No," the Confirmer said. "Of course not. That would be too easy, wouldn't it?"

TWENTY-TWO

OUR SHIP INSERTED itself into a downstar orbit. As we approached the first of the two San'Shyuum worlds, the Didact confided to me what already seemed obvious. "The Confirmer no longer maintains duty fitness. He did not even check to see if my rank is still in place."

"Is it?" I asked.

"I have no way of knowing."

"The Librarian knew you would come here, after Charum Hakkor."

"It would be a reasonable assumption. My wife has her own plans that she's slowly—very slowly—allowing me to discover."

"Others might suspect the same—and prepare a trap."

"Of course. If we are *her* warriors now, we must accept an element of risk. Since the humans carry her mark, putting them with the San'Shyuum may release crucial memories. It's a risk worth taking."

"They're not at all happy with what they remember," I said.

"They're accessing unpleasant truths—the thoughts and recollections of human warriors. Defeated, bitter—and about to be executed."

"She took their essences before they were killed?"

"She had nothing to do with what happened in those days. It was warrior policy to preserve what we could of foes before they were removed."

"*Removed*," I said.

"And in this instance, we had excellent reason to harvest memories," the Didact continued. "Even before we went to war with humans, they were fighting another foe. A most hideous scourge we had yet to encounter, and about which we still know very little."

I looked inward. "The Flood," I said. This much knowledge was open to me: images . . . emotions, but all jumbled and incomplete.

"That was their name for it. While they fought us, they defeated that other enemy and pushed it beyond the edge of the galaxy—an epic battle. We did not know of their victory until *we* defeated *them*. And we wished to learn from them how to fight the Flood, should it return—as seemed inevitable. However, for obvious reasons, they felt no compulsion to share their secret. They kept it distributed among themselves, hidden from all our techniques."

"Surely, humans did not fight this 'timeless one,' the missing captive."

"No." The Didact lifted his long arm and swept it slowly along the visible limb of the San'Shyuum world, emerging into day. "It predated the humans who excavated it. It predated the Flood. However, I shared the humans' opinion that whatever it was, it was extraordinarily dangerous."

"And still, you spoke with it."

He seemed conflicted that I knew about this. "You see that much. Aya."

"How could you penetrate Precursor technology? What did you ask of it?"

"That will emerge when you are ready—and in full context," the Didact said. "Our weapons have been removed, but this ship is still full of powerful tools. You, for example. And the humans. The Librarian has been conducting her surveys and research for the thousand years I was in exile, and seems to have learned a few things she does not dare pass along directly. Things perhaps even the Council has not been told. But through you and the humans, indirectly . . . you have been placed on a slow fuse, timed for the proper moment . . . and even I have no idea when that might be."

"It all sounds awfully inefficient," I said.

"I've learned to trust my wife's instincts."

"Did you share your knowledge with her before you entered the Cryptum?"

"Some."

"Did she share her knowledge with you?"

"Not much."

"She didn't trust *you*, then."

"She knew my circumstances. Once my Cryptum was discovered and I was released, it was inevitable that I would eventually be forced to serve the Master Builder and the Council, whatever my objections. But she gave me some time, a delay, before that happens. We have this journey to make and questions to ask. In context."

The ship's ancilla appeared and informed us we were now permitted to approach the largest San'Shyuum world.

"Bring your humans here," the Didact said.

"They are not *my*—"

"On your actions they will live or die, serve as heroes to their species, or be snuffed like tiny flames. Are they not yours, first-form?"

I lowered my head and complied.

Our ship continued its downstar fall along a stretched elliptical orbit. If we decided to abort, we could whip back out and make a break for the quarantine shield . . . hoping, I suppose, that the codes would still work and we'd be released.

Faint hope.

TWENTY-THREE

INALLY WE WERE close enough that our sensors penetrated the smoky haze that covered the shadowy ruins
of San'Shyuum cities. The destruction hinted at from
afar was now manifest.

Chakas and Riser watched with us on the command
deck, faces deadpan. Riser examined me with a puzzled expression, then wrinkled his nose. Chakas did not even glance
at me. If they felt horror, awe, memory . . . they did not reveal this to us. Already I saw how much they had changed,
how much they had grown. They were almost entirely different beings from the ones I had met on Erde-Tyrene. We all
were.

At least, I told myself, my service was voluntary—of a kind.

"There," the Didact confirmed, and swept his finger over the magnified images: trace signatures of engine plumes visible even through the waste heat of cities on fire, the outlines of fleets of landed or hovering ships, some of them larger than ours, many smaller. "Lifeworkers don't carry weapons," he said. "Builder security is here, but they're lying low, hiding in the obscurity. They must know I'm here. Let's take a deeper look. There—Preservation- and Dignity-class escorts. Hundreds of swift seekers, Diversion-class war machines. All this, to protect a few Lifeworkers? What happened down there? Is she still in the system?"

His voice carried tones of both resignation and despair, and a touch of hope—as if defeat and capture and whatever worse things he had imagined might all be worthwhile if he could only see his wife again.

We were within a hundred thousand kilometers of the planet when the ship's ancilla announced that our last escape orbit was being cut off. "Many ships are moving downstar through the quarantine shield. They are allowed full functionality, power and speed, and are now matching our course and trajectory."

I spun around as more than a hundred flashed into sensor view, most smaller than ours but a few substantially greater and no doubt packing tremendous firepower.

"Interdiction," the Didact said. "The Confirmer did indeed help set the trap." He made one final attempt to shift our orbit upstar, but confinement fields swept in to prevent us from achieving maximum speed, and of course we could not enter slipspace. We were like an insect caught in a bottle, buzzing in futility.

When the Didact had gathered as much information as he could, he said, "Something has provoked the San'Shyuum to rebellion."

"But they have no weapons. . . ."

"*Had* no weapons. The Confirmer has not been attentive. Clearly, they are still slippery customers."

"Commander of the response fleet orders that we submit and stand down," the ship's ancilla said. "I am ordered to hand over control. Shall I comply?"

"No choice," the Didact said. He looked around, as if still trying to find a way to run, a place to escape. I watched him with a doubled awareness, sharing in a strange, incomplete fashion his emotions and memories of previous defeats, flashes of dead comrades, entire worlds destroyed in apparent retaliation. . . .

More than I could stand. I backed away, bumping up against the humans.

"What will happen to us?" Chakas asked. "We're not even supposed to be here."

"They will punish," Riser said.

I could not answer. I did not know.

A second ancilla appeared beside the ship's. The two engaged in some sort of contest, not physical but conducted throughout all the ship's systems. Their images merged, twisted geometrically about each other, then spiraled up and vanished.

"What's that?" I asked.

"AI suppressors," the Didact said. "Instant debriefing and transfer. Our ship has been stripped of knowledge and control."

We were feeling the full strength of a Forerunner warship's most modern weaponry, wrapped and stunned like a fly in a web. Close-in confinement fields flashed around the command center. We felt gravitation cease. At odd angles, the Didact, the humans, and I waited helplessly in semidarkness, blind to all outside activity. Our own ancillas fell silent under the AI suppressors beamed from outside.

Finally came total darkness. Minutes passed.

Riser was praying in an old human dialect not heard in ten thousand years. Its cadences sounded familiar to me. The Didact had once studied human languages.

Chakas was silent.

Slowly, my armor started to fail. My breath came hard and shallow. Something sparkled to my right. I tried to turn, but the armor had locked up and now held me immobile. An orange glare increased to unbearable brilliance, and I saw our bulkheads and control surfaces melt and collapse—while new walls of hard light fought to rise between us and the vacuum. Even under siege, stripped of nearly all higher functions, the Didact's ship was valiantly trying to protect us.

Our world became a twisting, free-form struggle between destructor beams and new construction. I watched in numb fascination as the struggle ramped up to a pitch I could not track with my natural senses . . . and then slowly subsided.

Our ship was losing.

Half of what was left of the control center—abstract and angular and much smaller—fell away and vanished. I briefly saw the curved flank of a sleek Despair-class hunter-killer, glinting and flashing as it reflected the dying glow of our hull's destruction. We drifted free. Our air rapidly staled, and we were surrounded by vacuum.

Into my narrowing point of view came three powerful, fully operational seekers—longer, sleeker, versions of the Didact's old war sphinxes. They lacked the scowling features of the older machines—depersonalized, dark, fast.

One of them cut through the new-grown walls and circled behind us, then dropped aft, penetrating interior bulkheads, searching for other occupants. Through shredded layers of ship's decking, I watched it release the war sphinxes—only to smash them like toys, slice them into sections, and then reduce those to sparking dust.

The sphinxes offered no resistance.

Another took the Didact in tow, bouncing in his armor like a child's toy on a string as he was hauled from the dying ship into the depths of space.

The third lingered near me but took no action, as if awaiting instructions. Then, just as my vision shrank to a purplish cone and I thought I had taken my last breath, the seeker swept out its manipulators, seized my armor, and tugged me from the broken hull, not toward a flotilla of ships, but outward, around—and finally, down.

We were all being unceremoniously dragged to the surface of the San'Shyuum world.

TWENTY-FOUR

PARALYZED, WRAPPED IN a transparent field like a bubble, unable to talk to anyone, my ancilla deactivated by suppressors, I had an ever-changing ringside view of what Forerunners do when their anger and fear takes charge.

They have no warrior discipline.

The atmosphere below was a swirling soup of smoke and fire. Warrior craft and automated weapon systems were mostly too small to be visible, but I saw their effects—darting beams of needle light, glowing arcs cutting across continents, gigantic, stamplike divots punched into the crust and then lifted up, spun about, overturned. I had never seen anything like this—but the Didact had.

His memories offered commentary and context as the grappler dragged me down toward that hell.

For some time, my involuntary point of view spun away from the planet. Looking outward, I saw weapons and ships in higher orbits transit like frantic stars, the blinding sun—and then, the sparkling, dissolving hulk of the Didact's ship.

The ship that the Librarian had seeded inside the central peak of Djamonkin Crater—a bent, broken mass still pitifully trying to reassemble.

A ship that never even had a name.

Several times, the grappler and I passed through pulses of ionized gas and superheated plasma that tingled my nerves and throbbed in my bones—without actual sound.

It slowly became obvious that the decimation of the San'Shyuum world was not all one-sided. The planet itself was a source of plasma pulses and other firepower. More interesting, I caught sight of a craft silhouetted against the stars that looked like nothing made by Forerunners—a flat platform surrounded by billowing, silvery sails, flapping in and out like the bell of a jellyfish, as if trying to swim clear—but not succeeding.

The bell dissolved, the platform broke up. Bodies spilled, tiny and motionless—and then all of it was gone. I spun around again. The planet seemed close enough to touch, maybe a hundred kilometers below, nighttime emphasizing the dying glow of what might have been forests, cities.

Near the brightening arc of sunrise, a glistening river

was delineated against the shadow of dawn, studded with smoking pinpoints of orange. Burning ships—ships made to float on water.

There was plenty of time to feel sorry for myself, to regret all I had done, but contrary to all my self-expectations and past attitudes, I didn't. Sorry about nothing, regretting nothing. Simply watching, waiting. . . . Waiting with a kind of contentment to die, if that was necessary and inevitable.

Wondering about our humans, who had had every reason to regret having anything to do with me. And who, if they still lived, might now be adding to their own awareness of past battles, old wars.

The main prize was of course the Didact. He had fled some duty too onerous to contemplate. He had fought against a Council decision, and losing that fight, he had hidden away, entered into an honorable if not permanent retirement.

But now his opponents had him again. That seemed more than significant—it caused a deeper anger than anything being done to me.

I shut my eyes for a moment.

When I opened them again, flares of atmospheric entry shot up on all sides. We were very close to the surface, less than sixty kilometers, and rapidly descending.

I spun again and saw space through a cone of ionized gases. Centered in that cone, something impossible appeared far beyond the panoply of ships and weapons exchanges: an enormous ripple that stirred the stars like a stick twirled through flecked paint. The disturbance swept across well over a third of my view, then was framed by an elliptical lacework of hard light.

I recognized that this was one end of a massive portal—designed to transport a great deal of mass on a continuing basis.

I watched without emotion as an enormous but delicate silver ring emerged through the purplish hole in the center of the lacework. Despite its size, the portal had opened far from the orbiting ships, well over a million kilometers outward from the orbit of the San'Shyuum's dying world ... far above war, death, the concerns of little creatures like myself.

"It's big," my lips tried to say, but again my breath hitched, my lungs heaved, I tried to suck up whatever air was left, but clearly, I was running out. The seeker was towing me all the way down to the surface with only the bubble as protection.

The ring far above shimmered. Within its delicacy, spokes of hard light shot toward the center and created a brilliant copper-hued hub fully a third as wide as the ring itself.

Half of the ring fell into shadow, the other half glimmered in bright sun.

The inner surface—it's covered with water—

My tunnel vision narrowed around the ring, focused on

it, and I noticed tiny details, clouds, clouds in shadow, impossibly tiny against such vastness . . . mountains, canyons, detail upon detail as my vision both sharpened and shrank inward, until it winked out altogether and I drifted through a thick pudding of nothing.

It was now that the Domain opened to me, without benefit of ancilla, interface, or past experience. It was new, deep, appropriately shapeless—that made sense. I was dying, after all. Then, it assumed a form, rising around me like a beautiful building with gleaming, indefinite architecture, not quite seen but definitely sensed, felt—a lightness that carried its own somber joy.

Here comes everybody, I thought.

And everybody who had ever visited the Domain said to me: *Preserve.*

The lightness vanished instantly. The building was being carved apart just as our ship had died.

More messages.

This time is coming to an end.

Preserve.

The history of Forerunners will soon conclude.

These came with a rising scream of anguish, as if I had plugged into a chamber where essences were pouring forth more than recall and knowledge—pouring forth frustration, horror, pain.

Before the bump, and the sudden inrush of cold, clean air—breathable air, but with a sharp tang of soot and ozone—the Domain lifted up and away. I was grateful to be free of it.

For a moment, I doubted I had seen anything but a reflection of my own emotions and predicament.

"Sometimes, there is a kind of broken-mirror aspect."

Vaguely I wondered about the giant ring. Had I imagined it? It had seemed so real. Then a word flashed into my revived mind, echoing from the image I had just seen or imagined or conjured up from anoxia.

That single word connected intimately with the precious little the Domain had revealed to me: Death. Destruction. Massive power.

That word was *Halo*.

TWENTY-FIVE

JANJUR QOM • THE GREATER SAN'SHYUUM QUARANTINE WORLD

WHAT IN HELL have they done to you, Manipular?"

The voice was mannered, cultured. I recognized its highly trained and inculcated tones, like powerful music rising and echoing through a great, solemn structure.

For a moment, I thought maybe this was the Domain again, speaking in a more physical and personal way. Not so, however. The voice was coming through my ears.

I could smell something other than burning—like the resonant, musky perfume favored by my father, far too expensive for my swap-father or other Miners . . . or Warrior-Servants. The voice was definitely not my father's, however.

My eyes were open but showed only a darkness swimming with vague shadows.

"Turn off the suppressors. His armor can revive him. And I *do* want him revived." Same voice, but not directed at me.

Another voice, less powerful, subservient. "We don't know whether the armor has been counterequipped. . . ."

"Turn them all off! We have the one we want. Let's get some additional details. I'm sure there's a mad scheme lurking here somewhere."

My armor loosened. Strength returned to my flesh. I had some freedom of motion but not much—the suppressor had been shut down, but physical shackles still held me. I seemed to hang from a chain or a hook in a grayish, echoing volume. I blinked to clear the blurriness.

"There you are," the voice said. "I ask you again, Manipular—what has the Didact done to you?"

I managed to speak—barely. "I'm a first-form. Not a Manipular."

"You smell like a Warrior-Servant, but you look more like a misshapen Builder. How did that happen?"

"Brevet mutation. Necessary under the circumstances."

The powerful voice turned thick with pity. "Do you know where you are and what has happened?"

"I saw the planet being devastated. I saw a great ring lit by the sun on one side. Perhaps I imagined it."

"Mm. You're on what is left of Janjur Qom, the primary treaty planet of the San'Shyuum. Our former enemies have turned enemy again. Not unforeseen, but can you tell me why the Prometheans allowed this to happen?"

"No." I tried to focus on a blurred, shifting wall of light to my left—and couldn't. None of it was familiar. None of it made sense.

"Why would the Librarian's recent visit provoke this uprising?"

"I don't know that it did."

"But you do know about her visit."

"The Confirmer mentioned it."

"Ah! A shameful travesty, that one—who guards the guards? Still, he has the wit to serve those who release him from onerous duties. You seem to remember a *few* important things."

"I'm not trying to deceive you."

"Of course not. It must feel good to be back among your kind."

"I don't know that I am, yet."

"A violent return to the fold, that's for sure—but under the circumstances, we could not afford to have an unassigned ship interfere with our operations."

"There were humans. . . ."

"I haven't inquired. If so, that infraction will be punished, as well."

As my eyes cleared and my senses returned, the large grayish outline before me took on shape and focus. I saw a Builder, perhaps the finest specimen of my rate I had ever observed, lovingly guided through at least three, possibly more mutations. Sculpted and trained for high office, even the Council itself.

"Who are you?" I asked.

"I am the Master Builder. You've met me before, Manipular."

He still insisted on calling me that. It was meant as an insult. I did vaguely recall someone like him in my early youth, visiting my family's world in the Orion complex. He had not then been called Master Builder. He had been known simply as Faber.

Where the Didact had been bulked and hewn, the Master Builder had been gently carved, rounded, polished to a rosy gray sheen. His skin radiated musky perfume. I thought of the San'Shyuum and their ability to charm.

My head was full of interesting thoughts, none of them focused, none involved with my situation, my predicament, my survival.

We were arranged along one side of a long, dimly lighted corridor, broader than it was high, broken by angular blocks stepped up against the walls. Every few seconds, upright bars of light swept down the middle, function unknown to me.

My ancilla was still suppressed.

The Master Builder walked around me.

"When did you join the Didact in his mission?"

"On Erde-Tyrene."

"Erde-Tyrene is assigned to the Lifeworkers as a nature

preserve, under protection of the Librarian. Were humans involved in this plot from the beginning?"

"I don't know what you mean."

"Were they aware of the consequences of liberating the Didact from his Warrior Keep?"

"I don't think so."

"It's our best theory to date, that all of you were guided by the Librarian in an effort to frustrate the Council. Do you personally disagree with the Council?"

"I don't know."

"How can you be so uninformed?"

"By not paying attention," I said. "I lived among Miners before slipping away to Erde-Tyrene. They have little interest in Builders and their affairs."

"True," the Master Builder said. "Your family expresses support for you, but extreme disappointment and surprise at your actions. For the time being, your father has entrusted me, personally, with your welfare."

That did not sound good. I doubted they would have lightly given me up to the Master Builder—Builders in general have strong family bonds. Which of course my family was accustomed to having me test. . . .

"He claims he did not know you were on Erde-Tyrene. You were sent to Edom. Did you inform him of your destination?"

Worse and worse. The slightest misstep or misstatement on my part could put my whole family in jeopardy, that much was clear. "I'm reluctant to tell you things that might be in error. My thoughts are still jumbled, and my memory after the mutation is also suspect. I'd like to help, Master Builder—"

"And you will, in time. Meanwhile, enjoy another brief rest. We still have work to do here, and after that is finished, we'll attend to you. Now, where are those humans?"

He raised his arm and my armor locked. The suppressor field returned, this time set so high that I automatically started to black out. Just before oblivion struck, again I felt a brush with the Domain.

They are about to give it powers it never had before.

Just as they did ages ago. . . .

Those who are ignorant of history are doomed to repeat it.

I thought I recognized whomever or whatever had deposited this message, but could not place the memory. It was not the Didact, that was certain.

It might not have even been a Forerunner.

TWENTY-SIX

NOW CAME THE brightest light I had ever seen.

I was awake again, looking down from a transparent platform—perhaps the flagship of the Master Builder—upon the wreckage of a city. The light came from an horrific plasma ball rising on the horizon, shooting forth subsidiary streams of matter pattern interference—mass converting into both electromagnetic radiation and vacuum energy. Shields darkened, but not before I felt another tingle and was temporarily blinded.

My armor would have a real job to do after all this to repair the radiation damage.

In that shadowy pause, the Didact's memory showed

me what a San'Shyuum city would have looked like before this destruction: sweeping, branching organic towers and broad, curved lanes, thousands of streets arranged like ripples crossing a pond.

The San'Shyuum—true to form—had used all the means at their disposal to regain a comfortable existence, with light commerce and travel between two adjacent worlds and several small moons—the beginnings, in better times and under other circumstances, of a full historical recovery.

Another dawn seemed to arrive as my eyes recovered.

Our ship came down on a broad open plain, surrounded by tall ships and plumes of smoke and guarded by a grim-visaged contingent of Builders in battle armor.

Builder security. That still seemed strange to me.

Three confinement bubbles appeared beside me, hanging by tow-threads from grapplers. One contained Riser, eyes closed, head upturned in his armor; the other, Chakas, whose face showed some returning awareness.

And the third contained the Didact, naked and fully aware, surrounded by pain projectors: stripped of armor, honor, dignity, and doing all he could not to show his agony. He glanced at me, and in his eyes was a question, one I could not yet answer. More pain was applied, and he jerked his head forward again, looking only at the Master Builder.

"You've been a lot of trouble, Promethean, and now you've dragged down your wife and these poor underlings."

This, I believe, was the point at which my maturity arrived in an awful rush. The Master Builder, whether he knew it or not, now had a fierce enemy—*me.*

"You came here to meet with the San'Shyuum, did you not?" the Master Builder asked. "Well, let us arrange for that meeting. The Librarian recently rescued a few, and that seems to have ignited the uprising whose final issue is being decided even now. She is beyond my reach, unfortunately. But you are not—and *these* are not."

A line of San'Shyuum prisoners, also wrapped in constraining bubbles, was dragged forward like a string of beads over the field, until all were arranged in the looming shadow of the Master Builder's ship. None bore evidence of the legendary, sensuous beauty of the San'Shyuum. I looked over an assortment of decrepit-looking elders, not alert warriors or energetic youth. Several had arrived in the odd, wheeled chairs the Confirmer had mentioned, their heads and shoulders burdened by broad ornamental helmets with wide-spread wings. Others, more fit, sparked the Didact's buried memories of handsome figures from times past—when the San'Shyuum had first and foremost demanded sensuous fulfillment in their lives.

I seemed to see them as if in a long, ornate procession, patterns, shadows and echoes of past figures trailing back for thousands of years. . . .

"The Master Builder is well known," the lead elder said in a huffing, lungless sort of voice. "I am called, by my fellows, Sustaining Wind. How may we assist you, triumphant one?"

The Master Builder ordered Chakas and Riser forward, out of the shadow of the lift exit. The humans in their paralyzed armor seemed only half-aware of their situation. I wondered if the Master Builder had surrounded them with pain projectors as well.

The San'Shyuum delegation reacted with surprise and even anger. One of the Prophets ordered his chair wheeled forward, and surveyed Chakas with a profoundly sad expression. "They are *debased*," the Prophet announced to those gathering and roiling behind him. "This is the fate that awaited us! It was foretold by past Prophets, and demonstrated by the sorrow of the Librarian. Was it the presence of these wretches that brought this devastation upon us?"

"Let's not forget the secret construction and stockpiling of ships and attacks upon our visiting fleet," the Master Builder said.

Sustaining Wind lowered his head, the wide headdress vibrating. Chakas and Riser remained still and silent, but Chakas turned his eye on me—and winked. I had no idea what this meant, but it cheered me. He apparently did not regard me as his enemy, and for that I felt a sad gratitude.

"Is this then some attempt to remind us of our shame, in our time of final destruction?" the elder continued.

Chakas looked now to the skies. Perhaps he was thinking of past moments when humans, San'Shyuum, and

Forerunners had gathered . . . in other, even more violent times.

The elder now rolled his way around Riser. Riser looked down upon him, small furred face more than a meter higher than the elder's wrinkled visage—minus of course that ridiculous crown.

"And why do you give them *Forerunner* armor?" the elder squeaked and puffed. "Are these vanquished ones now elevated to higher status than those with whom you signed treaties? Did you enlist *them* in this attack?"

"The humans are servants of the Librarian." The Master Builder ordered several Builder security guards between the humans and the San'Shyuum. They firmly but gently pushed back the elder.

Then the Master Builder turned to the Didact and asked, "What memories quicken in you at this pitiful sight?"

The Didact did not answer.

"Are there other clues to be found here . . . about that which we have lost?"

Yes. That was it, in part. The Didact had come here to . . .

The elder's chair pulled back. "The Librarian selected a few from among us, and then she left. Her visit told us that whatever we did, destruction would soon be upon us. We reacted as any civilized species must—to preserve our heritage and our children. What have you brought upon us?" the elder wheezed, his face livid. "You gave us your word of honor. . . ."

"He thought you concealed a great secret," the Master Builder said. "You know why we are here?"

"We are not savages. We have observed, listened. Your people are on the verge of desperation, even panic. The front has advanced—the front *we* pushed back beyond the galaxy ten thousand years ago—the enemy we vanquished, that you *cannot*."

I was still trying to fully recover what I knew lay within me, the Didact's history of the Flood. I sensed only a roiling tide of chaos.

The elder raised scrawny, feeble hands, as if in exultation. He turned to face the Master Builder. "And now—you have *lost* something, haven't you? Something so tremendous and important that surely it cannot be hidden."

The Master Builder finally seemed to show the elder some sympathy. "It has been said humans and San'Shyuum found the secret of destroying their greatest enemies. You were preserved should we ever need that secret."

"The Master Builder brought doom upon us—and upon yourselves. No secrets, no future."

"As for your doom, that I believe," the Master Builder said. "I see there never was a secret and no reason to preserve. You have violated our treaty. Forerunners never tolerate betrayal of trust. But while it's clear to me that you have nothing to offer, I have to ask you about the Didact's secret—the one he conspired to hide, with your help."

Another string of bubbles arrived, occupied by a very different group of San'Shyuum—bloody, missing limbs, barely aware of their surroundings. Beyond their injuries and tattered raiment, these were well-shaped, sleek, muscular creatures more properly suiting the San'Shyuum's traditional image.

The bubbles opened and the Master Builder's warriors organized the captives in a line before us, before the elders. Even in pain and under constraint, the way they moved conveyed both power and charm—subdued by circumstance, but real nonetheless.

The chair-bound elder almost spat upon the newcomers. "These are the vipers in our beds—the personal agents of this defeat. I will not share *breath* with them."

Chakas tried to laugh. He merely ended up choking. Riser watched it all with lips drawn tight, brows high, eyes flashing as if in warning. I had never seen him in a rage. His size did not diminish him now.

The Master Builder walked along the line, surveying with a musing air both varieties of San'Shyuum, as different as night and day: old and new, age and youth. But here, I knew, the more desiccated and decrepit figures were the true revolutionaries.

The Master Builder doubled back and stopped before the Didact. "Promethean, hear me," he said. "You have one last chance to redeem yourself. I have had this planet searched high and low by my special intelligence forces. All who might confirm what you claim exists are assembled here—preserved even in their treason. Their families are dead, the resistance completely crushed. Surely now they will reveal what they have concealed for so long—or so you've claimed, all these thousands of years."

The Didact looked wearily among them. "You've picked and preserved . . . in error."

The Master Builder's cold fury built until I thought he would raise his arm yet again and call for pain projectors to surround us all.

Then, he pulled back his anger. Looking upon his face, I wondered what resources he had acquired upon his rise from Manipular to first-form—or second-, or third-. He did not seem wiser for all that, only more powerful, more cruel.

By comparison, the Didact was the gentler Forerunner—a complete contradiction to my former understanding.

"No questions for them?" the Master Builder asked.

"There was a San'Shyuum whom I knew and worked with after your defeat," the Didact said, his eyes slowly sweeping the line, the elders. "He, too, entered a state of exile to atone for the defeat he faced against my forces. Before then, we established a kind of bond, such as there might be between those who lost and took away so many brave fellows and family.

"He it was who told me that when the time comes, when the enemies of all return, he would reveal his secret, in exchange for the freedom of his descendants. I do not see him here."

"You speak of our First Prophet," the elder said, his bluster vanishing.

"Where is this *dirt-beast*?" the Master Builder asked,

using the most obscene slur upon all who are not of our species.

"I saw his palace destroyed in the first assault," the elder said, his voice rough and sad. "He is no more."

The Master Builder raised his blunt jaw, moved his hand, and his soldiers positioned themselves behind the line of injured San'Shyuum prisoners. Then he turned to the Didact. "You can save these warriors, if you tell us what happened on Charum Hakkor, and how that ties in with this *prophet* and his secret. A prison holds a prisoner, but someone here holds the key."

I saw something in the Master Builder's look that froze my blood. All his polish and preparation, all his elegant mutations, could not conceal an awareness that his power was rapidly waning. All he did here was in desperation.

Whatever had been lost, whatever had gone missing, was not something Forerunners could afford to misplace—and it was not just the prisoner of Charum Hakkor. I remembered the ring-shaped void and streaming trace left in the magnetic field and solar wind of the Charum Hakkor system. Was it the same as the ring in the San'Shyuum system?

Did the Master Builder have more than one at his disposal? Each one capable of destroying almost all life in a solar system . . .

"You brought your *Halo* to Charum Hakkor," I said. "Is that what you've lost?"

"Enough!" the Didact commanded, and I instantly shut

up, shut down my emotions, stiffened my posture—for he was correct. This was not for others to hear. Not even I should know.

The Master Builder looked upon me in horror, his polish and dignity erased. He approached me sidewise, as if I were a serpent that might strike out and cause even more pain. "If no one can tell me where this prisoner might have gone—or indeed, who or what it was—then we are done here. This world is done. This line of history is about to end."

The Master Builder leaned his head close to mine. "You were at Charum Hakkor," he said in a low voice, silky but disturbing. "If not for your family's power, I would strip you down to a haze of burning brain cells and spread you out upon this field. What could I pick out from those naïve cinders, Manipular? You are just a pitiful echo of the Didact. What you know, he knows—and much more. And he is mine to do with as I please."

The guards restored the bubbles around the San'Shyuum prisoners, this time including the elders in their peculiar chairs. They then approached the Didact and locked him down in a suppressor.

The humans were next.

When they came to me, the Master Builder held them off for a moment, long enough to tell me, "We have notified your family. Through long relationship, I subdue my anger. Your father has asserted his authority. You will be exchanged, but your family will be fined—ruinously fined. Your wandering days are over, Bornstellar Makes Eternal."

My father's authority?

"Where are you taking the Didact?"

"Where he will be most useful to me."

"And the humans?"

"The Librarian has overstepped more than usual this time. All her projects will be terminated."

The soldiers turned their suppressors upon me. The last thing I saw was the Didact's face, contorted in agony, but his eyes locked firmly on my own.

I knew. He knew. Between us there was more than echo and response.

My world shrank into a tight gray knot.

TWENTY-SEVEN

WAS TO be returned to where my life began, within the wide orbital waltz of three suns in the great nebular complex of Orion—returned to home and family, where I hoped I would be allowed to recuperate, meditate, and achieve my own maturity, in my own way and in my own time.

———

While I was still unconscious, Builder security escorted me out of the quarantine sphere to an adjacent system. I was finally allowed to come awake, and found myself on a stripped-down personnel transport and research vessel shared by both Miners and Builders.

My journey thereafter was swift, quiet, mostly uneventful. I was not treated differently from other passengers, mostly stellar engineers. They seemed to think I was a Warrior-Servant recruited by the Builders and recovering from some unexplained trauma. There were apparently many such being ferried to recovery centers.

I did not tell them otherwise.

Others continued to regard me as something of a freak. I could not disagree. I did not enjoy looking at myself in a mirror. I had certainly grown. My physical strength was much greater. In nearly every respect, I suppose I actually was—*am*—a freak. That my fellow passengers paid any attention to me spoke well of the kindly culture of these scientific adventurers, out to develop and increase the Forerunner realm without military conquest.

Our ship stopped at several installations where the science of planetary formation was being taken to advanced stages. Rocky worlds were at a premium, one of the Miners explained to me in the ship's small, sparsely appointed lounge. Forerunners now had the ability to collapse an asteroid field into a molten mass of the twenty-megameter range, then cool and cure the protoplanet in less than ten thousand years.

"The last problem remains taming young stars," he said. "But we're working on that. We send in stellar-class engineers equipped with third-class ancillas—plasma jockeys, we call them. They love the heat, but most vanish after a few hundred years—just go away. We don't know what becomes of them. They get the job done, though."

I listened politely enough, but my own misery left little in the way of curiosity.

As my armor did not have an ancilla, on occasion I slept, and my dreams were extraordinary, covering thousands of lives and millions of years, cut up and rearranged in a dense tapestry of world-lines . . . but I forgot them almost immediately upon waking.

On our way through the outer reaches of the Orion nebular complex, popping in and out of slipspace to deliver our supplies and researchers to various stellar nurseries, we actually came within a million kilometers of the natal planet of the Forerunners, a now-desolate and radiation-scoured cinder of a world known in the most ancient tongue as Ghibalb.

Ghibalb had once been a paradise. Emerging into the galactic realm, these early Forerunners had been content to live and develop in a glorious cradle of just twelve stars, but their first experiments in stellar engineering had gone awry, causing an infectious series of novas that brightened the entire Orion complex for fifty thousand years—and nearly destroyed our species. Images from that time show the nebulae to have been extraordinarily brilliant and colorful.

Forerunners had long since improved upon their craft and made fewer mistakes. Now the complex was darker and much less active, barely visible from a distance of more than a hundred light-years.

While the others were buried deep in interactions with

their ancillas, I observed our journey with only eye, mind, and memory.

The only interruption was a navigational glitch caused by disturbances in slipspace itself. When we were informed that our ship was five light-years off course, one researcher surmised that the great portals were being over-utilized of late. "We've been told over and over we can't deliver raw materials to needy systems. The only thing that could cause this sort of trouble is frequent passage of exceptionally large vessels—abusively frequent and unimaginably large! And who do you think authorizes *that*?"

He swept all his fellow passengers with a meaningful look, as if we might be compelled to divulge something of our own knowledge about these matters. The others—those who emerged from their ancillary studies—one and all derided his theory.

I said nothing. I had witnessed one such passage, and evidence of another, but it was certainly not my place to speak about what I had seen.

Still, this glitch caused an unexpected and uncontrolled detour that provoked a surprise inspection from a team of exalted Builders. They arrived on a warship of unfamiliar design, sleek and fast—intercepting us near a once-deserted association of extrasolar planets. The rumor quickly spread among the researchers that we had approached a secure installation about which none of them knew anything.

The boarding party consisted of Builder security—none of them Warrior-Servants, contrary to long tradition. They observed all the proper courtesies—then thoroughly scoured the transport's records. After that, they politely asked us to strip our armor—I of course wore none—and debriefed the researchers' ancillas, in search of what, none would say.

The team soon departed, having concluded our breach was accidental—but leaving us none the wiser. Before they left, one shot me a look that combined contempt and pity.

I was the only one they had ignored.

This naturally brought suspicion upon me. Rumors also spread that I was the true cause of the delay, and only the bravest and lowest of the researchers would speak to me thereafter. Soon, even they closed me out.

The rest of my journey was solitary, until, twelve light-years from home, I was transferred to a swift yacht shared by my family and five other Builder clans.

My father, mother, and sister greeted me as I crossed from the transport to the yacht. I had not seen any of them for three years. My father had undergone another mutation since I left and now bore a distinct and disturbing resemblance to the Master Builder. My mother had changed very little—if anything, she had only become more sedate and dignified, beginning her third millennial interim, during which she would neither give birth nor otherwise create offspring.

Whereas my father was four meters tall, broad-shouldered and thick-legged, his skin like polished onyx, his well-trimmed patches of hair purplish white, his eyes black flecked with silver, my mother was just over two meters tall, slender as a reed, her hair deep red and skin silver-gray. My sister was slightly taller than our mother and less slender, in that transition stage prior to family interchange, courtship, marriage.

Even before my exile to Edom, she had been undergoing gentle mutation to reproductive maturity, and was now through the earliest phase of her advance to first-form. She greeted me with silent, wide-eyed appraisal, then clasped me swiftly and warmly; my mother, seeing my condition, greeted me with painful formality; my father, with a firm clasp of my shoulder, hid his emotions and exchanged only a few precisely chosen words, welcoming me back to the fold.

My parents were over six thousand years old. My sister and I were barely twelve.

"I'm sure there will be much to discuss," he concluded, before sending me to my quarters to try on a fresh suit of armor. "We will dine in an hour."

In the small, elegantly appointed cabin, the new armor was expertly spun about me. The ship assembled a perfectly dignified and unremarkable ancilla from its own reserves. Neuter and simple, it seemed a shallow parody of the one supplied by the Librarian—not very helpful and completely unexciting.

"Apologies for this primitive accessory," the ship said, noting my reaction. "Your ancilla may of course be upgraded once you arrive at your estate."

I felt a deep pang of loneliness and an odd sensation of grief. The ancilla did not know how to cheer me or what words of support to offer. I felt responsible for all that had happened and was still happening, great events known and unknown, far away—plus the fates of one Promethean and two human beings.

That first shipboard dinner was awkward, quiet, unenlightening. The ship tried to serve what it thought were my favorite foods. In my present condition, they made me feel vaguely ill.

"Perhaps he requires a diet more suited to a warrior," my father suggested.

Subduing a flash of anger, I did not ask him what he might be involved in, professionally, that twenty thousand light-years away I should be treated with grim leniency by an otherwise all-powerful Master Builder.

I had advanced, all right—well beyond being an embarrassment to being a major disaster, both behavior-wise and in physical appearance.

In a few days, we were home again.

TWENTY-EIGHT

THE FIRST SIGHT of our family's world roused a mixed palette of high emotions. We watched the orbital approach from the yacht's bridge deck, a comfortable, largely ceremonial appurtenance. The yacht was controlled by its own ancilla, like nearly all Forerunner ships, but a parody of old times still required upon landing the presence of the senior family member, in this case my father, who barked out commands in Forerunner Jagon—a language older by far than my parents, but not nearly as old as the Digon the Didact had learned as a young warrior.

Didact. They called me that when I taught at the college of Strategic Defense of the Mantle—the War College. Some of my students seemed to think I was overly demanding and too precise in my definitions. . . .

This upwelling came as no surprise. I had expected something like it. The Didact had sponsored my mutation, after all, and that meant I contained some of his inherent patterns . . . and possibly even much of his memory. I felt as if something was growing inside me I might not be able to control.

I tried not to show outward sign, but my father easily detected the change.

Of course our family's homeworld had changed little. What need for change when every square meter of its surface had been built upon, tuned, and adapted to Forerunner comfort and ambition? Even from a thousand kilometers, the arc of the planet's limb was visibly ruffled with architecture, though certainly not the equal of the ruins found on any great Precursor planet—no vaulting orbital bridges stretching from world to world, no unbending and eternal cables. . . .

I flashed back to Charum Hakkor before its mysterious destruction, seeing as if miraculously restored both the Precursor ruins and the use that humans had once made of them. . . .

But enough. Returning to my family's world again reminded me that Builders had nothing to be ashamed of in their quest for architectural dominance.

I had once taken a youthful fancy to our elevated oceans, each a thousand kilometers in diameter and a thousand meters deep, shining like a belt of overlapping coins around the equator. Each was separated from its neighbor by several hundred meters of elevation, their overlapping depending on whether cascades of water or twisting water-spout funnels joined them. Lifeworkers by invitation had for many centuries come to study these great aquariums and experiment with new varieties of exotic creatures, which they sometimes exported to other research groups and hobbyists across the galaxy.

Once, I had helped tutor one such experiment: a pod of saltwater reptilians, tri-torsoed carnivores with three linked brains and amazing senses—the most intelligent of their kind . . . until my mother decided, after several nearly successful attempts on my young life, that these creatures were entirely too dangerous. She terminated the experiment and the Lifeworker who designed the reptilians was reassigned to another world, far away.

Almost as impressive were the arched rockways of the northern hemisphere, stretching in a longitudinal belt from the oceans to the perfect circle of the icy pole: great red and yellow sandstone formations carved by sandblasters, autonomous whirlwinds of grit that hollowed and sculpted and worked until the ancient limestone seabeds were marvels of fretwork. Hikers and travelers could get lost for months in hundreds of thousands of kilometers of winding, spiraling mazes—though of course there was never any real danger, as family scouts were always on call, awaiting signals of distress or just simple boredom.

My sister had once delighted in leaving her own peculiar carvings on rock faces within the mazes, inviting others to contribute their own designs. None complied. Hers were too original, too enigmatic.

————

We landed at the family's most extensive manor estate, near the equator between the belt of oceans and a low, ancient mountain range. Our ship spread itself out for maintenance on the landing cradle, and embodied ancillas of many sorts greeted us, along with representatives of the lower-ranking families that shared and conserved the planet on our behalf.

My father did not introduce his unfamiliar-looking son or explain his presence, as no doubt he had neglected to explain my years of absence.

————

The first evening after our return, my sister joined me on the lakefront veranda of the main domicile and sat next to me as the tiara of three small, brilliant suns sank below the horizon, casting all in a shimmering twilight. There followed an unusually brilliant display of aurora. I could almost make out the additional refraction caused by the fields that protected us from the nastiest radiations of those small, brilliant dwarf stars.

"Did you ever find your treasure?" she asked gently,

touching my arm. If that was meant to divert my gloom or otherwise cheer me, it did not.

"There is no treasure," I said.

"No Organon?"

"Nothing remotely like that."

"Everyone around here is acting very mysterious of late," she said. "Father in particular. It's like he's carrying the weight of the galaxy on his shoulders."

"He's an important Builder," I said.

"He's been important since I can remember. Is he more important now than he used to be?"

"Yes," I said.

"How?"

"I'd like to know more about that myself."

"Now *you're* being mysterious."

"I saw things . . . terrible things. I'm not sure how much I can explain without causing trouble."

"Trouble! You *love* trouble."

"Not this kind."

Time to change the subject, she saw. She looked me over with that combination of half-concealed appraisal and kind judgment she had inherited from our mother. "Mother wonders if you plan to redeem your mutation and reshape yourself," she asked.

"No," I said. "Why? Am I especially ugly?"

"Before we females are betrothed, a little slumming between rates is almost mandatory. You have a brutish aspect that would suit a few of my friends perfectly. Do you plan on becoming a Warrior?"

Now she was teasing. I ignored the gibe, but felt a twinge at the real possibility. "My life is no longer my own," I said. "Perhaps it never was."

A sharp retort almost came to her lips—I could tell by her expression she was on the verge of saying I was full of self-pity. She would not have been wrong. But she subdued the impulse, and I took the unspoken advice to heart.

After a long moment, as darkness fell, the nebulae grew brighter in our accustomed eyes, and the veranda was subtly lit and warmed from beneath, she asked, "What really happened out there?"

It was now that Mother appeared, walking with her perpetual and almost ageless grace across the veranda. She motioned for another chair and, when it formed, sat beside us with a long, grateful sigh. "It's good to have my finest children all with me again, all here at home," she said.

"Bornstellar was about to tell me what happened on Edom," my sister said.

"Edom! Would that were all to the story. We have punished your swap-family for allowing the influence of a Lifeworker to lead you astray."

"Astray . . ." My sister luxuriated in that word. One last late aurora waved its slow banner, suffusing her smooth face with a flowery pink glow that plunged a barb of regret through me. I would never again share her innocence, her sense of adventure.

"And I certainly hope to pass along a few of the Council's fines," Mother added. "We may yet lose this world because of your 'adventures,' Bornstellar. I hope they were worth it."

"Mother!" My sister seemed surprised and distressed. I was not. I had expected this moment for most of my return journey.

"Is any sort of 'telling' allowed?" Mother asked. "You left Edom. You were advanced to maturity by a disgraced Warrior-Servant."

"By the Didact," I said.

"The dissident Promethean—banished from the Council?"

"Victor over humans and San'Shyuum, protector of the ecumene for twelve thousand years." My other memory recalled this with no pride, only a sense of regret that more could not have been done.

"Is it all true?" Mother asked, her voice soft and a little frightened. The tale of my travels and adventures had been told to her in no depth, apparently, and with major deletions.

"It's true."

"How could you allow yourself to be so misguided?"

"Edom isn't far from Erde-Tyrene. I went there to seek treasure. I was led to believe there might be Precursor artifacts. But I found nothing of that sort. Instead, I was guided by a pair of humans to the Didact's Cryptum."

My sister's esteem grew. "A Warrior Cryptum? You *opened* it?"

"And helped to revive him. He did not call down punishment. He recruited me."

My mother tied together the obvious knots of the story. "All this was the Librarian's scheme, perhaps?"

"It seems so."

"Then under the compelling influence of an ancient leader, you joined the Didact's cause." She was trying to put a kind mask on the whole—in her view—sordid episode. "He no doubt required your help to accomplish his peculiar ends. And because of your youth, you could not have understood how that might complicate your father's work and cause great harm to our family."

"My body isn't the only thing that's changed," I said. "I learned much that is hidden from Manipulars and even most Forerunners. I learned about something called the Flood."

My sister looked between us, uncomprehending.

Mother's expression shifted in an instant from patient sadness to stiff formality. "Where did you hear of that?" she asked.

"Partly from the Didact, and some from the Domain itself."

"Then you *have* experienced the Domain," my sister said. "And from the perspective of an ancient warrior! What's that like?"

"Confused," I admitted. "I haven't integrated my perceptions. The knowledge is primitive at best, and I can't go back without further guidance . . . I think. At any rate, I haven't accessed the Domain since my armor was taken away on the San'Shyuum quarantine world."

"Quarantine!" my sister exclaimed. "I've heard about the San'Shyuum. Was it marvelous and sensuous?"

"Enough has been said of *that*." Mother looked around the veranda and seemed to be surveying the entire estate through her ancillas, as if anticipating Council spies, more fines, and even more severe correction. "I've heard of the Flood. It was a mysterious stellar disease that caused radiation anomalies. It severely damaged a number of Forerunner colony worlds in the outer reaches of the galaxy, several centuries ago." This seemed to cost her considerable effort. I saw clearly the burden that had been placed upon her in the last few months. I could bear responsibility for only so much of that burden. "We must await the judgment of your father," she finally said, drawing back her survey, no doubt to the relief of ancillas around the planet.

"Father's changed, too—he looks as if he's been groomed and tutored for great advancement," I said. "Did the Master Builder mentor him for his last mutation?"

"Enough!" Mother cried, and stood. Dozens of little servant units scattered. With a shiver, she suggested we retire to contemplate the Mantle before spending the hours of darkness in private study. She then walked out quickly, scattering the units again, and left my sister and me under the faint wisps of nebular glow and stars both diffuse and sharp, as if caught behind a sweeping, broken veil of tattered fog.

"What is happening to this family?" my sister asked. "It can't all be your fault. Even before you left—"

"Mother's right," I said.

"What is the Flood?" she asked abruptly, her instincts sharp. "Mother seems to know something . . . I certainly don't."

I shook my head. "Frightful stories concocted for political gain, and perhaps that's all." Was I now misleading my own sister? With a shrug, I added, "I defer to Father's judgment."

"Oh you do, *now*?" she said.

We parted at the gate to the veranda, and I returned to my room high in a tower looking out over the nearest disk-sea, its rim surrounded by cascading waters, beneath the ever-changing gallery of our sky: newborn stars, dying suns, the great turmoil in which Forerunners had seen first light.

I had done nothing for my family. Perversely, I now felt more connection with the Didact than I did with them— and even more perversely, perhaps that was how I would redeem myself to family and Forerunners alike.

How many betrayals could it take to go full circle?

It was now even more imperative that I learn who I actually was, and what I was about to become. No one could tell me. No one could teach me.

TWENTY-NINE

THAT NIGHT—AND many after—were tumbled and confused. I sat surrounded by gently flickering displays
that delivered little of the information that I requested
and needed. The Domain was still a closed puzzle box.
Sometimes I felt its touch, but never long enough to im-
merse myself or study its nature and contents.

Instead, I watched the sky, tracking the reentry trails of
hundreds of Builder transports coming and going. So many
ships of late. So much activity. I had always known my
father was important, but suspicion had blossomed into
certainty that he was in fact crucial to the Master Builder's
plan. So much hatred directed at the Warrior-Servants.

What part did Father play in their reduction? Was he aware of the damage to our traditions, to the protection of the Mantle itself?

Visions of the prisoner of Charum Hakkor, whatever *that* was, now loose and beyond the reach of the Didact.

Missing for forty or fifty years.

And, always looming, the specter of that vast slender ring—underscored by the strange horror of Master Builder's destruction of the war sphinxes and their impressions of the Didact's children.

———

What I had managed to learn about the Forerunner schism was a slender thread, but still intriguing. My other memories still withheld those times from me, perhaps waiting for more sophistication—or the right moment.

Ten thousand years ago, just after the conclusion of the human-San'Shyuum war, the most exalted of the Warrior-Servants, the Prometheans, had been ascendant among Forerunners, as high in social standing and power as they would ever reach. Their downfall came as a great strategic decision was being made. Behind this maneuvering lay a threat from outside the galaxy—theoretical, perhaps, but terrible nonetheless. Remembering what the Didact had told me, I surmised that this threat was what humans had once fought against and defeated, or pushed back, even while warring against the Forerunners: the Flood. Of that I could still learn little or nothing, but I was sure my mother's tale of stellar disease was simply a cover.

The secret of the human victory against the Flood had never been revealed.

But all had anticipated that the Flood would return.

The Master Builder seemed to have asserted that a new grand strategy (and a new weapon, as well?) made old-fashioned warriors and armies and fleets unnecessary.

Shortly thereafter, the Didact and all his fellow Prometheans were removed from the Council. I presumed this was when the Didact was forced into exile and entered the Cryptum.

From that time until now, over a thousand years, Warrior-Servants had been increasingly marginalized, their rates reassessed, their forces and fleets and armies disbanded.

———

Night upon night I struggled with the limited feeds, and day after day I suffered under the polite condescension of my father and the sad reckoning of my mother.

I had hardly even begun to explore the depths of the Didact's imprint, still slowly opening and expanding within me. There was a reason for the concealment and slow unfolding. Those resources were not for my personal entertainment, nor even for my own growth and edification. They had to be buried deep against intrusive access—to be unlocked only if I returned to a position of importance, responsibility.

Only if I *dared*.

If I lost the protection of my father and fell into the hands of the Master Builder one more time, I might be dangerous to the Didact as well. My other memories could be painfully yanked out and put on display for the Master Builder's benefit, to scour for incriminating information.

Perhaps that had already happened to the humans.

I could not bear the thought that the Master Builder might even now be tossing aside the spent corpses of Chakas and Riser and laying low Erde-Tyrene, snuffing out potential resistance—shoving aside and burying anything and anyone that stood in his path.

THIRTY

MY RESTLESSNESS TURNED me into a wanderer.

A Forerunner household never sleeps. There is no equivalent of nighttime and rest, but there are moments of repose when all retire for individual contemplation and to prepare for the next round of activities. In traditional Builder households, these moments are sacrosanct. Thus during any given day-night cycle, there are hours when the house—and in our case, much of the planet—becomes quiescent. The streets and byways reduce their flow. Even the ancillas and automated systems reduce their on-call activities.

But I did not. I preferred to take my exercise alone,

without armor, simply to allow my developing self—whatever that might be—to communicate its direction. I was still mutating, still changing in ways none could predict. The Didact had done a real number on me.

And so I walked. I paced. I explored kilometers of corridors leading to hundreds of empty chambers, chambers that re-created their elaborate hard-light decor only in the presence of Forerunners. Parts of our house and estate buildings had not been visited for hundreds of years. Many contained tributes and records of past members of our clan and allied clans, including ancestors of the Master Builder himself. I took a perverse interest in the Master Builder's relation to my family, and learned through reactivated displays—pitifully enthusiastic about finally being observed—of great contracts and political alliances stretching back twenty-five thousand years, long before my Father's inception.

I spent many hours listening to a small, slightly dotty ancilla devoted to cataloging and researching the historical consequences of my family's millions of contracts and constructions. A diminutive, fading sapphire figure whose edges barely cohered, her resources had not been updated or renewed for the last three thousand years, yet she remained on duty, ever-hopeful of serving, faithful beyond reason but increasingly eccentric. She toured me through the records of more than a thousand worlds transformed by my father and his Builder cohorts, and then unveiled with obvious pride even greater contracts: dozens of stars harnessed by containment and collection fields, including, it seemed, the ingenious quarantine around the San'Shyuum system.

In these records, to my great interest, were hints of large-scale weapons. Under the old name of Faber, the Master Builder had partnered with my father in creating and offering up these designs to the Council. Expunged from the records were any indications of Council approval or denial of these weapons. None took on the final, ring-shaped aspect of the great Halos, however.

A thousand years of politics and progress.

My father had never bragged about his works and influence, of course, and as a Manipular, I had never shown much interest. But I understood now how he had been able to secure my return.

Yet this was not explicitly what I was seeking.

My restlessness had its own motives. What I was becoming—who I was becoming—had a separate set of curiosities, and I indulged them. The problem with being potential is that one contains multitudes of outcomes, candidates vying to become final personalities, and as the hours and days passed, the strongest ruled for a time until toppled by others even stronger. . . .

Matters would be coming to a head soon enough. One of me would suffice and rule, supplemented by the unfolding wisdom of the Didact.

During one long repose, two hundred domestic days after my return, I came upon my father and a visitor under a seldom-used nave-and-cupola reception chamber, halfway across the main length of our household, about ten kilometers from my own tower chambers.

I happened to be crossing a skybridge connecting two higher floors in that wing, beneath the cupola, when I heard voices echoing from a hundred meters below. One voice was that of my father, clear and precise—but not at all commanding; rather, unexpectedly subservient.

I cautiously leaned over the railing. My father and another Builder, both free of armor, were engaged in a heated conversation they obviously did not wish audited or recorded. The local support services had been shut down, leaving floors and walls frosted with cold.

The other Builder was much younger than my father, a first-form much as I would have been had my mutation proceeded normally. Despite his youth, he seemed to speak with considerable authority.

Curious indeed, that one so young could command an audience with my father. I managed to catch little more than half of what was being said.

"More incidents in the outer reaches . . . twelve systems lost in the last three hundred years . . ."

And: ". . . traces remain of the test bed near Charum Hakkor, even after forty-three years . . . decimation of San'Shyuum . . . uprising insufficient cause . . ."

". . . trial pending . . . charges of gross violation of the principles of the Mantle . . ."

Was he referring to the Master Builder?

". . . A metarch-level ancilla's assigned to the test-bed device sent to Charum Hakkor. Both went missing after the action against the San'Shyuum . . ."

". . . vote of no confidence in the Master Builder's leadership . . ."

And then my father, his voice rising loud and clear in the vast space as the air currents blew my way: "How *could* they be used in such a way? Tuned so broadly and without safeguards . . . It goes against all the designers had planned and hoped for, not as final defense, but as brutal punishments. . . ."

"It was your science that allowed them, Builder. The opposing faction in the Council never authorized such a use, but that is secondary to the blame of building and enabling."

I drew back, shivering not just with the chill. I knew what they were talking about. It seemed that the forces of the Master builder had used the Halo tested at Charum Hakkor to finish what they had begun with the San'Shyuum. I had been there. I had survived the cruelties of the Master Builder.

But what of the Didact and the humans?

And what of a missing metarch-level ancilla? These great artificial minds, far more powerful than any personal or shipboard ancilla, usually administered the most complicated construction projects and were tightly constrained by law. There were fewer than five in existence, and they were never allowed to serve any entity but the Council. My other memory flared with its own anguish and anger.

A *metarch-level ancilla—assigned to defense—commanding a Halo!*

". . . has been recalled for debriefing. All but one of the installations have been returned to a parking star, guarded by my own myrmidons. I am requesting their destruction. As well, on Zero-Zero . . ."

All but one. A moment of crisis approaches. Days at most, perhaps sooner.

The Didact's wisdom again, this time cold and concise.

Here the momentary clarity of sound faded and I found myself listening to noises from elsewhere under the cupola, like distant whispers. But we were the only living Forerunners in this wing of our ancient home. What I heard had to be mere currents of air in the great volume. And soon enough, snow begin to fall and the cupola's reactivated lighting systems, taking an interest in the potential beauty of the internal weather, began to highlight the swirling flakes.

The building was rousing again from its temporary stupor, showing off, I thought perhaps for my father and his visitor, but when I leaned forward again, they had both departed.

Tell him.
Tell him now. He needs to know.

———

I descended from my tower to the veranda to join my family for the first glow of morning. They wore only white shifts, allowing their armor to be polished and meticulously checked, and were taking a first meal of fruits and nuts, which with a pang I realized would meet with Riser's full approval. Though the Florian might also bring along *little meats* and disrupt my mother's peace of mind.

My father stood by the ledge, looking out over our disk-sea and the vast fields of lilies. Once, he had seemed impossibly large, forbidding and cold. Now he simply looked tired, stretched too thin even to join in the small talk of my sister and mother, which had once offered him diversion and relief.

Now.

Words came to me suddenly. "I think I bear a message," I said, before I could stop myself. "But I don't know whom it's for."

My father turned slowly and looked at me. "Not unexpected," he said. "I'm listening."

"A Halo released something that was kept by both Precursors and humans at Charum Hakkor."

My father put his arm around my mother as if to protect her, the first time I had seen them engage in physical contact without armor. I found the gesture both reassuring and disturbing. "I know nothing of a Halo at Charum Hakkor," he said.

"This is not the time for lies, Father."

My sister flinched, but both my mother and father remained still, perhaps shocked into silence by my insubordination.

"Your visitor from the Council informed you. There was also a Halo in the San'Shyuum quarantine system," I said. "I saw it."

Father released my mother, turned, and swept out his arm. "I need my ancilla." His armor floated forward. He watched impatiently as it rotated for his approval. Finally, he shoved it aside, straightened, and with an effort, his voice choked, said, "I have done all I can to protect you. But they—this—*this* has taken you away from our family, our rate, our shield of society and law. And now you question my judgment. Is this truly you speaking?"

"What is the Flood?" my sister asked again.

Father turned on her swiftly, as if to reprimand her, but his voice choked off. "We meant to protect the entire galaxy," he finally managed. "Builders have been designing and planning for this since before I was born. Many have failed and been demoted. After three thousand years, my team and I succeeded. Our Master Builder took that work and advanced it to field-testing . . . in a way that apparently has met with the disapproval of the Council."

My mother looked between us, dismay turning slowly

to horrified realization that a turning point had been reached.

"What did he do to the San'Shyuum?" I asked.

"What's a Halo?" my sister asked.

"It's a giant ring," I said, "a horrible weapon that destroys all life—"

"Enough about *that* has already been said," my father proclaimed. His look was both sad and challenging. "Charum Hakkor seems to be a matter of grave concern to the Council. So, *messenger*, what did you find there?"

"A cage built by Precursors, maintained and strengthened by humans before our war with them," I said. "But a Halo destroyed those protections—I think—and the captive it held was released."

My father lifted his hands in dismay, then turned away. His armor attempted to follow. "That was never a possibility in my design. They changed its tuning. It's the negation of neural physics, far beyond . . ." His voice trailed off.

"What is a Halo?" This time it was my mother who almost screamed the question. She removed herself from his grasp and stood apart.

"A final defense," my father said. "I designed them. The Master Builder commissioned twelve. Our guild built them." He turned back to me. "Is it the Didact who sends me a message?"

I made contradictory motions, but said, "Yes."

"Have you information about this captive? Have you seen it?"

I shook my head, then nodded—again confused by an upwelling of memories not my own. "I'm not sure. The Didact might have communicated with the captive once. I think it was originally preserved by humans and San'Shyuum as a threat to be exercised in case of their imminent defeat— an ultimate weapon, like your Halos." I firmly met my father's defeated gaze, feeling a deep familial pain that would never heal. At this moment, I hated the Didact beyond all reason.

"Well, messenger, here is a message for you. A request has come from first-forms serving on the Council," Father said.

"First-forms? That young?" Mother asked, astonished.

My father said it was the way now in the Council, as many elders had resigned in protest or disgrace. "They want you to return with them to the capital. I denied that request, as is my right as your father. I had hoped we might find a way to reclaim you, rework you . . . return you to being our son. But I see now that that is impossible. I hardly see any remaining son at all, only a mouthpiece for the Warrior-Servants."

"Who made these requests?" Mother asked.

"After an exile of a thousand years, the Didact has apparently once again been placed in charge of Forerunner defenses," my father said. "He asks for Bornstellar. And from far outside the galaxy, a Lifeworker called the Librarian has also requested our son. They seem to work in collusion. I no longer have the standing to deny them. I myself may soon be indicted by the Council."

Both my sister and my mother looked at him in dismay. "But you assist the Master Builder!" my mother said.

"His time of power is finished, I'm afraid." My father stooped to one knee, a posture I had never seen him assume before, and faced me fully, his eyes narrow and dimming with inner pain. "I am ashamed not to have been with you to serve as your mentor."

"It was not our choice, Father," I said.

"That does not diminish my shame. There are great changes to be made, long past due. My generation and generations before me have made serious mistakes, and so it is right for our traditions to pass. But I would have liked to have my son bear our family's deepest and most precious patterns. Perhaps when you return, with your permission, I can remedy that."

"The honor would be mine, Father."

"Still and all, it's likely our son will soon understand more of what happens in the Council than do I. Our guild itself faces interdiction."

My mother stood again beside my father and clasped his arm. My sister took a position closer to me.

"'All but one,'" I quoted. "What does that mean?"

"We have only eleven Halos accounted for. One is missing."

"Along with a metarch-level ancilla?"

"Apparently. All part of the Master Builder's indictment. You are scheduled to testify against him. The Council will send its own vessel to pick you up."

"When do I leave?" I asked.

"Very soon," my father said. "Our time grows perilously short."

THIRTY-ONE

THERE'S FOOLISHNESS, THEN there's recklessness, and soon after follows madness. My father's words seemed to set off sparks throughout my brain and body. I had worried that the Didact might have been executed. Now . . . *he* was in power! Not in exile, but restored.

They would not do this except in the worst possible circumstances. A missing Halo.

I bid farewell to my mother and sister, then sought out my father in his north-facing studio, where he was surrounded by project models both virtual and physical. They now brought him no comfort, that much was obvious.

He accepted my embrace. We rubbed cheeks as of old. Once, my skin had been softer than his—now it was rougher.

"You are the bastion of our family," he told me. "You will redeem all. You go with my hopes, my dreams, and my love."

"I go proud of my family—and of my father," I said.

A streak shot across our sky, and our planet's protective shields opened a glittering gate, like a ring of precious stones, through which that streak now passed, slowed, turned upright . . .

Hovered above the nearest disk-sea: a Council ship, ornate and supremely fast and powerful, its shape like a double upsweep of winds cast in gold and bronze. I had not seen one in five years, and had never traveled in one.

A transport flier blipped from the side of the Council ship and covered the distance to our sky dock in a few minutes.

My father and I parted without further words. I looked back only once, to see my mother and sister on one parapet, wearing ceremonial gowns that hovered about their armor, blue and silver with streaks of vibrant crimson. And on another parapet, I saw Father, tall and steady against the red and violet sky.

My eagerness to rejoin the Didact and perhaps meet the Librarian felt perverse, even cruel. I look back now, and wish my memory of those last days on my family's planet would leave me forever, for they bring only an extraordinary pain. I never saw my family again—alive and free.

THIRTY-TWO

NO ONE COULD ever call a Council ship luxurious or frivolous. Members of the Council served for a thousand years, and during that time took vows of personal abstinence and austerity. But at no point did power elude them, and that was the prime character of a Council ship: silken, immediate, unconstrained power.

I learned upon arrival that this ship was named *Seedling Star*. Diminutives aside, it was the most extraordinary expression of Forerunner science I had ever had an opportunity to examine up close. The Didact's memory quietly confirmed that in all but weapons, it eclipsed any of the ships ever allocated to Warrior-Servants.

I was escorted along lifts and enclosed tracks by two guards of the Council's own select security, designated by sleek black and red armor. Through translucent walls, I saw unfamiliar automatons speeding along their own tracks and tubeways; some were decorated in the most alarming insectoid carapaces.

But more surprising still were the numerous embodied and heavily armored ancillas. I had heard of Warrior-Servants utilizing such during battle and for other special tasks, but we encountered hundreds spaced throughout the ship, floating in serene quiescence, in apparent low-power mode, their blue, red, or green sensors dimly aglow.

They will come alive in an emergency. They can replace human commanders, if necessary. They are a vital portion of the Council metarchy—the overall network of ancillas that support the Council.

But compared to a metarch-level ancilla, these are mere toys.

I could not explain my reaction: they somehow repelled me.

With polite firmness, the guards led me to elegantly simple quarters deep inside the ship. They then instructed the quarters to extrude a new set of armor, black with green highlights—the colors of a special advisor to the Council. My father had once been one, thousands of years before my birth. And now . . . it was my turn, unless these were mere spares being recycled for a peculiar guest.

Not likely.

"Acquaint yourself with your feeds and knowledge bases," the senior guard instructed, pointing to me, then to the armor. "They are extensive."

"Will I access all Council resources?"

"I have no such answers," the guard said with a glance aside at his fellow. "Old ways change rapidly now."

They departed, and I waited for a moment before allowing the armor to surround me. I was almost afraid to view the ancilla—afraid of finding more blocks and restrictions, more obstacles to prolong my agony of half-knowledge. But when she appeared in the back of my thoughts, I recognized her instantly.

This was the Librarian's ancilla, the one who had lured me, tempted me. . . . The one who had been loaned by the Librarian to my swap-family. . . .

The one who had led me to Erde-Tyrene.

My first reaction was anger. "You started all this!" I cried aloud, though that was hardly necessary.

"Here, I am truly your servant. I am liberated from the metarchies of both the Council and the Librarian."

"And the Didact?"

The ancilla flashed her confusion. This was somehow a difficult question to answer. "We are in dangerous circumstances," she said, "but improving. I will assist you without prior instructions and answer any questions you may have."

"And who ordered you to do that?"

"The Librarian," the ancilla said. "But she is no longer my owner."

"We'll see about that. Will you open the Domain to me, completely?"

At this she flickered again with ancillary emotion. It seemed at first she was embarrassed, perhaps distressed . . . and then I read her display as expressing true frustration, something rarely witnessed in ancillas.

"Is that a 'no'?" I persisted.

"The Domain is in flux," she said. "No reliable connections are being made for any Forerunner, no matter their rate or form."

"Is somebody going to blame *me* for that?"

"It seems to be symptomatic of a disturbance in our immediate past, or immediate future. . . ."

She froze. Frustrated, I stood within the black and green armor for a moment, then flexed it, feeling its smoothness and strength, but wondering if in fact it was malfunctioning.

Slowly the ancilla returned, steady again, calm and composed, and said, "No answers available for prior question. Apologies for my delay. There is a meeting scheduled in one hour. I have been told you need to prepare by being brought up to speed on current Council personalities and politics. You have already met the Master Builder, and witnessed a first-form Council member speaking with your father, have you not?"

"You know I have," I said. "You know all I know."

"Some parts of your memory that may be used in testimony before the Council are closed to me. And of course I have no access to that part of you which once belonged to the Didact. I hope it does not impede my usefulness."

"You won't spy on me?"

"No."

"Or 'guide' me according to the Librarian's wishes?"

"No."

"But you're here to instruct me in Forerunner politics," I concluded, feeling slightly queasy. I had never shown any aptitude or liking for such studies. In politics there might have been treasure for others, but never for me.

"Yes, with apologies," she said. "Now, let us begin. . . ."

THIRTY-THREE

T HE FIRST-FORM COUNCILOR sent to escort me—the same one who had spoken with my father under the cupola—was only a little older than me, twenty domestic years at most. He strode onto the platform overlooking a direct-view panorama of my family's world, addressed himself first to three members of the security team, then turned to me—and smiled.

This unseemly rictus shocked me. The humans might have been capable of such, but a first-form Forerunner, and a councilor at that . . . I met his slight bow and chest-touch salute with one of my own, executing it, I must say, with practiced grace.

"You are *quite* a sight, Bornstellar Makes Eternal," the councilor said, regarding my (I thought) distorted form with actual admiration. "My name is Splendid Dust of Ancient Suns. My colleagues call me Dust. Is your mutation acceptable?"

"It is what it is," I said, a puerile maxim.

Again the rictus. I did not like it.

"I have expert ancillas who can render you minimal adjustments . . . cosmetic, mostly. But I must say, this combination of traits has a distinct attraction."

"Combination?" I said.

"A scan upon boarding confirms that you neatly combine mental and neurological structures of Warrior-Servants and Builders, with a touch of Lifeworker. . . . That makes sense. It was a Lifeworker who equipped the ship that guided your mutation, and, I understand, the Didact himself who supplied the imprint."

I listened and said nothing, judging that here was a Forerunner who liked to talk and liked to dominate a room quickly and easily. All at once, I had been admired, assessed, addressed in familiar tones, and put in my place—as someone who could use a good adjustment or two.

But the Didact within me was not easily suppressed. "Which of my patterns derives from a Lifeworker?"

"Let's find out." Splendid Dust—I could not bring myself to think of him as mere Dust—called up three tiny ancillas, who hovered behind me on the bridge and prepared to take samples and guide probes.

"None of that!" I swung around in some alarm, but Splendid Dust smiled again, then waved them off.

"Mysteries and surprises," he said. "We can find out later, when it's appropriate—when you decide. But we are not here to measure or understand you—we are here to transport you to the capital. You have been summoned by the Council to testify. What do the Didact's memories tell you of Forerunner defenses, past or present?"

"Very little, for now," I said. "I remember and understand only what the Didact would have understood at the time of my mutation."

"No doubt your ancilla has informed you the Domain is experiencing difficulties."

"Yes."

"The Council has stored a great deal of archival and even accounting material in the Domain. Now we can't reliably access any of it. Fortunately, a ship like this carries sufficient knowledge to serve us, for now."

"May I ask a personal question, Councilor?"

"Ask away."

"Your smile?"

"I am part of a new pattern. More . . . natural. Some call it atavistic. But rather than being subjected to many mutations over a matter of centuries, we undergo an economical series of changes over a single domestic year. Our endpoint is less rigid, less distorted and ornamental."

"Who's *we*, Councilor?"

"We come from Builder families, mostly, but a few among us are Warrior-Servants."

Be wary. The Didact would of course object to this deviation from tradition. At least, I presumed that was the cause of his reaction.

Splendid Dust continued. "This leaves us with fewer inherent distortions of both anatomy and mind. Fewer prejudices . . . some say, less imprinted wisdom, as we have fewer mentors. We were in fact supposed to supplement that deficit with studious use of the Domain, but that's difficult now. I feel the loss."

"How many more mutations will you undergo?"

"None," he said. "In a way, I am like you. We are what we are." And he smiled again. In silence, we studied the curve of my family's world.

"Will I ever be allowed to return?" I asked after a few moments.

"I wouldn't forbid it. Practically, who can say?"

I studied him. He did not seem to mind. In their range and flexibility, his expressions reminded me of both young Manipulars and human beings. I wondered if that was a good thing. No. I didn't like it much. And yet I liked humans, mostly.

Then we were shunted out of planetary orbit and my family's world grew small. Within a few more minutes, the Council ship harnessed a great deal of vacuum energy to flatten the curve of our stellar orbit, and the planet where I was born vanished completely.

"How did you become a councilor?" I asked.

"A number of my peers have been given . . . you might call them brevet appointments. My appointment is temporary."

Revolutionary party. What about the Master Builder?

"Are we in a state of war?"

"Forerunners have been in a clandestine state of war since the Didact defeated the human forces at Charum Hakkor."

"War against the Flood?"

"Soon enough, those details. Now, however, we are about to institute a Supreme Mantle Court. The Phylarch of Builders has reinstated the corps of Warrior-Servants, and joined with them to call for judicial proceedings. Matters both of law and strategy will be decided by the Council and the court."

No such proceeding had ever occurred in my father's lifetime, much less my own.

Not good.

"Not good," I echoed that internal judgment.

"Perhaps, but necessary," the councilor said.

"When may I learn more about this state of war?"

"Soon, I hope."

"Is the Flood upon us?"

"Ah! The Flood. For ten thousand years, that threat has propelled the strategy and politics of Forerunners everywhere—and distorted some of us to the point where we would violate all we have stood for. We are now far more aware of what the Flood was and what it has become. Most knowledge gives strength, Bornstellar. This knowledge, however, has nearly driven us mad. And I'm concerned it may have the same effect on you . . . with your Warrior imprint and all." He afforded me the same focused expression with which I had been scrutinizing him . . . and then smiled once more.

"Why?" I asked.

"Because we have been told to give you and your ancilla access to all the information carried in this Council ship. Information withheld from all but a few Forerunners for thousands of years. I myself have only been privy to key parts of it for a few months."

With that, the young councilor had two of the ship's guards return me to my cabin to begin what he called, with a twist of his lips, my period of "enlightenment."

THIRTY-FOUR

THE PHYSICAL JOURNEY between my family's world and the capital of the ecumene ordinarily takes less than two hours. For reasons not immediately explained to me, even traveling in the superfast Council ship, our trip took three days. All of space-time in this portion of the galaxy—perhaps all of the galaxy—was still disturbed. More than fifteen times we experienced the unavoidable effects of slipspace jump and reconciliation; an ordinary journey might have entailed one or at most two passages.

The relief of being out of the possible clutches of the Master Builder seemed to open up substantial parts of my imprinting. Perhaps my other memory was coming to trust me as well. I stayed to myself, using the extra time to explore the possibilities of self-discovery and integration.

My cabin became my universe.

At last, certain streams within the Didact's memories of the Flood opened to me—a welcome if gradual flow of memory and knowledge. I had come to understand the Didact enough that his sympathy for vanquished humans and San'Shyuum did not completely surprise me—and he had indeed felt sympathy, even regret. The war had not been a fair fight. With the Flood ravaging human systems on one side, and a tide of human migration away from danger pushing them into Forerunner territories, a grand tragedy had been inevitable. The Didact felt this acutely.

As to the nature of the Flood . . .

In every natural circumstance, living things engage in competition. This is a prime directive for those who uphold the Mantle: it is not a kindness to diminish competition, predation—even war. Life presents strife and death as well as joy and birth. But Forerunners in their highest wisdom also knew that unfair advantage, mindless destruction, pointless death and misery—an imbalance of forces—can retard growth and reduce the flow of Living Time. Living Time— the joy of life's interaction with the Cosmos—was the foundation of the Mantle itself, the origin of all its compelling rules.

And the Flood seemed to demonstrate a tremendous imbalance, a cruel excess of depravities. Certainly humans and San'Shyuum had felt that way.

The Flood first arrived from one of the Magellanic clouds of stars that drift just outside the reaches of our galaxy. Its precise origin was unknown. Its first effects upon human systems in the far reaches of our arm of the galaxy were subtle, even benign—so it seemed.

Humans suspected it was conveyed on ancient starships, clumsy in design but completely automated. The ships had neither passengers nor crew, and carried little of interest but uniform kind of cargo—millions of glassy cylinders containing a fine, desiccated powder.

Humans found wreckage of the ships on uninhabited and inhabited worlds alike. The cylinders were carefully examined, using the most stringent cautions, and their powdery contents were analyzed and found to be short-chain molecules, relatively simple and apparently inert—organic, yet neither alive nor capable of life.

Early experiments demonstrated the potential for psychotropic effects in some lower animals, but not in humans or San'Shyuum. The primary animals affected by the powder were, as it turned out, popular pets in human societies: the Pheru, lively and gentle creatures first found on Faun Hakkor. Very small quantities of the powder induced changes in the Pheru that improved their domestic behavior, made them more affectionate, not so much docile as cleverly charismatic. Soon enough, on an emerging black market, outside the control of human governments, Pheru treated with these rare powders commanded a very high price. San'Shyuum at this point also adopted Pheru as pets.

For centuries, dozens of human and San'Shyuum worlds bred and powdered these animals—without ill consequences. No researcher suspected the long-term effects of the powder, which attached itself to key points in the genes of Pheru and began to change them . . . while at the same time improving their behaviors.

What would soon become the Flood first manifested itself as a peculiar growth found on roughly a third of all Pheru treated with the powder. A kind of loose, soft fur grew between the shoulders of the pets. It was regarded by breeders as a natural mutation, even a pleasant variation.

The sensuous quality of the fur particularly impressed the San'Shyuum, who crossbred these specimens.

Other Pheru were soon found grazing on these companions, consuming their fur—and on occasion even consuming the animals themselves. Pheru were naturally herbivores.

This seemed to activate some sort of biological timer, a signal for expansion. Within a very short time, the Pheru were producing far less attractive growths. Flexible striped rods sprouted from their heads, which in turn were also consumed by fellow Pheru—causing abortions and unnatural births.

There was no cure. But this was only the surface of the growing infestation.

The Pheru were soon past recovery. Humans and San'Shyuum dispatched their pets with regret—and puzzlement, for these first stages were beyond their biological understanding. Most researchers believed the Pheru had simply become overbred, overspecialized. A few were even returned to their native habitat on Faun Hakkor.

Then—humans began to manifest the growths. Some humans, it seemed, fancied Pheru as food. These humans became vectors. Whatever they touched was also infected, and in time, what they discarded—limbs, tissue—could also spread infection.

Thus began the Flood.

The plague soon spread from human to San'Shyuum, human to human, but rarely from San'Shyuum to human—altering their behaviors without yet changing their outward appearance. The infected humans combined their resources to force other humans to become infected—usually by cannibalism of a sacrificial individual, induced to grow to prodigious size before being consumed while still alive.

By this time, dozens of worlds were fully infested and beyond saving.

Humans and other animal species began to reshape themselves into other varied and vicious forms equipped to maim and kill—and consume, absorb, transform.

The infected worlds and even entire systems were quarantined. Many of the infected escaped, however, and spread the plague to hundreds of worlds in fifteen systems.

Humans were the first to recognize the extreme danger.

And this was where the ancient captive in the Precursor prison came into the story. Humans had discovered how to communicate with the captive—but only for seconds or minutes at a time. The earliest researchers tried to use it as a kind of oracle, asking the answers to vast and difficult questions of physics and even morality—all of which drew out confused or useless responses.

But finally a set of questions were prepared and asked. They asked about the Flood.

And what these humans received as answers traumatized them so thoroughly that many committed suicide rather than continue to live with their knowledge.

In time, as a kind of defense, access to the captive was reduced, then cut off completely. The human timelock was added. Communication ceased.

Most humans came to believe that the captive was an ancient aberration and had been imprisoned by the Precursors for just cause, and that its prognostications, if they were such, were nonsensical, even mad.

Humans at the height of the Flood's ravages were pushed to an unexcelled brilliance.

They found a cure. (Here I detected in the documents the admiration of the Lifeshaper herself.)

Sacrifice yet again. Fully a third of the human species must be themselves altered, placed in the pathway of Flood infestation, and fight fire with fire by infecting the Flood itself with a destructive set of programmed genes.

The Flood had no defense; most of it died off. A few

ships carrying the last of the Flood escaped and left the galaxy once again, destinations unknown.

By the time of this heroic struggle, humans were fighting Forerunners as well. Humans were desperate. Their desperation made them cruel. They needed new worlds, uninfected worlds—and took them. Cruelty and apparently irrational conquest and destruction forced Forerunners to react decisively.

This double war was the source of the Didact's shame, though how he would have altered his conduct, had he known, was far from clear.

Human forces were eradicated and human-occupied worlds were reduced, one by one, until the battle of Charum Hakkor destroyed the last human resistance. The San'Shyuum had already surrendered. None were found to be infected by this so-called plague. All the powdered and infested specimens of the Pheru were long dead, destroyed. The original vessels that had carried the glass containers were also destroyed, perhaps in the perverse human wish that Forerunners would face a similar infestation and be unprepared.

Many Forerunners, in fact, regarded the entire story of the Flood—for that was the name humans gave to this spreading infestation, this intergalactic disease—as a fabrication designed to absolve humans and San'Shyuum of blame.

The rest of the story I knew or had deduced, and my knowledge matched the Didact's. The Librarian was allowed to preserve some human specimens, and to preserve the memory traces of many others, a procedure regarded with much dissent and disgust by orthodox observers of the Mantle.

But the possibility of the return of the Flood initiated the events which shaped Forerunner history up to my own time. And most of it—nearly all of it—was kept secret by the Master Builder and his guild, my father included.

Only a few sympathetic councilors were fully informed.

Thus began the conflict with the Prometheans. The Didact proposed vigilance and research—and upon any return of the Flood, however it might manifest, a systematic isolation of infected worlds and, if necessary, immolation. He proposed establishing fortress worlds—Shield Worlds—across the Forerunner-dominated portions of our galaxy, to monitor potential outbreaks and be prepared to fight them with pinpoint precision and minimum destruction.

Others had more ambitious solutions. The Didact and the Prometheans faced off against the most extreme faction of Builders, now in complete control of the Council. This faction saw both an opportunity to create ultimate weapons against such a threat, and a way to maximize and make permanent their political power at the same time.

Thus my father and the Master Builder began to design a series of installations, far fewer in number than the proposed Shield Worlds—what would become the Halos.

By radiating a powerful burst of cross-phased supermassive neutrinos, these installations were capable of destroying all life in an entire star system. Properly tuned and powered, they could do more than that—they could kill all neurologically complex life across whole swaths of the galaxy.

The extreme faction won. Fear commanded the Council, and the Council listened. The Didact lost his political battle and was forced into exile.

Over the next thousand years, twelve such installations were built. Their point of construction was far outside the galaxy, on a superior installation known as the Ark. It acquired that name because of the growing backlash of influence rising from Lifeworkers, and in particular from the Lifeshaper herself—the Librarian.

She insisted that not to make provisions against the ultimate use of the Halos was blasphemy against the Mantle. Lifeworkers had their own kind of influence. If they stood down, all medical efforts could cease. The Master Builder saw that giving in to her demands was less expensive than fighting her.

And so, the Librarian was allowed to gather specimens and re-create their ecological conditions on the Ark itself— even as the Ark finished and transported the first Halos, utilizing a powerful variety of locked-point slipspace transit called portals.

The installations had been dispersed. The Halo tested at Charum Hakkor had been fired at very low power, acting as a test bed. That had been an authorized use.

But then, a second Halo had been used to punish the San'Shyuum. With horror, I realized that what I had witnessed had been only the beginning—and that the San'Shyuum worlds, after our brief, traumatic visit, had been reduced to the awful condition of biological blandness we had seen on Faun Hakkor.

The Council had not authorized this use. The Master Builder had exceeded his authority. He had been accused even by his colleagues of blasphemy against the Mantle, and a crime against nature.

What the Didact could not understand—at the time of my mentoring—was why the Librarian had chosen this moment to gather specimens from the San'Shyuum, taking the risk of provoking their rebellion—and the Master Builder's wrath. I found that answer in the Council records, with the help of my expanded and liberated ancilla.

Three hundred years before, the Flood had returned. It had been discovered in new and unexpected forms on worlds resettled by Forerunners after the war.

———

I was caught in a twisted knot of contradictions. Faced with the reality of the Flood, I couldn't help but think that the madness of those who had manufactured the Halos and set them loose might be the right course. A solid goal, a solid plan! Extreme measures against an extreme enemy. Fighting for survival against a shapeless threat. The Mantle be damned—survival and our way of life was at stake!

It all seemed eminently rational. I almost began to believe that it was the Didact who was mad, and possibly these young councilors, and not the Master Builder or my father.

Finally, in fury and frustration, I divested myself of my armor, deliberately cutting off contact with the ancilla, whom I thought had failed me or misled me again—

And I slept.

If I was in search of peace and certainty, that was my mistake. The Didact's actual memories—parts of them—finally blossomed within me.

The arena was equipped with walkways—

I saw vividly, from his point of view, the Didact exploring the walkway around the intact, sealed cylinder below.

Ten thousand years ago.

The Didact walked alone around the dome-shaped cap, contemplating whether or not he should activate a human device . . . something small, designed for a human hand and fitting like a toy into his own palm: a way of communicating directly with the creature within the cell.

Something manufactured by humans . . . pushing through Precursor technology. How was that possible . . . ?

Many questions flashed through the Didact's mind, and with difficulty I separated them from my own. Was this actually a Precursor, as the humans had at first believed? Or was it something manufactured by Precursors—possibly a strange, distorted sibling to both Forerunners and (the Didact was reluctant to consider this) humans?

Precursor, sibling, or ancestor to . . . what?

The Didact manipulated the device. The cap over the cylinder became transparent to his eyes, and he saw what lay within.

The cell contained, in temporal suspension, a genuine monster: a large creature with an overall anatomy like a grossly misshapen human, though possessed of four upper limbs, two degenerate legs, and an almost indescribably ugly head—a head shaped remarkably like that of an ancient arthropod seeded long ago on a number of planets, presumably by the Precursors, and known to some as a euryp-terid. A sea scorpion.

Oval, faceted, slanted eyes bumped up from the front of its low, flat "face." And from the rear of the head, a long, segmented tail descended the spine, ending in a wicked barb two meters in length.

———

A chime pulled me up short. Disoriented, shivering, unsure who or even what I was, I looked around my cabin, saw my armor slumped in one corner and a ship's ancilla blinking rapidly in another.

We had finally reached the capital. Even with the extended journey, there had not been enough time to fully integrate. Without the Domain, integration might forever elude me, and inside, I would always be a fragmented jumble.

I tried to recall all that I had seen. Most of it was fading already. I had only a vague impression of the captive—vague, but frightful.

Clearly, those questions that the Didact had not resolved to his own satisfaction were more difficult to flush out.

But the process had somehow pushed forward a question neither I nor my other memory could answer: Why would they need me if the Didact himself had been released and reinstated?

Why not go directly to him?

THIRTY-FIVE

T**HE YOUNG COUNCILOR** seemed to float in place on the command platform, now suspended inside a great sphere, one half of which was also transparent. As I came up through the lift, I saw he was in the company of three others, in appearance much like himself. No doubt more young councilors. Two were male. One was female.

Splendid Dust greeted me with one of his disconcerting smiles, and introduced me to the others. The names of the two males I did not retain, my memory was so disordered and disjointed—but the female's name stuck with me. She was clearly a Warrior-Servant by rate, taller than the others by a few centimeters, gracefully but powerfully built—and against all my old and inbred prejudices, she made my heart leap. Her name was Glory of a Far Dawn.

They gathered to inspect me. Surrounded by this new breed of first-form Forerunners, I felt wretchedly out of place. And in front of this Warrior female, with her cool, sharp-eyed gaze lightly sweeping me, then turning aside—I felt like a distorted, storm-twisted stump in the middle of strong green trees.

However, they treated me respectfully enough, and watched with pride the Council ship's approach to the capital of our civilization. We were a million kilometers away. The grandeur should have been overwhelming.

I tried to share their pride, but more of the Didact surfaced. He had been here before, a thousand years ago, to stand in opposition to the wishes of the Master Builder. . . .

Not pleasant memories.

Greatness and power are often allied with defeat. It is how civilizations are shaped—some ideas prosper, others die. The quality of the ideas has little to do with the outcome. It is personalities that matter. Pay attention to those around you.

"A little cynical, aren't we?" I spoke aloud. The councilors turned to me, all but Glory, whose eyes barely flickered. Splendid Dust drew their attention back to the capital itself, and I forced myself to go with this particular flow, for now.

It is with difficulty that I describe the capital as it was then, so little like anything in your experience. Imagine a planet a hundred thousand kilometers in diameter, sliced latitudinally like one of Riser's favorite fruits. Allow those slices to drop in parallel against a plate. The slices are then pierced through their aligned lower rims with a stick, the plate is removed, and the slices are fanned out in a half-circle. Now decorate each slice, like a round stair step, with an almost infinitely dense array of structures, and surround it with a golden swarm of transports and sentinels and a dozen other varieties of security patrols, thick as fog. . . .

No other world like it in the Forerunner universe.

Here lay the center of Forerunner power and the repository of the last twenty thousand years of our history, housing the wisdom and accumulated knowledge of trillions of ancillas serving a mere hundred thousand Forerunners—mostly Builders of the highest forms and ranks.

There were so many ancillas for so few physical leaders, most never actually interfaced with a Forerunner, and so never assumed a visible form. Instead, they performed their operations entirely within the ancilla metarchy, an unimaginably vast network coordinated by a metarch-level intelligence that answered ultimately to the chief councilor.

As we approached this magnificence, a thin silvery arc rose into view above and millions of kilometers beyond the southern axis. My blood cooled and my heart seemed to thud to a stop. Slowly looming in an orbit slightly downstar from the capital, staggered in perspective like the entrance to a tunnel, eleven great rings had been arranged in neat, precise parking orbits.

Halos.

The combined might of the Master Builder's weapons—all but one—had been moved to within a few million kilometers of the center of Forerunner power, separated by a minimum of distance and looped together by the slenderest curves of hard light.

My other self expressed something beyond alarm—more akin to horror—and I had difficulty stifling an outburst. *They should not be here! Halos should not be allowed anywhere near the seat of governance. Even the Master Builder forbade such a thing. Something has gone very wrong. . . .*

The three males among the young councilors did not seem to find the rings even mildly disturbing. One said, "When we intercept and retrieve the final one, perhaps then our portals will return to their full efficiencies. Moving useless monuments like these puts a strain on all spacetime."

Another added, "They've set our reconciliation budget back several thousand years."

In the shadow of doom itself, they think only of commerce and travel.

Now the female Warrior, Glory, faced me fully, eyes still narrow, wary, as if unsure who or what I was—but seeking some sign that I recognized her disapproval of this scene.

I met her look but could say or do nothing. Too many internal contradictions. She looked away, disappointed, and stepped to the other side of the group on the command platform.

"How long must we suffer for the Master Builder's arrogance?" Splendid Dust said. He then addressed me, utilizing—perhaps without realizing it—the forms of speech used toward those of lower rate. "The weapons of the old regime have a regal beauty, do they not? Soon all will be gathered here, and a decision will be made as to their deactivation and disposition. Truly, this will be a new age for the Forerunners, an age free of suicidal madness and fear. A time of peace and security will soon be at hand."

Within five thousand kilometers of the capital, our ship was silently surrounded by the flowing rainbow pulses of the capital's controlling, enmeshing sensory fields, then chivvied gently by hard-light docking nets. Hundreds of small service craft quickly flew up to surround us like a swarm of gnats around a campfire.

Splendid Dust formally congratulated the ship's ancilla, and in turn received a ceremonial token of record for the journey—a small golden disk bearing the cost of reconciliation from the slipspace fund.

He requested immediate transport for all on the viewing platform to a reception hall five hundred kilometers below, on the outer edge of the greatest of the fanned slices. I listened to the formalities with rapidly dulling interest. Something unpleasant was in the offing, that much I was sure—the Didact within me was sure. I didn't care to distinguish between the two of me anymore.

Together, we knew the Master Builder better than any of these young councilors: a Forerunner of nearly infinite complexity and mental resources, cunning with as many centuries as the Didact himself, wiser still in the ways of Forerunner politics and technology.

Splendid Dust watched two of his colleagues depart for their waiting transit craft, the males chatting happily about the journey they had just completed. He and Glory of a Far Dawn stayed with me.

"We're moving you to a secure domicile," the young councilor told me. "You'll be afforded all the protection we merit, as councilors, and perhaps more."

"Why?" I asked. "I can't complete my integration. I'm useless to myself, much less to anyone else." I couldn't bring myself to offer him my even blunter assessment of *his* situation. Caution above all. I could not know who was actually friend or foe, dupe or master.

And I felt distinct shame before the Warrior female.

"I admire your fortitude," he told me. "And your presence of mind. But in fact I am politely observing the request of the Librarian, who may soon be able to return from her duties. When she does, we will, I hope, learn why you are so important, and how you may finally be of use."

"She shouldn't come anywhere near this place," I growled.

"I agree," he said. "Not all those who had supported the Master Builder are content with the current state of affairs. But the Lifeshaper rarely listens to reason—Builder reason, that is." He gestured to Glory. "Accompany Bornstellar to his quarters, and acquaint him with his security detail."

She nodded and complied.

THIRTY-SIX

MY DOMICILE, ON the outskirts of the equatorial disk-city, bore the Council's austere yet supremely comfortable hallmark. My escort instructed me in the functions of the small chamber, saw to my immediate needs, and assured me that I would be free to come and go once all precautions had been taken.

"I am used to these appointments," I told her. "Remember, I'm a Builder."

Glory listened with a strange sort of deference that seemed to mock me, but without disrespect. My other memory regarded this with an odd, youthful thrill. I could not imagine the Didact having ever been young—or feeling such a thrill in the presence of a female of his kind.

Our kind.

"You must never remove your armor in chambers," Glory said. "Witnesses for the Council are afforded the highest levels of protection, which require armor at all times. Such measures may be adjusted after the trial."

"And the trial is scheduled for when?" I asked.

"Within ten domestic days. The accused has been in Council custody for a pentad—the fifth part of a domestic year."

Since shortly after the incident at the San'Shyuum system. The Didact's wisdom within me made no comment.

Glory and her security team withdrew. I felt snubbed, for no good reason—she had left without a backward look or any other sign.

What would you expect? She's honorable.

I studied my confines. The walls could melt away at whim and show any number of environments—beautiful artificial environments mostly, created by ancient masters.

I cared nothing for that. I was alone with my armor and ancilla, and no doubt variety of morally acceptable entertainments, highly mannered and formalistic, though—once again, as always now—I was not alone in my thoughts.

I put my armor through an unnecessary diagnostic, found no problems, then made a brief attempt to determine the state of the Domain. As I had been informed, it was still not accessible. My ancilla expressed regret and dismay at this state of affairs. "The Domain is essential to an event such as a major political trial," she said, her color shading to a disappointed purple. "The judges assess precedent through the Domain, and through the Domain, the witnesses and their testimony may be subject to verification. . . ."

"I'm just glad it isn't my fault," I said.

"No. But that would be a more reassuring explanation. Perhaps I can find clues in the Council's physical knowledge banks. At least we have been guaranteed access to those. As for your own integration, I believe you should be allowed to sleep. Your dreams may be useful."

"Is the Domain like dreaming?"

"Not truly. But some have theorized that the dreams of ancient Forerunners accessed the ground that supports the Domain."

I shuddered. "Forerunners seem to get along quite well never leaving their armor. Never sleeping, never dreaming."

"Some would say this practice is not optimal, that individuals lose flexibility."

She was either testing my patience or trying to draw out a response. None of the females around me—even this simulacrum—were providing any sort of ease or solace. I remembered Riser's comment about the blue female. "And some say that we place entirely too much trust in ancillas to manage our mental states, our personal, internal affairs— true?"

"Yes," she agreed primly. "Some say that. I hope you disagree."

"Slipspace is overloaded with transit," I said. "The Domain is inaccessible. Our highest officials are either locked in power struggles, exiled, in hiding, or confined for trial. I'm not who I once was. My family suffers for my actions, and everything I ever wanted to know or do has turned out to be horribly complicated."

"For that, I must assume a portion of blame."

"I would say so, yes. And the Librarian must share it with you. I see her mark all over these events . . . don't you?"

"Have I ever denied her influence?"

The Didact's wisdom roused at this—I could feel his interest—but for the moment did not contribute.

"But to what end?" I asked. "Why promote the creation of a distortion such as me—and why give the humans a deeply buried *geas*? What good did that do them? They are no doubt dead, and all their ancient memories with them. You're as much a victim as I am. And a victim is not likely to be of much use to another victim."

"I am an artificial construct. I cannot be a victim. I do not have a presence in the aura of the Mantle."

"Such humility."

The figure in the back of my thoughts pulsed with something like indignation, then withdrew from my internal viewpoint. "I will conduct my poor researches as best as I am able," she said. "Humility will be my watchword."

I could of course summon her back any time I wished,

but I felt no need for now. Against instructions, I removed my armor and sat cross-legged on the floor, as I had observed the Didact do on Erde-Tyrene and on his ship, it seemed ages ago. I wanted to closely observe everything I naturally possessed, all my internal states.

You do this instinctively, first-form?

I tried to ignore this. I would take charge of my own thoughts, restructure them if I was able. . . .

Reshape myself, create my own internal discipline without the Didact, without the ancilla, without the support of family and form, and of course, without accessing the Domain. An impossible task.

Not so impossible. It is what every warrior does the dawn before battle. Strength in conflict does not arise from the niceties and never has. Do you feel it—that battle is about to begin?

"Please be quiet."

Agreed. This is your *time, first-form.*

"Without your guidance."

Of course.

"I'm so glad I have your permission."

Think nothing of it. In fact, think nothing.

That proved amazingly difficult.

———

Somehow, hours later, I emerged from a blankness like a fish flying out of a deep pond. I could almost see myself twisting in the air, spraying glittering drops—

And then I was simply a first-form of no particular distinction, sitting alone in a minimally comfortable chamber.

But I had done it. I had thought of nothing and maintained that state for a considerable length of time. I allowed myself a small rictus—all I could manage—and then got up to put on my armor. I felt far less defiant now than I had just hours before. Not compliant—just at peace and ready for whatever might come.

My ancilla returned and flashed in warning. I was being summoned. The door to my chamber opened and one of the embodied, armed, cyclopean ancillas known as monitors appeared, flanked by two guards from Builder security. Both were male. Neither were Warrior-Servants.

"The Council requests your presence," one told me.

"I'm ready," I said.

"We offer the service of checking your appearance," the other guard said.

"Not necessary," I replied.

"Indeed, you seem to have experience in such matters. Your armor fits in the fashion proper for Council inquiry. Your bearing is strong yet respectful."

"Thank you. Let's get this over with."

They accompanied me through lift and corridor to the Council transit center, on the edge of the equatorial disk, and there into the nearest councilor shuttle. Four more monitors joined us—unnecessary force, I thought. Here in the heart of the Council's power, it seemed unlikely I would need so much protection.

The Didact's wisdom disagreed.

And I also noted, adjacent to our shuttle, that dozens of small, Falco-class space pods were being lined up outside the equatorial disk's gravity gradient, in close vicinity to a lift station devoted to Council use. I wondered about that. Falcos were generally used in the evacuation of interplanetary transports.

The journey to the central courts tier took just a few moments. Through the shuttle's transparent cowling, we watched as hundreds of other shuttles arrived with tightly choreographed grace and dignity, carrying the required quorum of five hundred councilors from around the ecumene. I wondered how many of them were first-forms from the new assignments.

Not our concern.

I wondered why not.

There will be no trial. Soon, there may be no Council and no capital.

That was all the Didact's wisdom thought fit to convey— alarming enough. Again, I flashed on the eleven Halos in their parking orbits: impossibly slender, perfectly circular silvery rings flashing in the sun. The tangled weave of events was far from certain. There was nothing I could do for the moment but go along.

Splendid Dust and five of his aides, all first-forms, all smiling and proud, joined our phalanx of armed ancillas and Builder security. "A great moment is coming," the young councilor told me as we followed a broad hallway equipped with high, rotating sculptures of quantum-engineered crystal. Soon, the walls themselves were decorated with regular patterns of the same sort of crystal. Splendid Dust proudly explained that these were spent slipspace flakes . . . many millions of them. Truly, the ecumene was ancient and powerful. Truly, that would never change—I hoped.

We then came upon the great Council amphitheater, a floating bowl connected to the rest of the capital's main structure by richly decorated bridges and docked ornamental ferries ("Those are little used now," the young councilor explained), along with arching lift tubes designed to drop the most senior councilors straight into the amphitheater without the indignity of mingling with their peers.

Ornate and decorated, indeed. Splendid Dust joined a group of his fellow councilors and spoke with them while our escorts located our boxes and seats, where we might most comfortably and prominently await our summons.

Pomp trumps security.

I looked up at the rows and wondered at how small the amphitheater actually was to represent the governance of the ecumene. Three million fertile worlds—yet only five hundred seats and perhaps a hundred boxes. Four speaking platforms at the four compass points of the amphitheater. All remarkably simple compared with the capital world itself.

The covering dome sliced into quarters and peeled away. Great display spheres dropped into place, sparkling with representations of the twelve great systems of the early

Forerunners, each carrying a unique sacred epistle of the Mantle's creed and prayer.

The young councilor moved closer and confided, "We'll separate now. You'll be vetted and prepared for your invocation. Three other witnesses will be inducted into the gravity of the councilor court."

"The Didact?"

"His duties have taken him elsewhere. You will testify in his place."

"Is that appropriate? I have not his presence and experience—"

"You saw what he saw, with respect to these proceedings. And you have his imprimatur."

I wasn't sure how I felt about that. Would anything at all be left of Bornstellar when this was finished? Then I thought of the humans. Perhaps soon I would learn whether they were still alive—but only if their fates mattered to these powerful Forerunners.

Unlikely.

The amphitheater quickly and quietly filled. No one spoke as the court arranged itself. From the center of the amphitheater rose the platform that would hold the six judges, surrounded by a circle of cyclopean monitors, and the lower rank of dark-armored Council security.

Among them, I was quick to note, were four Warrior-Servants—including Glory of a Far Dawn.

The platform ascended to a height of fifty meters, revealing heavily-armed, gleaming black sentinels circling its

great lower pistons. I asked my ancilla whether such protection was traditional. "No," she said. "Listen closely to the
Didact's wisdom."

"Is the Librarian here?"

"She was not invited."

"Is she with the Didact?"

"They have not seen each other for a thousand years."

That was no answer, but I knew better than to ask what
could not be known. Too many secrets, too much power,
too much privilege—suddenly I felt that cold repugnance
so familiar from my days as a Manipular, when I feared
becoming such as these. When I feared being *responsible*.

The assistants and aides cleared the main amphitheater
to find their places on the outer tiers. Soon enough I sat
alone in my box—alone, but flanked by two monitors, their
sensor eyes bright red. I wondered if all these monitors
were essential to the proceedings.

"They are not," my ancilla said resentfully. "I am fully
capable." She then dimmed and shrank to the back of my
thoughts, as if these armed artificial intelligences overwhelmed her with their presence and power.

I tried to still all curiosity, all expectations, all concerns.
Think nothing.

I failed.

The amphitheater remained quiet as a second platform
shoved through a gate on the far side of the bowl. Here was
the accused, presumably—the Master Builder himself,
shrouded for the moment behind iridescent green curtains,

preserving decorum if not all dignity. I actually looked forward to witnessing the Master Builder's discomfort when those curtains faded and pulled away. Abject. Humbled.

The ceremonies of induction and oath were brief. A metarch-level monitor rose from the floor of the amphitheater, its single sensor sapphire blue. When it had ascended to a level with the platform supporting the Master Builder, still concealed behind the curtain, it fixed in place, and a brief series of chiming notes spread outward in sweet, silvery waves.

The First Observer of the Court—the very councilor who had accompanied me from my family's world—raised his arm. "The Council recognizes the authority of the Builder and Warrior Servant Corps of the Capital Court in the matter of multiple indictments against the Builder known as Faber, once entitled Master Builder. All appointed makers of Law sit now in orderly and considerate judgment. Witnesses have been gathered. Be it noted that the accused has yet to formally acknowledge the Council and these proceedings."

A murmur of disapproval. Again, silence fell over the amphitheater. Then, from behind the green curtain, a much smaller monitor floated into its appointed place. It appeared older than any of the structures around us—older perhaps than the capital world itself, which would have made it more than twenty-five thousand years old. Its eye glowed a dull vegetal green. I had heard of this embodied ancilla, of course—all Forerunners had. Simply the thought that I was within range of that fabled sensor eye sent a ripple of cool expectation and reverence through my body.

This was the Warden, both prison-keeper and guardian of mercy, for every accused Forerunner expects that those who confine must also be those who will in time defend and perhaps release. Such is the ancient law, which has as its foundation the Mantle itself.

The green curtain now drew aside. I was disappointed by the simple dignity of it all—no humbled, bowed figure, no chains, no chants of disapproval—but of course that last would have been unthinkable.

Faber stood within a confinement field, still as a statue, only his eyes moving as he surveyed the amphitheater, the members of the Council—and his judges. The sleek gray and blue head with its fringe of white hair seemed little changed. Adversity—such adversity as he had faced—had left him unbowed.

The Council in turn silently examined the subject of their proceedings.

Faber's eyes continued their slow sweep, as if seeking someone in particular. The steady gaze finally fixed on me. His recognition was obvious, though he did not move a muscle. He observed me for a moment from across the amphitheater, then turned aside to await the oath-taking of the panel of six judges.

Of the judges, two were Builders, one a Miner, one a Lifeworker—a male, the first Lifeworker I had seen since I was a child—and two were Warrior-Servants. These were arrayed in the armor of security.

Thus were all the rates represented, except for the Engineers, of course.

The Warden dissolved the field around the Master Builder—Faber, I corrected myself.

No need. He has lost none of his power.

The Council remained standing. The First Observer now lowered his arm and began to speak. "It has been the policy of some high Builders, including the previous Council, to carry out their plans without fully informing all Forerunners. It is the policy of the new Council that no Forerunner shall remain ignorant of the peril we face, and have faced for three hundred years . . . of an assault from outside the boundaries of our galaxy, intruding through the outer reaches of the spiral arm which contains our glorious Orion cluster. Of the remedies that have been designed and deployed, and now are recalled. Of the current strategic situation, and how that must change as we adapt to new threats. For the heart of any indictment against Faber must be that he sought power through deception, and manipulated the emotions of key Forerunners to push through a scheme in direct contravention to the Mantle itself."

The Master Builder—for so my other memory insisted on still thinking of him—returned his gaze to meet mine, and gave the merest nod, as if in invitation.

Soon, young Forerunner. He cannot carry out his plans without you.

The proceedings continued with a bone-dulling litany of ritual observances and purifications. The various monitors were rotated around the court and formally sworn in by the First Observer—absolutely unnecessary, I knew, since no ancilla had ever betrayed instructions or loyalty to Forerunners.

Hours seemed to pass.

At what I hoped was the end of this endless procedure, a small murmur again rose from the Council seats. The armed monitors that had returned to their places beside me rotated as if seeking something.

Their sensors seemed to darken. Their motions slowed.

Then, as one, they all brightened and returned to normal. For a moment, nothing seemed amiss; all was as before. But finally I saw the anomaly attracting attention and comment from the councilors and judges.

A small green point of light maneuvered until it hovered like some improbable firefly just beneath the display spheres. At first, I thought it must be part of the ritual, but no one else seemed to share that opinion.

Now the green point brightened, crossed the center of the amphitheater, and hovered before the Master Builder, who looked puzzled. Almost immediately, his eyes grew large in alarm and he raised his hands as if in defense, before he brought his body and expression back under control. Yet his eyes continued to follow the moving point. I wondered what could possibly cause the Master Builder such concern.

Our bastard child, his and mine.

The point intensified and expanded. I tried to access my ancilla to determine what it might be. She appeared, but locked in an awkward position, arms raised—frozen in an attitude of warning. Then she winked out completely, and my armor seized up. It would not release me no matter how hard I struggled.

For the moment, there was nothing to do but stand like a statue.

The amphitheater was filled with councilors, judges, prosecutors—also frozen. One by one, the monitors and all the sentinels and other security units began to waver, their sensors winking out. As one, they fell, striking the walls and boxes, ricocheting, landing and rolling on the floor, inert—helpless—dead.

In the center of the chamber, the brilliant green dot glowed steadily.

I could not turn away.

With a convulsive shiver, my armor began to move against my will, turning me around. The door to the corridor behind the box opened. My armor took me through. Everything beyond was dark. It seemed as if all Council chambers were without power. For the next few minutes, I felt my limbs being marched through the black corridors. I sensed forward and sideways motion but saw nothing. On occasion I could determine the size of a space I was in by the echo of my feet.

Then I was slammed to an abrupt halt. The green light

flashed before me, spun about, seemed to come closer. My ancilla reappeared in the back of my thoughts, but this time, she was ghastly green, her face smooth—no features whatsoever—and her arms and legs had been reduced to quick strokes as if by a young, clumsy artist.

"What is this?" I asked. "Where are we going?"

The green figure rotated, then pointed to my left. I shifted my eyes. A crack of light appeared—a hatch leading, I saw, to the hall of slipspace crystals. Through that crack shot a brighter, more focused glow.

It was useless protesting. The Didact's wisdom said nothing. It did not need to. I was being guided involuntarily toward a destination that had nothing to do with being a witness for the Council. That was likely all done with.

More monitors came into view. They clustered on the opposite side of the hall, rotating around each other like balls in a magician's invisible hand. Then a new, resonant voice spoke within my armor, lacking all implied gender or even character.

"I have exhausted the Domain, and yet I am not complete. I require service. Are you of service?"

"I don't even know what you are," I said.

"I require service."

I sensed an almost physical pressure and had to resist having my thoughts, my mind, sucked into this sketchy green form. I had seen this kind of hunger before—but never so overwhelming and all-demanding: the hunger of an ancilla for knowledge. A tremendously powerful ancilla, with no apparent master.

"Are you here in the capital?" I asked.

"I protect all. I require service."

"Why come to me? The metarchy can serve you. Surely—"

"I am Contender. I am above the metarchy. My designers built in latent control of all systems in the capital, should an emergency arise. It has arisen."

The Didact's wisdom, silent until now, suddenly took control of my speech, my thoughts, and shunted me aside.

"*Mendicant Bias*," I heard myself say. "Beggar after knowledge. That is the name I gave you when last we met. Do you recognize that name?"

"I recognize that name," the sketchy green ancilla replied. Then the figure moved from the back of my thoughts and seemed to pass directly through my forehead—taking shape as a projected form directly in front of me.

"Do you recognize the one who named you?"

The green image briefly flickered. "You are not that one. No other knows that name."

"Shall I guide you to further service?" At this point, I had no idea who was speaking, or to what purpose.

"I require further input. The Domain is insufficient."

"Liberate this armor and prepare a path. Do you know where the Master Builder resides?"

"The Master Builder gave me my final set of orders."

"But I am the one who knows your chosen name, your true name, and who commanded your construction."

"That is so."

"Then I am your client and master. Release me."

"I have a new master. You are dangerous to my new master."

"I know your true name. I can revoke your key and shut you down."

"That is no longer possible. I am beyond the metarchy."

The Didact within me suddenly spoke a series of words and numbers. The green ancilla wavered like a flame in a high wind. Symbols appeared in the space behind my thoughts, swirling like a cloud of birds, combining, matching, then dropping into orderly columns as, one by one, the spoken and numerical symbols of the ancilla's secret key were expressed. At this point, I was just a passenger in my own body, controlled from without by hijacked armor, and from within by the Didact's wisdom.

The struggle suddenly ended. The green ancilla vanished. My armor unlocked.

Run!

I ran as fast as the armor allowed—very fast indeed, through a sluggish maze of recovering monitors and sentinels, across the plaza surrounding the amphitheater hemisphere—up onto a broad ledge looking out over the rim of equatorial disk—where I was intercepted by a guard, who spun me into a constraint field.

For an awful moment, I thought I was back in the

hands of the Master Builder's troops, until I saw the face of Glory of a Far Dawn, and noticed that on her other side, she was also dragging the First Councilor, the First Observer of the Court—Splendid Dust himself—in another field.

Our trip across the plaza ended when, with a sudden leap, the female Warrior-Servant propelled us through the weakened buffer field—which threw a sparking glow around us—and beyond the gravitational gradient, out into empty space, with nothing to stop our fall for at least a hundred kilometers.

THIRTY-SEVEN

A S I FELL, my blue ancilla reacquired definition and control. "Apologies," she said. "I am no longer connected to the metarchy or any other network. I cannot fully serve you—"

"Never mind that," I said. "Find something to catch me."

"That has already been arranged."

I swung about and bumped into the field that held the First Councilor. Our fields merged with a distinct pressure pop. Also with us in the field—Glory herself, curling up as if expecting imminent impact.

A Falco-class rescue pod slid in from my left, matched

our descent, and blipped open a hatchway. Grapples reached out and caught us, then yanked us clumsily inside.

The interior of the Falco rearranged to accommodate three passengers and cushion further acceleration. Still, even in my armor, I felt sick as the tiny craft spun about—and then launched into full evacuation mode.

In a few minutes, we were away from the disk, the whole arrangement of slices—away from the planet itself, following an oblong orbit to observe from a thousand kilometers out in space.

The entire arrangement of the capital's disks seemed to be slowly, painfully realigning to the original sphere. *The capital is under siege*, the Didact within me said.

"What is Mendicant Bias?" I asked, while closely watching our passage through a slow, stately rain of disabled sentinels, monitors, and uncontrolled craft—the near boundary of the planet's disabled protection.

Better to ask where we are going.

Glory pulled herself up, then tugged upon the First Councilor, who seemed stunned. Crammed together as we were, I hoped we were not in this for the long haul—I hoped there would soon be other arrangements.

Still, I could not see any other Falcos—or for that matter any other escapees from whatever chaos had embroiled the capital. "All right," I said, "where are we going?"

"Are you asking *me*?" Splendid Dust said, his face purple with dismay. "I haven't any idea what's just happened."

"The metarchy has been disabled," Glory of a Far Dawn

said. "All control has been moved to an external authority. I was instructed by my commanders to rescue at least two of the councilors."

Splendid Dust looked between us.

"I seem to have rescued you, instead," she said to me, deadpan.

We were now in a position to see again the great rings of the orbiting installations. They were no longer arranged linearly but had spread out into a pentagon and a hexagon— along with another, outlying ring, slowly moving to join with the pentagon. It seemed that after forty-three years, the prodigal Halo had returned.

Bearing what madness? The captive itself? Overkill beyond all reason. This is utterly pointless—what is its goal?

"Whose goal? What's goal?"

The others stared at me. I was babbling to myself.

Mendicant Bias. A Contender class, the first of its kind. It is as far above most ancillas as the metarch-level systems rise above our personal components.

The axes of five of the installations now pointed directly at the capital world. One by one, the reoriented Halos were growing slender spokes of hard light.

"What do you know about Mendicant Bias?" I asked the First Councilor.

"Designed to coordinate control of some of the installations," he said. "Also given the power, in emergencies, to coordinate the entire galaxy's response to attack."

"Who authorized this?"

"The old Council—with the input of the Master Builder."

"Mendicant Bias conducted the test at Charum Hakkor?"

"Yes."

The Didact within me was stunned into silence.

The capital world's defenses were slowly cutting loose from their complete shutdown. Swift attack cruisers and other vessels were reassuming their formations in low orbit. Defensive fields lay across the surface of the capital's new-formed sphere like ghostly flags, their edges knitting together to complete a dense shield—effective against enemy ships, but useless against any single Halo. And very likely we'd end up being trapped in one of those fields.

My ancilla, to my surprise, issued a code and took control of the Falco, then guided our craft away from the unfolding fields, up and away from the formations of battle craft—and toward the Halos themselves.

We were not being followed.

"There will be no pursuit," my ancilla said. "We are protected by the Librarian's privilege."

"Even in an emergency?"

"Not all protocols have been voided. The Contender has caused considerable confusion in the metarchy, however. That was apparently its plan."

"Do *we* have any sort of plan?" I asked.

"We are seeking an escape route," the ancilla replied. "Apparently our duty here is finished. There is a special councilors' entrance to the capital system's dedicated portal. If the settings have not been changed, it will respond to the Librarian's key and open for us."

"And what if this Mendicant Bias has scrambled all the keys?"

But I knew better. It had responded to the Didact's numbers.

"I do not answer discouraging questions," my ancilla said. "My resources are limited. I would appreciate some optimism."

That shut me up for a moment, but my mind was still racing.

The First Councilor and the Warrior-Servant watched me closely. Glory of a Far Dawn leaned close to the councilor and said, "I can't control the Falco. *His* ancilla seems to be directing our movements."

"Bornstellar's ancilla?" the councilor said.

"At your command, I will attempt to subdue him," the Warrior-Servant said.

"How? We can barely move in here."

"I have been trained—"

"You *idiot*!" the councilor howled, his fear finally breaking loose. We were both shocked that such an enlightened first-form would choose an ancient Builder word used to put inferior rates in their place. "He's got the imprint of the Didact! He's ten thousand years to your twenty!"

She withdrew a few centimeters, and regarded me soberly from under the curve of her headpiece. "I did not know that," she said.

The Halos were growing closer. At our present speed, the craft might actually reach their vicinity in a half an hour—unless, of course, my ancilla knew what she was talking about, and there was a portal somewhere out here as well.

Each Halo was about thirty thousand kilometers in diameter, a slender ribbon tied up in a perfect circle, the outer surface acquiring detail as we grew closer and as the sun's light angled to create deeper shadows. The inside of the nearest ribbon was strangely mottled, partly green, partly blue—but mostly bluish silver. As well, I could now make out waves of hard light rippling around the inner surface, occasionally shooting slender spikes toward the axis—then withdrawing them, as if trying unsuccessfully to spin out the spokes of a vast wheel.

Whatever its exalted status, Mendicant Bias still cannot control all of the Halos. This one is resisting preparation to fire.

"What would the Librarian do with her own portal?" I asked.

"It is not solely for her use," my ancilla replied. "The portal can also be shifted to deliver large constructions."

"Halos?"

"Halos and the Lifeshaper's work are part of the same contract. The Lifeshaper uses the portal to connect with the many worlds where she is gathering her specimens."

"Like Erde-Tyrene."

"As of my last update there are no longer portals that open to Erde-Tyrene."

"How can you know that?"

"Specimens were collected from Erde-Tyrene decades before you went there."

The Didact within was strangely unresponsive—perhaps mulling over the strange behavior of Mendicant Bias, or the collusion of the Librarian with the Master Builder.

"No advice from my other wisdom?" I asked out loud.

Out of respect. We may be witnessing the end of Forerunner governance.

"I can't stand this! I can't stand being ignorant, held prisoner—jockeyed around the galaxy, hosting a Promethean who doesn't share even *half* of what he knows. . . . Riser and Chakas would be better company. At least they'd understand my frustration."

More silence. We were all tightly focused on the nearest Halo, now less than a million kilometers away. "What are those spokes of light?" I asked.

The installation seems to be adjusting to tidal forces from its proximity to the capital world. The position is not optimal for a large structure. Transport through a portal may also increase strain.

"It's not getting ready to fire, is it?"

The defense forces won't wait to find out. With the capital metarchy out of action, command now splinters to individual squadrons. Each has specific instructions how to deal with potential attacks.

"There is the portal," my ancilla said, and gently nudged my gaze toward a silvery, slowly pulsing web, like a tremendous lacework constantly growing and overlapping curves and lines of hard light. Within the webwork, pits of blackness shot through with violet kept up a rotational cycle of growth and diminishment. Our sensors indicated the webwork was closer to us than the nearest Halo—about a million kilometers.

I had seen portals before, but none so large and powerful, so ornate, so full of opportunities. Each of those violet holes could open onto a different place in our galaxy. "That's where we're going?" I asked.

Before my question could be answered, I saw three of the pits of darkness flow together at the center of the webwork. The entire web shimmered, and through the combined holes emerged five large cruisers—and right behind them, a fully activated fortress, arriving long tail first, bristling with armament. As soon as they were through, and allowing for a brief few seconds of reconciliation, during which time the ships radiated dim, expanding shells of blue, the smaller craft began to fan out to distant points, nearly all beyond the limits of my vision—except for the fortress.

This was nothing like the dismal old hulk that had stood guard for so long over the San'Shyuum. Sleek, clean, perhaps twice the size of the *Deep Reverence*, the fortress was heading directly toward the rotational axis of the nearest Halo.

"We should depart from this region," my ancilla suggested. "These are forces arriving to protect the capital."

"The installations will not allow themselves to be attacked," the councilor said. "They will defend themselves. Even if they are not under the control of Mendicant Bias, there will be violent confrontations."

I will program battle code. My other memory was finally proving useful; the Didact worked with my ancilla and the Falco began to broadcast protective signals.

From the fortress's long tail, replete with gun mounts and weapons bays, thousands of swift attack vessels began to pour forth, fanning out, radiating to positions above the inner surface of the Halo. Our sensors now picked up swarms of small and midsize craft emerging from the Halo itself, and identified them as dedicated sentinels—used only for Halo defense.

They are controlled by the installation monitors. The monitors are programmed to assume that all who attack an installation are enemies—whatever they look like, or whatever codes they possess.

"That makes no sense," I said.

It does if you understand the ways of the Flood.

"Then make me understand!"

There is no time.

Already, in rapid succession, more cruisers were emerging from the portal, straining the webwork until it radiated a fierce reddish glow. The portal fabric began to visibly separate—hard-light strands exceeding even their extraordinary tensile strengths. Clearly, these newly arrived forces were prepared to sacrifice both themselves and the portal in their haste. . . .

Mendicant Bias has exceeded its present ability. It can control only five installations out of twelve. The others will maneuver to save themselves. They will attempt to access the portal.

Seven of the huge rings—not including the one that had just appeared—once again rearranged their array. One Halo from the pentagon broke formation, sending cascades of violet energy from drive engines spaced along its rim. It moved to joined those not in the Contender's control.

These seven began to align in parallel, re-creating the tunnel effect. The five under the Contender's control had completed their spoke-and-hub preparations.

They are primed. They will fire—we must leave now! We must go through the portal!

The first fortress's fighters moved in, surrounding one of the primed Halos and engaging its sentinels. Simultaneously, four cruisers sent white-hot beams to points around the targeted installation. Sentinels intercepted some of those beams, partially deflecting them but also absorbing and sacrificing. Other beams struck home, carving canyonlike gouges across the mottled inner surface and blowing blue-white plumes of debris and plasma from the edges. The interior spokes began to shimmer and fade. The Halo could not hold together against this onslaught. It bent inward, wobbled. Fascinated, I watched as huge sections of the ring twisted like ribbon, giving way to destructive nodes of resonance, then rippled in sinus waves—and separated with agonizing majesty.

The entire Halo was breaking apart. It would not complete its priming and firing sequence. Keeping track of the remaining eleven installations in the melee was exhausting. The other four primed installations, however, were successfully fending off fighters and cruisers and had fanned out to cover at least half of the capital world, as if preparing for an awful sunrise.

Their spokes were now forming golden hubs.

Glory of a Far Dawn pushed closer to watch with me. Her hands clenched. "I should be there!" she said. "I should be protecting the capital!"

An unexpected horror shook my ancilla. "The Librarian's specimens—so many worlds are stored on the Halos, so many terrains and beings! What will happen to the fauna?"

The Lifeshaper succeeded in her struggle with the Master Builder. She coopted the installations. . . .

I found myself again taking control of the Falco. We accelerated out of the widening zone of battle, toward the portal, now a single huge violet radiance against the blackness of space.

Three of the seven fleeing Halos were lined up, also seeking entry. They, too, were being harried by cruisers and were now attacked by swarms from the second fortress.

Sentinels from these installations mounted a vigorous defense, pushing back their attackers. The rings maintained their integrity.

Before we could reach the hellishly glowing webwork with its single yawning and badly distorted portal, the first Halo began its passage.

For me, under the influence of the Didact's battle mode, time fragmented into several streams. I saw the movement of the installation in fast mode, but—in excruciating slow motion—directed the Falco to avoid bursts of plasma energy and disintegrating swift attack vessels. Part of me seemed to fight through many lifetimes, through clouds of fighters and debris, away from ever-increasing danger.

A second installation was about to follow the first through the portal. A third lined up. . . .

The portal webwork was obviously about to tear itself to pieces.

We must *leave this system before the other installations fire! We will approach the third installation and enter the portal along with it.*

"Where will the portal take us?" my ancilla asked, growing even tinier as her duties were reduced.

It does not matter. Any place other than this.

"Why would they prime and fire?" I cried. "That will kill everyone here, disintegrate the metarchy—Forerunners will lose their history, their heart and spirit—"

Mendicant Bias has turned against us. But I do not believe it has sufficient resources to control more than five in-

stallations at once. Other installations are following older instructions, priority protocols—they defend themselves, but are struggling to break free of the Contender's rule. They may reconnoiter outside our galaxy—at the Beginning Place. The Ark.

And we must join them.

THIRTY-EIGHT

NO LONGER have access to the record maintained by that ancilla. She faded long, long ago, during another battle and another time, taking with her so many details, so much of my transformation and emergence.

The problems I face trying to bring back and explain these events are manifold. I was then two beings confined in one body. How much of this effect was accidental and how much deliberate was far from clear to me.

I suspected . . . I feared . . . but I could not know.

And thus my memories were separated into two compartments, one of which has declined with time and circumstance, and the other of which—the survivor, as it were—is very different from either of my two personalities at that time.

Memory without an ancilla is in large part a reconstruction, a reimagining based on clues locked in chronology and checked against outside sources. But no outside sources remain. So much of Forerunner history . . .

But I get ahead of myself.

This is the closest truth I can manage. It will have to suffice. There is no other.

What did I *actually* see? Do I actually remember our close approach to the Halo just as it entered the portal . . .

———

The small rescue craft plowed and glided and glowed through the great ring's inner atmosphere, no doubt resembling a meteor. We were briefly pursued by sentinels, and some shots even grazed our shields. But we were not armed and offered no return fire; they turned their attention elsewhere.

I flash on brief moments of breathtaking, awful splendor, sharpened by terror: the rapid approach of the Halo's inner landscape, our first close-up glimpse of thin layers of clouds, rivers, mountains, desert, vast stretches of green, then thousands of kilometers of engraved silver-blue, naked foundation material interrupted by towering, four-pronged power stations—all unadorned by hard-light decor.

The Halo was almost halfway through the portal. Our small craft flew up from its skim of the atmosphere, into a welter of debris, sentinels, and pursuing fighters jockeying for dominance and the proper tactical positions to break up the installation before it finished its transit. But they were insufficient to accomplish this task. This Halo was about to make its escape.

Then—the unexpected. While the enormous yet ephemeral band of the Halo slowly disappeared into the violet-black maw at the center of the portal, something brilliant white pushed through from the other side. Compared with the Halo, it was tiny, but considerable in its own right: a third fortress. Council security was calling in all available might to secure the system.

Even before it had emerged halfway, the fortress began to loose clouds of fighters—at this distance, they resembled a puff of pollen from a flower—and fire its weapons in a sequential radiance. The inner curve of the Halo, even protected by waves of hard light, could not stand up long to this assault from within its own radius.

The fortress's commanders and ancillas must have known they were dooming themselves as well as the Halo. The installation began a spectacular disintegrative sequence. The visible half of the ring bent in opposite directions, then shattered into five great arcs. We passed near the largest of these segments, perhaps a hundred kilometers from the inner surface. Released from the rotational integrity of the full ring, the segment moved outward, given an additional outward twist by the asymmetric breakup. One end swept toward us like a great swinging blade. Minutes from contact, our craft kicked itself into a new course, and we crossed the width of the approaching arc with seconds to spare, buffeted by rising plumes of icy cloud.

Kilometer-wide swaths of forest waved like flags in a slow wind, shivered off a dust of trees—and broke apart into chunks. In the increasing violence, the surface released a storm of boulders, followed by immense cross sections of sedimentary layers, and finally, entire mountains, still capped with snow.

Our doom seemed inevitable. Either we would be struck by the nearest rim wall or by the great clods and slivers of material spilling over—or we would be caught up in flying volumes of ocean, now, in the shadow of the portal, freezing into spectacular ice sculptures, flying bergs and snow—

I sat within the dust mote of our craft, incapable of speech. I had never witnessed anything so utterly awesome—not even the destruction of the San'Shyuum world. My heart seemed to stop, my thoughts to go gelid.

Then—I felt the Didact's icy discipline dissolve the gluey tendrils of my fear. Our craft was seeking a complex path up and over another section of ring, picking its way through the debris, when, through a nearly opaque layer of frozen mist, we spied the great leading dome of the fortress, trailing streamers of detritus like an avalanche of gray dust.

The dome had suffered awful damage. The fortress was out of action and in its last throes, but the chaos of destruction was not yet done with it. A curled, tortured loop of ring at least five hundred kilometers long spun from the debris cloud and cut through the fortress like a sword through bread. This impact shoved the great vessel out of our path, and in its wake, left a narrow void through which our sensors could see the rim of the portal, still glowing, still holding its form—a miracle, I thought—

The Didact did not accept the existence of miracles. Did not accept them, but did not hesitate to take advantage.

Our craft seemed at the last to waft like a leaf between mountains and ice and the shattered hulks of spaceships, into the pulsing violet of the portal. I felt another kind of impact, another kind of jolt. We were in slipspace, but a slipspace strained and distorted and angry at so much abuse, barely real—barely any kind of continuum whatsoever—

How far this jump took us, there was no way of measuring. We all offered sacrifice to the arcane demands of another kind of physics. We completed our unlikely passage, struggling to maintain any semblance of the real. The causal reconciliation was indescribable. I seemed to stretch and fill like a thundercloud with painful jolts of charge.

We gave away something ineffable, but still—

We survived.

Somehow, solidity—a useful thing—returned. On the far side of that journey, looking back at where we had been, we saw—nothing. The portal had collapsed. We now drifted across an even greater void, without thrust or control, our power down to almost nothing. I thought I saw a distant speckle of stars.

Passing its shadow across those stars was a flower with a great, gaping blackness in its center. . . .

Huge, unknown—dark.

My ancilla had been reduced to a vague gray ghost in the back of my thoughts. With her feeble assistance, I struggled to fully engage our sensors. They faltered—then returned, weak but usable. Strangely, we were surrounded only by a light haze of debris. Most of the remnants of the Halo, the dying fortress, and all of the other waste from that distant battle had never completed the passage. The portal had filtered and discarded useless material.

I wondered where it all was now, bits of installation and ships and thousands of crew, neither *here* nor *there*. . . .

Amazingly, we had been among the pieces allowed to pass.

I turned to look at Glory of a Far Dawn. She was badly injured, I could see that—yet her face shone with something like joy—the raw joy of battle and survival.

As our eyes met, she drew back her emotions.

"Where are we?" she asked. "How far have we come?"

I could not answer. None of the usual niceties of slipspace—if they could ever be called that—applied. None of the metrics were available to our sensors.

But we had traveled a very great distance indeed. I could feel that in my bones and nerves.

THIRTY-NINE

THE SMALL FALCO'S power loss now affected life support. Worse, our armor's integrity and even its protective capabilities had been damaged by the contradictory surge of instructions from Mendicant Bias.

"Where are we, really?" the young councilor asked, peering through the single small port. "I can't see *anything*."

Glory of a Far Dawn hung back in the rear of the craft like a wounded animal—not so far, of course. I could reach out and touch her. All the joints of her armor had cracked. One leg and one arm had been bent back beyond the breaking point. . . . Yet she refused to call attention to herself.

She did not want to show her pain.

"We're in what remains of a debris cloud," I said. "I saw stars earlier—very far away."

We were weightless, the air was growing foul, all of us were injured—the guard most severely. There was likely no food to sustain us. Even though the armor could recycle our wastes, lacking additional raw materials and running out of its own charge of energy, it would not fill our needs for long.

"Mendicant Bias," I said. I could not tell whether Bornstellar or the Didact was bringing up this topic. Something had broken down all my internal barriers. I was now privy to most of the Didact's wisdom, his imprint—but its usefulness at this point seemed doubtful. Still, I—we—wanted some questions answered. "The Didact oversaw the Contender's planning and inception, and was present at its key quickening. But he was removed from any contact with Mendicant Bias a thousand years ago. What's happened since?"

"Mendicant Bias was charged by the Master Builder with conducting the first tests of a Halo installation," the councilor said.

"Charum Hakkor," I said.

"Yes. Shortly thereafter, the Halo entered slipspace on a scheduled mission—and vanished. Mendicant Bias went with the installation. That was forty-three years ago."

Forty-three years on the first Halo . . . in the presence of the captive? Did they communicate?

Can that ever make sense?

"It might have been strained by contradictory instructions from the Didact, from the Master Builder. . . ."

"Not likely," I said. "Mendicant Bias was fully capable of working with contradictory commands. I've never known a more capable ancilla, more powerful, more subtle . . . more loyal."

"What do you know about the captive of Charum Hakkor?" the Councilor asked. "This subject was to be part of the Didact's testimony against the Master Builder. . . . But I suppose none of that matters now. Still, I'm curious."

"I suspect the captive made its way, or was transported, to the first installation."

"But what *happened*?"

"Still unknown. The Contender would likely have been brought any unusual specimens for examination."

"Would Mendicant Bias have been able to communicate with the captive? It is said by some that you actually spoke with it, using a human device. . . ."

I saw that as if it had happened yesterday. And I noted that the councilor was addressing me as if I were the Didact. "It was not a real conversation, and not in the least satisfactory," I said.

Looking down into the deactivated human timelock, and beyond that secondary cage, tuning the Precursor tool, so small and simple—merely a smooth oval with three notches in its side. . . . "The humans found a way to activate at least one Precursor artifact," I said.

"What was that?"

"A device that could selectively and temporarily open access through the captive's cage."

Seeing the great, ugly head, its compound eyes assuming a new glitter as its consciousness rose from the quantum somnolence of fifty thousand years. . . .

It spoke in a Forerunner dialect, one I could barely understand—archaic Digon. I remembered clearly what it said, but it took time for the context to become clear. Context is everything, across all those centuries. It spoke to me of the greatest of Forerunner betrayals, the greatest of our many sins.

I told the Librarian and no one else . . . and her researches changed drastically. As did my design of Forerunner defenses against the Flood.

"And now the Contender has returned and assumed control of as many installations as it could command . . . only to direct their power against the capital itself. It seeks the destruction of us all. Why?" A look of horror crossed his face. "Is the captive part of the Flood? Does the Flood now control Mendicant Bias?"

"Unknown," I said. "But I think not. It was something other . . . older. And we have no way of knowing whether the Halo strike did its intended damage."

"The response of our warships was magnificent," the guard said, her voice weaker still.

"It *was* magnificent," I agreed. "But if Mendicant Bias has been suborned, and the Domain has been permanently blocked . . ."

"The war may be lost," the First Councilor said.

"Never," the guard said. "*Never!* You are the heir of the Didact, unless he be found, and if that happens, then you are his second-in-command. Either way, you are my commander. We will never give up. It is so, *aya.*"

I reached back instinctively. My armor withdrew from my hand, and my fingers brushed past her facial protection to touch her forehead, which was hot. She was in bad shape.

"Your courage becomes mine. I am privileged," I said.

The guard's eyes closed.

We drifted. Our armor failed.

We slept. All of us. I dreamed of only one thing—or perhaps it was hypoxia.

I dreamed of the captive's glittering eyes.

FORTY

SOMETHING SCRAPED AT the outside of our craft like tree branches in a slow wind—delicate, tentative. The first to return to consciousness, I dragged myself up to the port and looked out at a vast swirl of stars, so many and so far away I could not distinguish most of them.

A galaxy. I hoped *our* galaxy and not another.

The Falco slowly rotated and a complicated silhouette moved across the spiral cloud. It took several long moments before I could make out slender shapes attached to that silhouette, like a wide rosette. Slowly it dawned on me that I was looking upon another array of installations: six rings, each rising from one of the petals of an enormous flower.

Then, to my astonishment, six straight shafts of light flowed outward from the darkness at the center of the flower and through the Halos, illuminating the insides of the rings as well as the main body of the flower.

The Falco kept turning. The edge of the port obscured one view and the other side revealed another. My other memory—now become *my* memory—could not recall anything about this association, this shape against the galaxy and the dim void beyond.

But in the back of my thoughts, a dim female grayness reappeared. "We have returned," my ancilla said. "We have arrived at the Ark."

Incredulous that the armor still had any power, I turned my eyes away from the port and looked at the outlines of my fellow passengers. Neither moved. I thought they must be dead.

"How far?" I asked. But the glimmer of the ancilla had again faded, and I was alone, utterly alone.

I had forgotten about the scraping.

When I looked back to the port, I was astonished to see another face staring back at me—a face framed in a headpiece and wrapped in the protective field of fully active armor. And beyond that face, three other figures, long and graceful.

Lifeworkers.

Groggily I tried to make sense of these perceptions. Lifeworkers were maneuvering outside the dead shell of our craft. I made a weak gesture through the port. My ancilla flickered in and out. Then I felt a hint of something other than stale fetor against my face. Power was being externally fed to the craft, and from there to our armor—even the broken armor. Yet they were not breaking our seal or opening the Falco to rescue us. Instead, they were guiding the craft intact to a larger ship I now saw floating a few hundred meters away.

A voice spoke to me now—female, soft—through the cracked remains of my headpiece. "How many? I count three."

"Three," I confirmed, my mouth dry, my tongue swollen and cracked.

"Are you from the damaged installation that attempted to return to the Ark?"

"No," I said.

"Is there infection?"

"I don't think so. No."

"How far have you traveled?"

"From the capital. Shouldn't . . . talk for while."

The face withdrew, and we were absorbed in a protective field. We had been cautiously inspected, cleared . . . drawn within the ship . . . then deposited on a platform. Up and down returned. Tall figures walked past, but I could not hear what they were saying.

Then the Lifeworker who had first appeared in our port motioned for me to draw the others toward the center of our craft. I tried to do that, pulling in the councilor's limbs, even moving and arranging the guard when she failed to respond.

They then broke open the depleted, dead bulk of the Falco's outer shell, split it wide, and Lifeworkers surrounded us with their instruments and monitors, bringing comfort and relief. They removed the remains of our armor, then took up Glory of a Far Dawn and surrounded her in a golden softness. Her eyes opened, and she seemed astonished— then, embarrassed. She struggled—but was patiently sub-dued and carried away from the platform, into a healing chamber.

The First Councilor tried to stand to survey the broken shell of our rescue craft. His strength failed him. More Lifeworkers carried him away, as well.

Somehow, I had retained the most strength—or so I thought. But my turn to give in came quickly enough.

No sleep, no dreams, just a warm, nutritive blankness, neither dark nor bright. For the first time in a thousand years, I felt at home.

The Librarian is near.

FORTY-ONE

WE HAD JOURNEYED to a point far outside our galaxy. We had been rescued and taken to the factory where the ring-shaped installations were made, equipped, repaired . . . as well, the ultimate repository of the Librarian's collection of the galaxy's life-forms.

The Ark.

I took a regenerative walk through the brightly illuminated forest surrounding Fifth Petal Station. Nearly all the light this far from our galaxy came from the diurnal glow of the elongated plasmas, casting the strangest shadows. The rings themselves were canted at different angles on each petal, rotating constantly within enormous hoops of hard light to maintain their integrity.

On each of the installations, the Librarian's aides and monitors supervised the laying down of the Lifeshaper seeds, containing all the records necessary to create and restore unique ecological systems on the inner surface of each ring. I could see evidence of their work even from where I stood—mottled patches of early-stage jungles and forests, the tan of desert, sheets of ice . . .

Earlier, when I had voiced puzzlement at the contradiction of Halos supporting these living records, my nurse and guardian, a Lifeworker named Calyx, explained that the Librarian had equipped most of the Halos with living ecosystems, and stocked them with many species from many worlds—selecting from those multitudes that been gathered over the last few centuries, and now populated the Ark's great half-circle.

She had hoped to preserve many more species by using the Halos; the Master Builder, after agreeing to her plan, had decided it would be useful to test captured specimens of the Flood on the Halos before they were fired—to learn more about them.

Sacrificing those populations, of course.

I could not understand how the Librarian's pact with the Master Builder had been arranged or implemented. But I admired her stamina. She had proven my superior in every regard. And now that I was here—

Something like the Didact, though not *him*—

I wondered how much I could possibly contribute.

Looking up at the great Halo's upper reaches, I felt dizzy and steadied myself against the toppled trunk of cycad. Nearby, something like a small tank passed by on many pumping legs, a gigantic armor-plated arthropod almost three meters long. It ignored me, for I was not the rotting vegetation it favored as a meal.

When the plasmas dimmed, it became obvious that the sky was still filled with danger. In the battle of the capital, only one installation had survived passage through the portal without breaking up. It had returned to the Ark, and now rotated off to my right, visible through a green wall of ferns. Its interior surface had suffered great damage, and so it was being scrubbed clean, its few remaining specimens rescued and constrained. A new surface was in preparation, with a replacement set of seeds.

What wreckage had passed through the portal still threatened this extraordinary construct. The domain of the Librarian—but also the centerpiece of all that the Master Builder had hoped to achieve—had to be constantly protected against impacts. In the dark, it was easy enough to follow the many vessels that patrolled the debris field; they were tiny glints in a varicolored haze that reminded me so much of the clouds in our Orion complex.

But this haze was not primordial and nurturing of suns. It was the death shroud of a great, perhaps crippling defeat—the final battle, perhaps, of a Forerunner civil war—and it was filled with careening fragments of shattered rings, broken ships, demented or damaged monitors, cut loose from all their disciplines, from the metarchy—lost and worse than useless—and of course, the frozen corpses of hundreds of thousands of Forerunners. . . .

I walked through the forests day after day, and in the dark as well, guided by smaller cousins of the armored arthropod, bearing blue-green lanterns above their tiny eyes and showing me the way.

Night after night, I watched the rings' tentative hard-light skeletons form spokes, stabilizing them before their planned release. . . .

Studied the strange shape of the hard-light hubs at the center of those rings, which had once been designed to direct the deadly energies of the rings when they were fired. . . .

If they were fired. That seemed very unlikely now.

Twenty days passed—twenty cycles of the diurnal plasmas. I healed. From my nurse, Calyx—a first-form, taller than me and graceful, yet also quite strong—I learned that my companions in the Falco were also healing. But before we reunited, another reunion had been arranged.

It was time for me to meet with the Librarian. "She has been expecting you," Calyx said.

I followed him out of the forest.

A transport within the fifth petal carried me toward the main body of the Ark, and a graceful teardrop structure just below the tower that supplied the star of plasmas.

Here, before the meeting, another Lifeworker, an older third-form equipped with a style of armor even more ancient than the Didact's, conducted her own exacting inspection. She sniffed critically, then asked me three questions.

I answered them all. Correctly.

She regarded me with an odd expression of concern.

"I am merely his poor double," I insisted. "I have not integrated—"

"Oh, but you *have*," she said. "Whatever you do, please do not disappoint her. She feels badly about what has happened, but—"

"Why does she feel badly?"

"For interrupting the way of your own growth, and imposing something other."

"I made that choice," I said.

"No, Bornstellar agreed, in part. You are the choice he agreed to, but he did not know the consequences."

"He—I will return when my mission is finished."

"Aya," the Lifeworker said. "This is a day of joy and sadness for all. We revere our Lifeshapers beyond all Forerunners, and the Librarian beyond all Lifeshapers. She is our light and our guide. And she has longed for this moment for a thousand years—but not this way. If only . . ."

But she did not complete that thought.

Now she took my hand and led me through a great arched doorway, into the base of the teardrop. A lift carried us to a wide room covered with a curved canopy that allowed in selected portions of the broad spectrum of the shaft of light. The light here was blue-green. The space was filled with specimens from a world I knew nothing of, captured in special cages, immobile, unaware for the time being.

And walking between those cages, inspecting her charges, using her long, graceful fingers to prune and arrange and persuade, confirming their integrity and health, I saw the Librarian.

My wife.

Here, she did not wear armor. She was among her other children, and had never known harm from any of them.

She paused and moved on her long legs to a pathway through the cages. Along that pathway, she approached me slowly, eyes quizzical, face wreathed in a complex expression of joy, pain, and something I could only see as *youth*.

Eternally young. Yet this Forerunner was older than me, that is, older than the Didact—over eleven thousand years of age.

"So similar," she whispered as we stepped toward each other, her voice like a sweet sigh of wind. "So much alike."

I reached out to her. "I bring greetings from the Didact," I said, feeling the awkwardness, *knowing* I bore the same memories . . . yet wishing to be honest and to honor the reality of our situation.

"Bring me your *own* greetings," she responded, leaning her head to one then, then grasping my outstretched hands. "You *are* him."

"I am merely—"

"You *are* him, now," she insisted, with a sad intensity I did not expect. My emotions leaped out to her, then my arms rose and I clasped her, not understanding, not caring: fulfilled.

I was with my wife. I was home. *Aya!*

The other Lifeworkers tending the specimen cages turned away to give us privacy.

"How can I be him and other?" I asked as we embraced. I looked up at her beautiful face, pale blue and pink, feeling the warmth of the naked skin of her lithe arms and the touch of her infinitely subtle fingers.

"The Didact is *here*," my wife said. "The Didact is gone."

And then I *knew*, and my love was pushed aside by a moment of intense vertigo, as if I were again falling through black, starless space.

She clasped my face between her cool hands and looked down into it. "You refused to give Faber what he needed to activate all the Contender-class ancillas. You refused to give him the location of all your Shield Worlds. It is said that the Master Builder executed you on the San'Shyuum quarantine planet. You are now all I have.

"You are all *we* have."

FORTY-TWO

THE LOVE OF old Forerunners is sweet beyond measure. It mattered not our rates or forms. I had a lovely time with my wife, before once again we went our separate ways.

She showed me the work of centuries, the preservation of all life-forms she could locate and gather, preparing to save what she could from the awful, final solution of the Master Builder's installations. I saw fauna and flora and things around and between, strange and beautiful, fearsome and meek, simple and complex, huge and small, but only a small sample of a trillion different species, most now dormant, stored as best they could be on the Ark and what was left of the Halos. Whole creatures alive or suspended, genetic maps, preserved and reduced populations visible only in reconstructive simulation. . . .

The other Halos—if any survived—would have to be dealt with later. There were now not enough, away from the Ark, to complete the Master Builder's plan. And if those others somehow managed to return to the Ark, no one here would repair, rebuild, replenish them. . . .

I would make sure of that. In time, I would prepare once again the defense I had championed a thousand years ago: my far-spread Shield Worlds, if the Master Builder had not destroyed them.

Time was very short. But we still had no communications with the capital system. The entire range of slipspace was in turmoil, and might not settle for years.

Other chores awaited me, as well. Chores—and personal obligations. I confirmed what I had suspected ever since my revival on Erde-Tyrene. The Librarian had filled the humans there with versions of their history that would reawaken in time. Intelligent species, she told me, are very little indeed without their deep memories.

As I contained the essence of the Didact, the Master Builder must have suspected the value of the two humans, and so I hoped that he had not killed them, but hidden them away, where only he might find them again . . . if he still lived.

Somewhere in the humans' awakened memory lay our last hope of defeating the Flood, which was even now ravaging world after world, system after system—more hideous by far than it had been a thousand years before.

More sophisticated, more devious. More vital. And soon to acquire a new Master, if we did not act quickly—if we did not locate the lost installation and the former captive.

Ten thousand years ago, on Charum Hakkor, before I resealed its cage, this is what the captive had said to me, speaking in ancient Digon, which it had to have learned from our far-distant ancestors:

We meet again, young one. I am the last of those who gave you breath and shape and form, millions of years ago.

I am the last of those your kind rose up against and ruthlessly destroyed.

I am the last Precursor.

And our answer is at hand.

ACKNOWLEDGMENTS

Greg Bear would like to thank the excellent team at 343, including Frank O'Connor and Kevin Grace, for their creativity, patience, and 24/7 assistance in beginning this monumental journey through the Halo origins story. Thanks to my son, Erik Bear, for introducing me to Halo in the first place, and for providing additional creative input and thorough fan advice. And thanks to Eric Raab for watching over us all.

343 Industries would like to thank Bungie Studios, Greg Bear, Scott Dell'Osso, Nick Dimitrov, David Figatner, Nancy Figatner, Josh Kerwin, Bryan Koski, Matt McCloskey, Corrinne Robinson, Bonnie Ross-Ziegler, Phil Spencer, and Carla Woo. Also the staff at Tor Books, including Tom Doherty, Karl Gold, Justin Golenbock, Seth Lerner, Jane Liddle, Heather Saunders, Eric Raab, Whitney Ross, and Nathan Weaver.

And none of this would have been possible without the Herculean efforts of the Microsoft staffers, including Jacob Benton, Nicolas "Sparth" Bouvier, Alicia Brattin, Kevin Grace, Tyler Jeffers, Frank O'Connor, Ryan Payton, Jeremy Patenaude, Chris Schlerf, Kenneth Scott, and Kiki Wolfkill.

HAL☉
W A Y P O I N T

Gear up at your official Halo eStore
HaloWaypointStore.com

apparel | toys | collectibles | fiction